# Hot Soles in Harlem

# Hot Soles in Harlem

by

Emilio Díaz Valcárcel

Translated by

Tanya T. Fayen

Latin American Literary Review Press
Series: Discoveries
Pittsburgh, Pennsylvania
1993

The Latin American Literary Review Press publishes Latin American creative writing under the series title *Discoveries*, and critical works under the series title *Explorations*.

Library of Congress Cataloging-in-Publication Data

Díaz Valcárcel, Emilio.
    [Harlem todos los días. English]
    Hot soles in Harlem / by Emilio Díaz Valcárcel; translated by Tanya T. Fayen.
        p.  cm. -- (Discoveries)
    ISBN 0-935480-61-7
    I. Title. II. Series.
    PQ7439.D498H3713  1993
    863-dc20                   92-21226
                                      CIP

Cover illustration by Noel J. Torres
Cover and Book Design by Barbara Alsko

*Hot Soles in Harlem* may be ordered directly from the publisher:
Latin American Literary Review Press
121 Edgewood Avenue
Pittsburgh, PA  15218
Tel (412) 371-9023 • Fax (412) 371-9025

## ACKNOWLEDGEMENTS

This project is supported in part by grants from the National Endowment for the Arts in Washington, D.C., a federal agency, the Commonwealth of Pennsylvania Council on the Arts, and Saint Joseph's University.

The translator wishes to acknowledge the assistance of the Millay Colony of the Arts, Steepletop, for a month long residency.

# Hot Soles in Harlem

# 1
●

IN GENERAL, the atmosphere is warm and cozy, tensely friendly, but you get the impression that it hangs in a delicate balance, that perhaps one word too many would bring the bottoms of the bottles crashing down from the ceiling in a menacing manner. Or, just as when you gaze at a lovely goblet and sigh and your very breath brings it down crash; you reach the dizzying heights and when you try to kill the wasp that stings you, you flounder and you kill yourself; just so the atmosphere of Dutch's bar presents itself, he understood intuitively, still feeling the motion of the airplane, fasten seat belts. Listening to the music and feeling Aleluya's gaze penetrate to the marrow of his bones, it is upsetting for the recent arrival to think about it all too much because he begins to assemble arbitrary images and instead of wanting, for example, a bed, he thinks of a bicycle, an experience that tires him terribly. The world begins to tangle itself in a thoroughly irrational manner and to explain it all to himself the word *mogolla* (muddle) pops to mind, the most meaningful of the ample lexicon of his sunny island. He clings tightly to several elusive and simple phantoms

> rainfall on banana leaves
> oxen plowing
> a woman nursing her newborn
> an old drunkard cursing
> a mayor with a flashy tie
> rivers of sweat
> airport

and, fearing that he might bury himself in complicated internal meditations, he held onto the word *burundanga* (hodgepodge), the veritable vibration of his soul. Why try to communicate this to his friends? Instead of beer, he could say icebox or, worse yet, ambulance. The words could break the mysterious equilibrium—suspended by a mustache hair—of the drinkers' convention and a catastrophe accompanied by the music of police sirens could beat against the pub sweaty with darkness. Let not a pin drop, for it would be like a bomb; let no one toss a cigarette butt because the TNT which daringly awaits beneath the pavement of Harlem would explode apocalyptically. But, immediately, the temperature eases, the air clears (the flies fly about tamed by the smell of summer beer). The miraculous death of the atmospheric density encourages the recent arrival:

"Could I get a cheap hotel, something not too fancy? It wouldn't have to be anything out of this world, a room with a shower or even if it didn't have one, but that I could get by with until I find work, even if it were only a bed, but cheap?"

Aleluya studies, part by part, clause by clause, the question constructed—or deconstructed, if you prefer—with a circumspect attitude, but he doesn't allow himself to pronounce an easy sí—yes, straight to the point—but he embarks upon a lengthy mental review starting from the East Side to the west flank of Central Park, evaluating the cross streets beginning at 95th street. From here on down, there are zones of unbreathable bourgeois contamination: white whites, filthy rich Jews, ex-Italians, Germans of suspiciously Aryan extraction. From the border at 95th he continues upward till his memory finally arrives at 140th, widely overshooting before linking up with the vividly dramatic South Bronx, cradle of many ghetto delights, a garden where rats' nests flourish (music for the recently arrived: guitars without strings, hump-backed Picassoesque musicians) but he reflects that you don't need to go so far.

"There's a vacant room," he says, pushing the bridge of his horn-rimmed glasses with his index finger. "If they didn't rent it today. In any case, don't worry, there will be a rational manner to resolve each and every one of the problems that will be coming up for you, that is to say, arising."

The mulatto's verbosity distorts the few images the recent arrival has of the world with which he is cautiously dealing: there are holes and treacherous bumps in life. He says "thanks a lot" supposing that the moment has come for the demonstration of some measure of gratitude between compatriots. He smiles self-consciously, feeling like a jerk, a half-wit, an asshole, with his eyes of a dangerous blue, sitting there, right there in Dutch's bar, that tortured Alabama soul. Aleluya skips the joyful gratitude which, had it been allowed to run its ineffable Boricuan course, would have ended in a torrent of tears. Fire-eating apostle, Aleluya is God's commissar in the Barrio.

"Dino Calabrio has an explosive temper," he says, "but he's all right. He could have made his fortune by associating with the other Sicilians of his generation, but he has remained honest. He's the super. He's been there twenty years. Maybe more. Ever since the time when the Barrio was overrun by Italians. Thousands of his compatriots became integrated, moving upward, but he remained here after we had begun to arrive. When Dino Calabrio gets nostalgic, he praises us for our 'Latino' roots or he sings '*La donna é mobile*'."

Then Mongo Santamaría hurls himself at his drums with a dazzling display of white teeth in his black face, showing that he's gone over to disco, expressing himself as he sweats acetate, vibrating in Bigote's and Dutch's and perhaps even in Aleluya's post conciliar skulls. The recent arrival notices that the music tortures Bigote, cruelly weakens his knees, transforms him into an outline whose edges fade out with every vibration: radiations from a planet ruling within the depths of every one of us: all of this emanates from the mysterious planet of Africa. Nevertheless, Bolo appears to be frozen deep within burning depths—he lives in a more classical age—with all the lyrical serenity which this implies—he's lost in a jungle of guitars and dances: *milongas, pasillos*, and torrential *tangos*. Mongo's beat is slow but charged, as Dutch points out in his disconfederated accent, and the initial pacumpah, pacumpah settles into a more relaxed and tolerable, comfortable and smooth umpampah, umpampah. The trumpet and sax appear to adhere with alarming rigidity to the notes written and permanently inscribed upon the staff, but Bigote points out astutely that from time to time the trumpet lets out an anarchistic moan. With clear holding power throughout the number, spontaneous and carelessly lumpen, the chorus adds a defiant naturalness, a certain marijuanality to the band. But the musical enterprise cannot stop there—no, Mongo, no, you Santamaría of the Trinitarian name—, the silence shall not fill them with the fierce, disturbing expectation with fills all post-musical silences. Another artist of the circle which appeals to the Harlemnian sensibility must ascend to the proscenium of the jukebox and Dutch, completely stepping out of his conservative role as bartender, puts several coins into the slot. Bolo shouts to the skies for more drums and nigger's racket; he shouts without changing expression, but his words, pronounced alveolarly due to the defectiveness of his missing teeth—sad irony, lamentable contradiction—are bitten off by a new, whistling form of speech. Without a doubt, disco does not entirely meet with Bigote's approval, who considers some of the Barrio's musical phases uneclipsed. Tito Puente doesn't really bother him, but he realizes that Tito is out of date with his carefully orchestrated big band, his calculated and precise movements encased in a formalism which excludes any dynamic freedom. Even what appear to be improvs on sax and trumpet and drums were perilously similar to the unchangeable lines on a map, cartography for classy-cal mentalities. He discovered unimaginable defects in the period in which the "King of the Kettledrum", with enviable confidence and aggression, set his course, somewhere within the last few years of the forties. A retrospective view of the drummer could not help but move Bolo, now that the disappearance of *milongas* had made the King an "old timer" at the very least. He said this without being able to prevent the escape of an excessive amount of slightly phonated air, an excuse for a *vidalita* at the very least. Gerardo (the recent arrival) notes a noticeable difference in the number runner's pronunciation when he articulated letters like m, n, l, a, e, i, o, u, but the astute Aleluya understands that all these sibilant sounds come out sadly due to the incompleteness of his ancient phonic apparatus. No stranger to human suffering, he did not even smile, nor did he say I'm sorry, brother, for this fetid and slobbery air—ascendant flatulence—, for this ventilator vexed by uncontrollable f's and s's, the unraveled specters of phonemes, but instead constrained himself to lifting his small African cranium in order to hear better. Without knowing what to say in the midst of this torrent of music, suddenly aware of his estrangement, the recent arrival seeks refuge in such well worn expressions as

raise crows and they'll pluck out your eyes

no one was born to be a stone

such is life

the sleeping shrimp is carried off by the current

The pornographic implications are not lost on the group when Santamaría's lead singer becomes inspired behind the chorus singing

Hey, baby, you like-a the salami

a line directed toward the chick, babe, *chamaca* already mentioned in the song in a suggestive context. Bigote leans forward and clap-claps his hands to celebrate the witticism. Quite apart from the fact that such a phrase signifies, according to Aleluya, the vocal expression of the sublimation of a repressed libido, his love of stylistic analysis compels him to analyze the line:

hey/ba/by/you/like/a/the/sa/la/mi

which leaves him frustrated because of what it might have been with one more syllable: the beloved hendecasyllable of the Golden Age poets, but it satisfies him to realize that this vulgar, blatantly lumpen creation could be considered a major work of art for purely quantitative reasons, and he constrains himself to commenting: spicy vocals and a spicy rhythm. And he immediately thinks of the subject peoples south of the Rio Grande, burdened by their conflicts and their inhuman repression and deprived of the constant erotic sublimation of being successful at creating a mighty civilization—as suggested by the father of psychoanalysis—which instead causes untold suffering and dissatisfaction. Thick books with titles like *The Function of The Orgasm*, for example, circulate widely north of the Rio Grande, a fact which strikes him as somewhat excessive. He thinks: "Part of the divine plan" (along with his tendency toward materialistic analysis, Aleluya displays a propensity to derive meaning in the direction of divine explanations of reality, a fact which completely crosses his circuits, since he understands the two systems as being complementary and completely antagonistic). He is nonetheless delighted by his friend's directness and simplicity: Bigote limits himself to questioning the legitimacy of Mongo's followers, revealing considerable concern—in an obviously southern English, assimilated from the black Dutch—that he had abandoned his calling as a drummer after having tried out with relative success in several bands. Bolo offers number 235 to his compatriot who enters smiling. Immediately, Aleluya thinks circuitously that this is not the beat of the music in question, but he couldn't swear that it was 3/4, because he is weak in math; in any event, he is obsessed by all disciplines which relate to time-space phenomena, and this problematic is clearly demonstrated in music. In the meantime, without charm or specific motivation, Dutch serves a group of retirees, sickly old men inclined to speak in monotones and deaf to music. Gerardo contemplates his off-brown bag held together by two turns of twine. Bigote says to him:

"If you don't like the Barrio, you could move to the Bronx or lower Manhattan. Long Island is falling and we're starting to invade Queens. We're filling up almost all of the West Side. One day we'll have the whole city."

Aleluya smiles ironically: "Obviously. When we control the means of production."

"In the city alone, we have close to a million."

"Not long ago, some official said the same thing. The city will be ours. They pay him to talk nonsense. We would have to become Wall Street big shots, take over Canal Street. If we haven't been able to resume control of our own country, we'll take over the nerve center of the empire! Don't dream, brother."

Gerardo finds that Aleluya has an alarming capacity for dashing buckets of cold water over other people's enthusiasm. Bolo looks at him ironically. His sixty ironic years observe the implacable and proper young man.

"Are you a preacher or a politician?"

"I see no contradiction. Well, we'd better go, we don't want them to rent out a room which could very well be yours."

"Yes," says Gerardo. "Is it far?"

The other doesn't like the laziness implicit in the question, but he recognizes small wrinkles of weariness beneath Gerardo's eyes. A weariness that, perhaps, transcends mere physical appearance, that carnal shell where hides a spirit as strong as the next, comparable to a German, for example, or perhaps to a Chinese (although the suspicion exists that Buddhism and other oriental religions leave a special mark, a delicate spiritual erosion caused by the ongoing struggle of the spirit against the flesh and by the pressure of the material against the pillars of the pagodas). But he has no desire to mollify himself with such reflections.

"Are we walking or not?" he asks cuttingly.

"Okey," replies the recently arrived bilingual Gerald.

$$\frac{2}{\phantom{+}\bullet}$$

T HEY SAY there's one rat per person," said Aleluya at the corner of 120th. "Divine ratified commandment: be fruitful and multiply, my son. Look at the blacks. This is Lexington. It's further up. Almost on the corner. A great avenue, eh?"

It smells of rancid fried lard, of onions and rotten garbage. Two rows of mailboxes on the wall. In the darkness he could make out hearts crossed by overly sharp arrows, arrows knives daggers that correspond to specific offensive defensive uses. The elevator was completely dented, battered with a thoroughness worthy of better goals, a box of long dead motion.

"Someone should make an anthology of the things they write on these walls," says Aleluya, pointing toward the wall. "Here, people speak plainly. The craven use the bathroom to release their resentment. Not by means of a bowel movement, but with a simple ballpoint pen. The specialists use magic markers. Imagine that the Latin American capitalist X meets with his North American counterparts in a sumptuous hotel on the East Side. They intimidate him, he feels secretly humiliated, they have a tendency to poke fun at his English, comment on his native coloration; those blond haired fellows live with such self assurance it's irritating. The capitalist X who, when you come down to it, is nothing more than an intermediary servant of the host group feels cramps by the time the desserts are served, says 'beg your pardon', 'please', etcetera, goes to the bathroom and while he defecates ponders heroically, so that before he leaves he takes out his Parker and writes on the wall in a shaky hand: 'Down with...them'. Then he returns to the banquet, convinced that he has performed a heroic act of national liberation."

"That's all right," says the recent arrival. "With a pen!"

Then Aleluya knocked lightly three times on the first door. Everything that he did assumed the ponderous quality of a ceremony, of public ritual. Tying things together, Gerardo remembered a small rural altar with a few tall candles, a ten year old *peon* who, every Sunday, attained an enviable position as a rude altar boy. The priest, his back to the gaping rustic congregation, drank—he alone, without inviting anyone to join him, without directing so much as a glance toward his flock—the contents of a truly lovely cup that must have weighed at least a pound. So much effort to lift it, all for one swallow. And, in some way, he associated the face of his childhood priest with that which appeared in the just opened door: plump, with a dark five o'clock shadow, atop a stout man in an undershirt and heavy corduroy pants, as hairy as a monkey. Behind his back was an entangled Dantesque scene of old chairs, tables without legs—which could be identified by the archetypal characteristics of all tables: the horizontality independent of whatever distance mediated between it and the floor—broken mirrors, tattered curtains, confused piles of cloth which might be sheets and bedcovers and tablecloths, a suicide victim's undershirt with a hole in the left hand side, the edges of which were scorched, stockings, shameful handkerchiefs—everyone knows why—, panties converted into fetishes by lonely men, sheets saturated by nightmares and historic fornications—verifiable by the existence of children in the building—and, over it all, the dusty layer which coats everything with a greyish color and struggles against the faint light from a bedside lamp rescued from the final fire. All of this smells dry, muddy, turbid, aggressive, sneeze-provoking; it tickles one's throat, burns ones tonsils like acid, outrages the most virile lungs. As if that were not enough, Aleluya was so proper and meticulous and correct that Gerald was vaguely infected, soiled from the heart on, consubstantiating himself with the malodorous chaos, perhaps his conscience was a mattress that had been repeatedly wet by immigrant children, a box spring that had lost its bounce or a tablecloth offended by ancient coffee stains. Thus, he felt completely humble and defenseless, his freedom of expression imprisoned in the mousetrap of the mulatto's rapid fire verbosity. The wind of a Septembrian storm blew through the holes in his brain, but this too would pass, he sensed without naming the problem, without thinking about it at all. Nor did he try to understand the shyness he felt as he climbed the stairs. The super shoved and opened the third door on the third floor.

"More than twenty disreputable characters have come to rent it, but I've got enough with the Pollack on the fourth, the transvestite and the family that hasn't paid their rent for the past six months. They don't understand Mr. Levine's situation, that he'll die of starvation if they don't pay on time. Well, this is the room. Understand? Let me see your arms. That's a prerequisite. Uh-huh. Okay. I don't see anything. Even though there are people who shoot up in the legs. You can rent it."

"I have to see it first."

"Well, then, look at it, shit!"

Gerardo paused between Calabrio and the door. Aleluya saw in him the perilous calm of the angered *machetero*. He saw blood, rivers of blood down the stairs, Dino Calabrio's face laid open, the howl of police sirens, serious accusations in legal jargonese. Murder on 126th Street. Aleluya could serve as a peace maker, a mediator in defective human justice, but not a muscle of his face nor a saccharine softness of his eyes nor a word would ever betray him; no show of weakness would ever undermine his public image as a militant apostle.

"It's his nature, brother", he says, severe, motionless, friendly. "Go on, look at the room, that's why you came."

He found a chair, a sway-backed brass bed, a recently installed, clean washstand, deserving of better surroundings. The guillotine style glass window, from which one could see the fire escape in the foreground, seemed normal to him because it looked out on the street, on the windows of the building across the way. There were holes in the partition, covered with squares of tin, and he was immediately struck by the idea that he could reopen one in case there were a girl on the other side to spy on in moments of solitude. To judge by the number of patched holes, voyeurism is an activity that is perfectly compatible with human dignity. "Bob and Nellie did it here", he read beside the window, imagining prolific outpourings, secret communication in the dark, in the sweat of the lovers who had tangled in this bed.

"Doesn't it have a bathroom?"

Aleluya and the super exchanged a perplexed look in the face of such an incongruously bourgeois question.

"What do you expect?", Calabrio shook his head from side to side. "The Waldorf-Astoria? The famous Greek privateer lives with his honored wife, the widow of you know who, on Fifth Avenue, with a marvelous view of Central Park and dozens of servants. Oh, it's right out of a fairy tale! They won't let him show himself at the entrance or stop on the sidewalk. There're a lot of people who'd like this room with its bed, chair and sink."

"There's a common bathroom on every floor, Gerardo."

Despite the tight discipline he maintained over his logical apparatus, it was impossible for Aleluya to avoid certain lapses into free association. He repeated the word "common" and imagined the happy period of early Christianity with its still warm communism, fresh from the oven, pure and tender and soft, utterly rejecting the subsequent sclerosis, the crowded processions of candelabra and vestments. Common, of the community, he said, for the benefit of all he should help to keep the place clean, but when they inspected the bathroom they realized that there wasn't room for one more piece of paper. They even found a page from the NY Times announcing the devaluation of the dollar. The chips of soap were relics from the Museum of Natural History. Surprisingly, the shower didn't drip— not even when Gerardo turned on the faucet—but Calabrio assured him that he would take care of it soon, that for the time being, he could wash himself in the magnificent sink or in the swimming pool at the Commodore, the Sicilian added maliciously, but Gerardo ignored this with a shrug of his shoulders, thinking that it really didn't matter how dirty it was if he weren't going to eat out of it. That shit was covering the world was a fact that could be deduced by reading the papers, so there was no reason to get into a hassle over it; he would buy himself a basin to compliment the functions of the sink.

Aleluya was waiting while his dim-witted compatriot completed the contract. He realized that in this, as in any developed nation, a man's word is worth infinitely less than a pig's grunt or the swan's discordant song, for which reason it was necessary to deal with the whole gambit of contracts and signatures and seals and so forth. Calabrio said shit when the tenant timorously sketched his signature, then he crumpled the damage deposit in his hands and disappeared down the stairs.

"If you come in late, walk softly, Gerardo; I live in the room below yours," says Aley.

"Don't worry. Unless I come in after one drink too many."

"Do you drink a lot?"

"Not to excess."

"'Socially', eh? If you have further problems of the spirit, don't hesitate to consult me."

He captured the precise sense of this "further" which suggested the existence of problems which weren't necessarily those of the spirit.

"I'm hoping to run into my cousin Antulio. He knows the city, too."

"On the island of Manhattan alone there are more than three million people. Plus four million more who come in daily to do their shopping and business. You can imagine the rest. You may run into him in ten years by accident. Well, I must return to my labors. It would be best if you rested now."

Return to my labors. As if he didn't know any other expression. Aleluya turned with a precise motion, without allowing himself the least sideward fluctuation, and began to sink down the stairs, as if he were floating.

Gerardo dropped onto the bed, took off his shoes and fell onto his back. On the wall next to the bed he discovered an electrical outlet. To plug in a radio. But he immediately felt goose bumps all over because once, when he was a child, he'd played with a bare wire and a spark had jumped out and caused a short circuit. The incident had unleashed mysterious forces, established strange connections. He knew this because that night an electrical storm had been unleashed which lasted over two hours and had terrorized the entire neighborhood.

$$\frac{3}{\textbf{.}}$$

T HE DOMINICAN, Atila Piña, told him that he'd come for the same reason but no dice. He had a mustache and long dark sideburns and kinky hair and the youthful recipient of his words imagined banana covered mountains *merengues* Cibao Saint Peter of Macoría Rafael Leonides, things he'd heard talk of on his island—the smallest and most eastern of the major Antilles—an abundant Dominican population lives there

small merchants
bartenders
plumbers
maids
house painters
night watchmen
whores

soapbox orators
Third World spies
and the astronomical distances not withstanding he could imagine Laotians and Thais and Cambodians and Vietnamese of indistinguishable appearance living together in a city like Saigon, because the Ecuadorian, Glauco Hermosillo, also spoke up saying that he'd come for the same reason as the others but that so far no dice; his words floated on a puddle beneath his palate, melting as though he were making a hot chestnut jump on his tongue. The Argentinian, Macedonio Perusso, interrupted, speaking with an easily recognizable accent thanks to the innumerable *milongas* and *tangos* that the radiant island of Borikén had consumed for years and also thanks to the innumerable second-rate actors actresses in commercials of unmistakable Buenos Airean precedence who prosper from the radio television unimportant magazines of the aforementioned island. White-skinned, black-haired, hawk-faced, he shut out the Ecuadorian as he talked, the Ecuadorian who dragged his short stubby body, his anti-Hellenic nose and who radiated vexation with a skin color that was not of his country (oddly enough, Gerry's wasn't either!).

The Brazilian, João Braga da Cunha, chubby and brown haired, his hands in the pockets of his wide pants, agreed, smiled. His huge country, lashed by cruel droughts, furrowed by fabulous rivers and entangled jungles where the indigenous peoples maintain archaic cultures, weighed upon his conscience. Braga da Cunha was conscious of the wave of colorful advertising put out by travel agencies: Río, paradise on earth, carnivals; Brasilia resplendent in a jungle of rags; the folklorically dancing Carmen Miranda carried to every corner of the globe by Hollywood; Pelé, covered with sweat, kicking the ball; monstrous, inconceivable, tortured country; cinema nova; sertão.

Slight, with a huge head—giant glasses—the Japanese, Asho Jodoka, had a bag at his feet where he kept goods of unmistakable origin: the Nikon camera, the pocket Sony television, his Generalzubi ElectroKoda shaver, and a Japanese-English dictionary prepared by Tashio Okasama. He smiled without the slightest provocation, as though he were deliberately ignoring the fact that his companions were suffering from unemployment. But Asho Jodoka, spiritually molded by ancient Samurai doctrines, knew that his laughter was involuntary, that the black humor of thousands of carefully adminis-tered *hara kiris* had left this historic mark, this perennial smile upon the faces of his compatriots. And to please this group he barely murmured smilingly mor hir tin tair no untirstan toyota u taki mazda u taki no ki ri lei son Fujiyama.

The Chinese man, Tai Ken, smiled amiably shaking his extem-poraneous pigtail. Nevertheless, Tai Ken felt an ai-so-lei-shun from this enormous city of steel glass rock, and at night he would recreate his Cantonese childhood—before his parents' disastrous flight to Formosa—, the slow crystalline rivers, the tender, metaphysical dragons of his childhood, and the family dragon, Ton, captured and tamed by his father. With serene joy, Ton offered his long fiery tongues to the entire Ken family as central heat on cold nights. With slight bitterness, Tai Ken stated Confucianly itz aul don, song don, still anticipating that the Arab, Alí—fez, caftan, dromedary skin sandals—would begin his Koranic litany. Because right now his words would secrete a fathomless resentment. Shortly before, Alí had expressed, in a desert-like voice of wind through date-laden trees, his conception of a wealthy America, open to all peoples, an international oasis which would attract the nomads of the entire planet, far, in his case, from Berber stores and camels doomed to obsolescence (while, in America, there was a Ford in his future), far from depressing inaesthetic dromedaries whose nightly coughing made it seem as if an anti-Allah demon were blowing his terrible apocalyptic trumpet in the very center of Mecca, also far from the filthy Medinas (he didn't say a word about the Levees and Dunes) and from the hateful petroleum which serves only a small group of the privileged, but which couldn't quench the thirst of the dusty Bedouins and their mounts. But his illusions were shattered like a castle built upon the sands of the Sahara, because no sooner had he entered the factory where he hoped to find work than the owner, Moses Levy, began to shriek stridently at the sight of the applicant's aggressive dress. The Arab Alí recognized in the gesticulating bald man with his bulging forehead and hooked nose his ancient enemy number one, inexorable Zionist cabalist, Talmudic patron of the Six Day War, brutal speculator who, in his ancestral greed, was incapable of understanding the truly heinous significance that the often possessed and repossessed Wailing Wall contained for the sons of the Prophet Ishmael, supporter of Golda and the One-Eyed

Dayan on the land snatched from the Musulmanic soul. Alí gripped
the Koran tightly inside his jumbled pocket and hurled age-old
epithets and would have whipped out his beloved cutlass—if Immigration had not confiscated it—to behead his Israeli enemy with
lyrical precision. An instant intuitive Arab warrior, Alí was thrown
out of the enemy's factory by force, cursing between clenched teeth
Allah halvah all thah muttah.

Through his small, sharp Pelopennesian eyes, the Greek, Spiro
Octapoulos, looked at the young man with his curly reddish hair, his
frightened blue eyes and heavy worker's hands bronzed by the sun and
the salty Caribbean air. The young man felt his personal, internal,
churning breeze blow through the interstices of his delicate brain. He
had just finished listening resignedly to the words of the foreman of
the factory, a bald, chubby American who told him simply, "No, I'm
sorry, my lad". The Cuban, Fulgencio Guerra, said Havana-esquely
that this city is rough, *mi socio*, it bunns for them that wokk hadd and
for the white colla wokker. No' jus' de ceetee, says the Dominican,
Atila Piña, de ho' contree. The Brazilian, Braga da Cunha, commented that ther se less hopp in e eslumm do Brasil, *fina carioca dansa
do Minas Gerais, candombe* an' *bossa* an' *nova E pirhuana ne' er
coum doon do mautahn.* You would have been saved, *che*, intervenes
Macedonio, if you were a musician, you'd be rollin' in the dough,
*pibe*, but if you were a soccer player like Tostão, out of sight! Glauco
Hermosillo said, in Ecuador eets worse then anywheah, haff-breeds
an' sambos bye god they sons of beetches United Fruit, ayayai cow
sheet in they poor shacs oh thinking of his country divided by the line
which bore the nation's name: he could put a foot on either side and
the line would rise secretly to his crotch, placing one testicle in the
northern hemisphere and the other in the southern hemisphere;
innumerable tourists who take photographs of this tortured belt of the
globe, beautiful names: Quito, Guayaquil, by God! The Japanese,
Asho Jodoka, interrupts, hirohitally, cutting him off, Amerika it iz
fokt and Spiros Octapoulos, suspecting that his friends could barely
understand him, pronounced every word carefully: Aristodoto assix
Amerika, oucanni maggine thee resstis, skairsitti kalamari marathon
octopus costagavras. Oh, brother! exclaims Atila Piña, and the young
man with the blue eyes and the curly red hair says in Puelto Rico, it's
the same: we let 'em fock us in the real. Tai Ken stated, ah soo, no pan

tzon. No bols ei tir, spit Jodoka. The sharp, black and lashy eyes of Octopoulos hurled sparks of the Olympic lightning, likki swarrum gnattos, thanatos raggidous anthropos raggidous, kronos stoppodos kursis, he ended, looking at his wrist watch. ¡*Pucha*! exclaims Macedonio, look at what time it be, *che*. Where do you live? Le sing ton, says the Chinese, Tai Ken. And Jodoka comments, pointing into the distance, iko tat wai, tir mai om mai boi. I live in the Village, says the Cuban, Fulgenico Guerra, not in the best, mind you; the truth be told, Manhattan has been hurt by all the riff-raff, tú. I'm going to Rico, where they still speak Spanish and it isn't cold, tú.

The Rican looked at Guerra, but he wasn't thinking about anything. He felt a weary irritation and a clear discomfort or perhaps the desire for time to run wild like a horse. He felt a rubbery dizziness, like a *guanábana* ready to fall from a tree and, at the same time, the firm bulge of his ex-machetero's muscles, that could be merciless when necessary. Macedonio seemed to sense something: "What's happening with you, *pibe*?"

"Nu ting. Om feelin' lo'."

Tai Ken, the Chinese, looked at him fraternally, agreeing: this is what a shake of the head means in the Far East, codified mystery of universal gestures, perhaps not so much with what the words meant, but because of the unusual nature of Cantonese phonetics in that to one not initiated into oriental languages it would seem to be possible to represent these words in perfect ideograms charmingly traced by an enlightened citizen of those distant lands. "Om feelin' lo'", a phrase probably coined during the period of the venerable Sinanthropist and strictly preserved into the Chou dynasty—to the joyous politico-religious satisfaction of Confucius and Lao Tsu—on through dynasties such as the Ching and, unless there had been some error on the part of the most learned Sinologists, even the subsequent Han dynasty would have accepted such perfect diction with the unmistakable flavor of his country and the successive and ineffable Tang and Ming would have acknowledged with a precise sense of justice the entire historical import that these simple, but profound words carried, in accordance with the Chinese outlook and tradition created during the aforementioned Chou dynasty. And, strangest of all, this expression had developed on an island smaller than the treacherous Formosa—a deformation of the word Fermosa with which the Gallicians had baptized it centuries before—so distant from those latitudes, located precisely in the antipodes—if they had not been extirpated from the throat of the planet—and situated in the Caribbean Sea, truly, the sea of darkness. It was clear that Tai Ken meditated intensely and profoundly for a few seconds, basing himself every second on the fragile structure of the yin and yang lotus, supposed to be deliciously contradictory in a perpetual and not always secret motion of approach and retreat, moved by an impulse as vulgarly explicable as that of electrical connectors: the female part that waits despairingly until the male connector joins it to achieve the mysterious cosmic equilibrium?, the Hellenic androgyny?, the Anglo-Saxon gay power? The subject was an enigma founded precisely in the dynamic possibilities of every dialectic. Nevertheless, the polyglot  Rican was far from perceiving the quietly electric current which his phrase had provoked in the mind of the exiled post-Maoist, the simple and perpetual symbols of an imagination enriched under the shelter of such yellowly romantic rivers as the Hoang Ho and the Sung-Koi and of such glorious legendary spots as Yenan. Was Formosa an unobtrusive geopolitical appendix of the continental mother country? Was the Caribbean island not only a geological appendix, but also ideologically, politically, culturally, historically torn from its mother, that is, from the continent from the Rio Grande south/Tai Ken's four seconds of intensive thought reached a rapid conclusion for the one, a slow one for the other—Belg Son concept of time, thought the Chinese—and Tai Ken looked at his watch and said by means of a metaphorical and allegorical statement what he thought of the Caribbean country:

"Fo kin."

Perversely secretive, with open semantic occultism he wished to contain in this brief statement all the tragedy which, nevertheless, the Rican was not certain that he understood. Tai Ken understood the ancient ill in its entirety: regions governed by thick shadows, stupid movements that march against cosmic harmony, giants that exterminate delicate dragons—symbols of all the loveliness and tenderness imaginable—foreign spirits dedicated to patrolling unknown seas. A sweet memory fluttered in Tai Ken's soul: a forest of birch trees, boats floating softly upon a river reddened by the newborn sun—a planetary occurrence which the Japanese had appropriated in a typically imperialistic manner to create the national metaphor par excellence—and he laughed softly to himself at the gross simplifications of his enormous country which were promulgated by the West: duck a la orange, acupuncture, Fu Man Chu, Kung Fu, the Wall, *The Good Earth* and other bits of nonsense spread through the West by men of a historically funerary color. How could he return, not to Lexington Avenue in this city of skyscrapers, nor to the traitorous Taiwan, but to his Cantonese village? Would his compatriots in New York give up their dry cleaning establishments and their restaurants serving fake Tzechwan food to aid him in these moments of forced unemployment? Anyone with a smattering of Confucian readings would realize that his case was not the same as that of the young man with blue eyes and the large peasant hands who looked at him attentively, blinking his eyes, the handsome white whose homeland happened to coincide cosmically with his by adoption through the miracle of a phrase necessarily drawn from the history of both countries: Om feelin' lo'. Despite the fact that all these whites were as much alike as drops of water in a spring thundershower. On the other hand, every Chinese is as clear as a pool, an uncontaminated pond, the river flowing down from the heights of the mountain Tsing Ling! Looking into their faces is to read an open book, to decipher the clear message of the lilies at dawn, to see oneself in the crystalline waters of the Yellow River. The men of the West were identical in their external appearance and in their minds, produced on an assembly line. And, all this aside, he was here, concretely in Spanish Harlem. Moved to the roots of his flowering cherry tree, he said to the young man who looked at him in fascination:

"Lau-tse?"

The youthful Rican could not escape a strong magnetic wave of overpowering attraction, and said rashly:

"Hor-ri-bil."

This went down easily for Tai Ken, except for the articulation of this abstruse sound, not to be found in the tongues of his country, this disastrous "rr" which, to date, western man had not been able to eradicate, carrying with it, as with all its horrors, an inconceivable physiological aberration which tended to deteriorate the stability of the voice box and of the tongue—sacred organ, delicately reproductive within limits—with this useless, ridiculous and forced multiple vibration, which did not naturally follow the lyrical meanderings of expression one could expect from men who had achieved a certain cultural development which, although misled from its very origins, had its merits. His Chinese ancestors had ferociously eliminated the inexçusable sound, for which reason his first ancestor, the aforementioned venerable Sinanthropist, still kept, even to this day, his skull in a state of perfect health. So, do the westerners laugh until they cry when a Chinese says "lich" instead of "rich"? Confucius knew better than that. Infinitely more than the Cretins from Crete and the other Greeks, that gang of sodomites and charlatans adored by the barbaric peoples who sucked, not only from Athens, but from Sparta, a culture which by all accounts ran counter to the secret rhythms of nature. Them and their gods! Zeus, clearly, was a cuckold dedicated to raping any nymph who happened to fall into his ferocious Olympic Mediterranean claws. All this mythological garbage had anchored the Western world in a maremagnum of shitorum inconfessablis, thought Tai Ken in a Latin learned from the Jesuits. These guys who finally liquidated one Christ and afterwards spent entire centuries crying over it and, to top it off, this avalanche of philosophers engaged in proving the premise that the world is not the world, that the thick steak that they devour exemplarily is not a steak but its ideal image. Reality is not reality, but its complete opposite: in the meantime, they digest and, within a reasonable period of time, expel from their bodies, with vulgar materialism, the image of the steak swallowed with such obstinate idealism. And he immediately remembered his small Hispanic neighbor on Lexington, a little girl deformed by a counterhuman culture, reciting her absurd tongue twister near Tai Ken's window: "Around the rough and rugged rocks/ the ragged rascal ran."

The first time he heard such a suicidal monstrosity, Tai Ken locked himself in his room, horrified and trembling from head to toe. To exorcise the threat, he converted it to a more mellifluous and civilized sound: "Alound the lough and lugged locks, the lagged lascal lan." It was a question of simple and necessary peaceful coexistence, he thought now, looking sympathetically at his little neighbor's compatriot, equally misled. The Boricua remained at his side, gazing at him with the serenity of a genuine Buddhist monk, taken by an ataraxia which could only be achieved in the self-respecting pagodas which did not open themselves up to the tourists' cameras as, he thought, happens in the Shinto temples of today's deplorable Japan.

The blue Rican eyes scrutinized him with tranquil fascination. At this moment, did a mellifluous forty ton dragon hover beside the young man to favor him with his blessing? and, when all is said and done, who invented gunpowder, the compass, China ink? The Boricua came over to him and embraced him warmly while a honey sweetness flooded his soul. The word "sugarwater" flowed into his graceful tropical Antillian mind, and he feared that a rock candy would appear somewhere in his body, the uncomfortable actualization of all the sweetness appropriate to his homeland's latitude.

"Ciao", he said warmly in parting.

Tai Ken responded with mysterious solicitude.

"Lin-chao."

F ANTASTIC METALLIC WORMS
perforating the darkness;
hurtling to a stop with a clatter
of scrap metal,
agonized metal,
metal turning furiously against metal,
the cars smash into each other
disappear into the sinister caverns
Flatbush Bronx Brooklyn Queens,
red lights blink
before the men women children who
fill the platform "with all my love",
the velocity disfigures
the jumbled faces in the expresses,

windows from train to train create
a magical illusory game,
kaleidoscope,
frozen rapid motion
> Jesus Saves
> Love
> Tom y Margarita
> Fuck

advertisements for rye bread, airlines; heat noise fuse in a detestable clump while the mini-skirted girl swaying her hips on the stairs above oh to be the loving cloth that covers her you know what, you immediately fall into the coldly programmed burning heart of the myth

TIMES SQUARE!!!

OH!!

UGH!!!

movie marquees, the greasy smell of the fast food joints, mouthfuls of spiced air, greasy corn-on-the-cob steakhouse turnovers pizzeria the store windows display hard core underground porn, sex shops rubber phalluses, vibrators whips leather straps, horsily human harnesses you stand surprised

THE MOST BEAUTIFUL GIRLS IN EUROPE
ONLY FOR MEN
DEEP THROAT
THE HONEYMOON KILLERS
Two years of unparalleled success!

curvaceous effeminate youths caress each other on the billboard of a movie theater, films about monsters from outer space abound, westerns, at the corner of Sixth Avenue the girl in a bikini offers you an enormous cold Fanta, further on you face expensive show windows glassware shining doorways, completely extravagant, you don't realize that from the other bank of the Hudson you could see Manhattan as an ordinary model crammed with rectangles beneath the perpetually grey sky, stair-stepped roofs, the ever present pointed Empire State Building, the shiny flat-topped United Nations building, you wouldn't really see the streets but long grooves like incisions from a knife between the mechanical geometrically aligned boxes, shimmering in the distance it's like a city given over to terror and desperation,

which one flees like the plague, the anthill of Brooklyn outside with
its low irregular houses, the somber Bronx raised in grey black stone,
the green breathing stain of Central Park stretched out in the center of
the island, the trees bushes crushed by the industrialized quality of the
air; a motley dirty aimless multitude walks jeans slacks shorts wide-
brimmed hats, miniskirts bare midriffs
PIZZERIA NAPOLES
    you immediately recognize the combined smell of baked dough,
tomato sauce, mozzarella. The black-haired counterboy—scars of a
tropical smallpox on his pointy face—looks at you for a minute,
smiles.
    "Hot, isn't it?"
    You say yes. That you've walked half of New York looking for
work, you know, I got here three weeks ago. You bite the steaming
corner of the triangle of pizza.
    "They've wiped out more than three thousand jobs in the last
three years," the counterboy serves an Italian ice to a greedy black
boy. "The street is hard."
    "I have a license. I could drive a taxi."
    "Don't get into that," the scar-faced fellow shooed the large
healthy American flies. "They hold them up, they kill them. And you
don't know the city. What are you gonna do if they ask you for the
Bowery, Canal Street, Bleeker Street? Aren't you doing anything
now?"
    "I help out in a market, La Placita. And also at Dutch's bar. A
black American. But I need something sure that's not dangerous.
They stabbed a guy."
    "Where?"
    "In the chest."
    "No," the counterboy laughs. "In what part of the city?"
    "He died on the spot. On upper Lexington. In Dutch's bar."
    "Did you see it?"
    "Dutch told me after the police left."
    "So you weren't a witness?"
    "I wasn't there. I wasn't a witness. He turned white. As black as
he is."
    "Who are you talking about?"
    "And he shook. Dutch. I already told you. The police asking

questions without really caring."

"They're like that," says the counterboy, ringing up the register. "I know them well."

"One kicked the dead man."

"There's no compassion."

"The dead man was lying on the floor."

"A long time?"

"He had the knife stuck in his chest. About two hours."

"Until the coroner came."

"In a puddle of blood. With the knife stuck in to where it says made in Japan."

"Wow, man."

"He insulted this guy."

"He killed him for that?"

"The guy didn't want to give him something."

"Oh. Of course, the drug."

"They left him lying there. This guy pulled his knife out and stuck it in up to the hilt. The coroner came afterwards. That's when I showed up. The people were calm, like a horse had died."

"It depends on the horse. Some are worth a fortune."

"Nobody cared. When they carried him away, Dutch washed the floor. Then he put *salsa* music on the jukebox. Willie Colón, Ray Barreto, Eddie Palmieri."

"Do you like *salsa*?"

"Some of it. Then a black woman arrived and began to yell. The dead guy was real young, thin and he had a goatee. The woman got on Dutch's case and ripped his shirt. She was the dead man's sister; she said he was her brother."

"They call each other that even if they're not brothers. Soul brothers, you know. But, maybe so."

"When I went to play a song, my shoe got stuck. I had just washed the floor."

"Lay off it, man."

"The blood smells bad. Dutch got drunk. He said he wasn't upset about the fucking stiff, that's what he always says, but because he'd have to go to court."

"No one likes to drink where someone's been killed."

"So drunk he could hardly stand. Dutch says it doesn't matter.

That this was the third one in two years."

"Dutch's bar is no playground."

"But there're always customers. They never stay away. The first one was an Irishman who was a policeman. They were watching him. Four shots. The second one, knocked on the head with a pipe. He was putting the make on a Latina and kaboom!"

"What a jungle, man!"

"There're so many wounded that Dutch doesn't even count them. One day, this chick came in and started flirting with him. Dutch took her into the corner and they were real tight, you know, getting down, and this guy came in and tried to clean out everything in the register. Dutch gave it to him with a chair and left him lying there bleeding on the floor."

"And the chick?"

"They worked together. He gave her a kick in the ass and 'bye-bye, baby'."

"So much violence. You'll see. You haven't been here long."

"Three weeks. But I already know."

"Four men caught a student on the subway; they raped and choked her. At one in the morning. The politicians want the electric chair again, but that won't solve anything. What's your name?"

"Gerardo."

"I'm Miguel. When they invented it, it didn't work right. It burned some parts of the condemned or it roasted them. They didn't die all at once. But they've perfected it. They're great at that."

"In the three weeks I've been here, I haven't been able to see my cousin."

"People move away and you never see a trace of them again."

"His name is Antulio. I went to his address, but no luck."

"Hum. And if he moved to Brooklyn, I'll warn you. You have to think twice about catching the subway. At full speed, it takes about an hour. You can imagine the rest. Brooklyn is nothing but a city, and they even speak English different. You know, the people from there."

"That's what they've always told me about Brooklyn."

"On the subway the people look at you, and when you look back, they look away. That's why most of them have newspapers. So they don't have to look you in the eye. They're afraid to look at each other. Like they're ashamed. After a while, you start to talk to yourself on the subway. That's how you know if someone's been here a while. And laughing to yourself, too."

"That's true. I've seen a lot of that."

"We're the only ones who laugh and carry on."

"And we talk a lot on the subway."

"We're not as serious as they are, you know. You have to know how to live life."

"Of course."

The counterboy smiles at the girl who appears disruptively, transparent nylon blouse the disturbing fringe oh, oh the delicious coppertone fringe of her waist bellybutton island, the island oh, tight faded jeans they call them denim pants in other places, and you, Gerry, you look, you can't help it because it's been a long time since; you look your crotch violently restrained by the denim cloth, spongy padded triangle raising itself a little toward you when the girl eases her buttocks onto the stool and lets her stubborn rebelliously bare feet hang, the dyed blonde hair over the tanned white oval, small Czech or Polish nose (how are you to know!), you realize that your crotch is activating calling telegraphically for the one you see, called violently to attention, reminding you with sharp recognizable discomfort that for a long time you haven't been close to what do you call it, take it off, take it off, wherein to enter a certain moist environment ay. And it turns out that when she's introduced to you her name is Shirley, a *bien chévere* chick, says Mickey, you discern the smooth stomach breathlessly, the beginnings of the two slight posterior half moons marked by a coldly white shadow burning where the luxurious sun of Broadway New York City USA has not been, you look briefly into the depths of the blouse where light conical thick pendulums jiggle which graze the cloth freely, her thighs flatten slightly against the stool, you suddenly realize that you've scarcely even looked at her face, that you sound her, you trap her in your mind like fish in a violently flung net; an embracing gaze in which you capture until death her strong, strangely regal, erotic image, but a tall thin muscular figure enters your field of vision and pauses beside Shirley, his fingers ringed with white metal stroke the faded WASP hair (if it is, perhaps it's Slavic); the young man combs a round Afro which from a distance makes him look like a long pin with an enormous head, wearing pre-faded jeans and the lone star flag of Borinquen sewed on the left shoulder of his

denim jacket (!), Newyorican badge patent pending, and the brief
Newyorican show of affection is enough to make you decide to face
the hard interminable Broadway wilting beneath the August sun at
four pm you arrive at the corner of 86th street after an exhausting walk

FIRST NATIONAL CITY BANK

CHINA GARDEN

Tzechuan Foods

a melancholy discomfort in looking around you, wide sidewalks
to your left extend to the western limits of Manhattan, Broadway
(although it's been mentioned already!), the West End, Riverside
Drive!, what a lovely street! from which you can make out the heavy
colorless Hudson, sailboats, ferries, ships, beyond the long narrow
park filled with old bums absorbed in their newspapers as with old
unresolved battles. You come to Amsterdam Avenue which extends
bordered by buildings of the same size and catastrophic age (except
the new multi-level cooperative on 88th), the Alcoa aluminum hangs
over everything that catches your upward moving gaze below, construction sites surrounded by chain-link fence where the bulldozers
grunt pushing frightening masses of post-industrial garbage

BODEGA LA ISLA

DOMINICAN RESTAURANT

fruits tropical vegetables gasping in open boxes on the sidewalk;
when the cars, trucks, motorcycles, buses, pushcarts, bicycles bow
reverentially before the blush of the traffic light; feeling vexed, you
cross the length of this moment of crackling heat, you leave behind the
old three story homes, vaguely manorial porches, stairs with wrought
iron railings, resonant hallways of dark wood, pointed roofs, garrets
as mysterious as the old people peering from their windows, teenagers
playing jumping afros jeans, apathetic trees—how few remain, you
think with your head full of leaves, militant chlorophyll, sap, burning
resin—when you suddenly recognize the intersection of Columbus
Avenue and 88th,

BROADWAY CASINO

VIBA DON PEDRO ALBISU

RICHIE RAY AND HIS ORCHESTRA

you go down 86th, land on Central Park West; to your left
stretches Central Park with its promontories covered by groves of
trees, plazas crammed with a multicolored multitude, balloons, pairs

of lovers beneath the trees, old folks sunning themselves on the iron benches, young Latinos make the air resound with their drums. You board the enormous dark blue thirty five cent bus, Shirley's braless breasts dance in your tranquil excited memory, to speak with total frankness, wouldn't you throw her down beneath a mango tree in an enclosure smelling of manure (if any still remain); Shirley naked firm beneath you, your hands ringed with white metal stroke the straw-colored hair (or Polish or Czech, it's the same thing); you reject this denigrating scene with secret pensive sadness then you see her against the walls which line the road that crosses the park behind which the treetops crowd and peer out, hey baby pull down your panties and give it to me, you think give me what but you're not referring now to anything in particular, forcing yourself to toss the erotic nude image from your head, you would make her come four times, better nailed than a tack in a board, baby, you think with your blood at one hundred degrees (centigrade, naturally); on the seat in front of you a lamentably ancient black woman observes you without joy or hatred looking away and holding tightly to two plastic bags from Gimbels department store; Fifth Avenue glides beneath the wheels; huge apartment buildings, solemn porticos, important liveried doormen, extensive terraces upstairs with colorful umbrellas; leaning forward, twisting your neck, you discover flowerpots in bloom, where are the garbage cans, honey, the elegant garbage? American Beauty. The Metropolitan Museum of Art on your right, do you have to wear a jacket to enter? Chakit, as the Cuban Guerra says,

LEXINGTON AVENUE

the bus purrs people get on get off, strange how one gets used to places, a Harlemnian nostalgia overcomes you for a few seconds and you almost shout down with the elegant neighborhoods!, you think all of this with the calmness which certain hours impose on you; the ancient black Old Grand Dad smiles on a huge billboard, children playing in the stream from a fire hydrant beautifully assaulted by the neighborhood, you will throw yourself into bed before going to Dutch's bar, with what you earn you don't even have enough for cigarettes, you don't earn much more at La Placita but there at least um hum, Caty, this egg needs salt. She's not thin and firm like Shirley, but over the proper weight, light skinned with indigenously straight black hair, you have to content yourself with what the boat brought;

dark bars with dark customers, wood impregnated by generations of whiskey fumes; the light wounds your sensitive pupils born in a certain dazzling latitude (it's not the light, but the overwhelmingly grey quality of this sky); you know you're too shy to think to excess, humble as a dog but knowing in the depths, in the depths of a place in
  your head, that if they poke you a bit, just a little bit they'll find
  a certain steel
  better said, a certain metal
  a certain incalculable fortitude
the next thing you know you're asking yourself when you'll get back to your room, Jesus Christ, to the sonorous lonely spaciousness of your room. Before Dutch. B.D. and also A.D.; your brain's call for rest doesn't bring up the image of your narrow and sagging bed but
  a pair of dusty shoes
  certainly well worn,
  dusty shoes that walk far
  without stopping
  walking
  shoes
  dust
  melting asphalt
  walking
  but, rather, hallucinatingly

$$\frac{5}{\phantom{x}} \cdot$$

**W**HO IS WHO? The Polish fellow. Black eyes round livid face. Flattened boxer's nose that was never, caftan three-quarter sleeves deliberately dirty cream jeans. With his white disheveled albino Polish mane and his room rocking with

Baez
Joplin
The Rolling Stones
Soul Train you make me feel brand new

Gerardo gazing sleeplessly rudely awakened the blinking light of the bar on the other side of the street red light, yellow, violet shadow. From the roof, in the darkness, hang romantic bananas, mangos, many intensely green leaves, dampness; finding a wild fruit hanging over his noble face, once more the stream beneath his bed so that if he rolled over he could put his hand into cool water and dampen his serious forehead, his brow of the total man, his blue sweetly solitary foreigner's eyes. Useless, the Pole always has his music going, he'd already told him and nothing, not listening, much less understanding. Gerardo wasn't up for violent measures right now, not yet, but he knew that his punch connecting with the Slav's chin would be like lightning. When he couldn't take it anymore, then.

Obviously the aforementioned character wasn't the only one. What could he say about this ineffable creature? The young man with the deliciously copper skin, the bright red curly hair. With his huge wide green eyes shadowed by long blonde lashes. He moved, leapt, pranced about on tiptoe with the agility of a ballerina. Gerald looked at him that way. Like a cat at a mouse. Or something like that. Almost treacherously. Not without a certain degree of sympathy. As one would look at a yucca sprout which grows where the soil is hard as a bone and the sun scorches it. Almost protectively, but with a certain control, almost moved. And then, what could he do if he were put off balance, struggling with expressions like

Everyone has a right to

Tell me who you hang out with and I can tell you

thinking about the name of the lovely youth, Tom Kress, who arose looking toward the interior of the pitiful room on the second floor, gazing cautiously over the heads of the other strange characters, less colorful than he, Tom, Mr. Kress. Whose door, let it be said in passing, was directly across from Gerald's

MR. TOM KRESS

and

MRS. ANNE COUVERT

With astonishment, he'd watched Mrs. Anne Couvert arrive in the morning, a fleeting narcotic vision, huge red roses decorating her lilac dress, slender, tall, hair flowing like a midnight waterfall (forgive me) down her thin delicate vulnerable shoulders, looking into the mailbox one afternoon she'd seen Gerardo, her big eyes had been fixed on him—as dazzlingly grey as were the intentions of the confused but resolute Boricua at that moment; Anne's bangs covered her eyebrows so that her eyes were as they say feline in their strange electrifying gaze, her emerald green outfit, knickers, the V back, her arms adorned with sinner's serpentine post paradisiacal bracelets. The next step would be to knock on her door while the young Mr.

Kress was absent, naturally, thought the Boricua. With any excuse. To borrow a needle, ask her for the time, tell her it was hot out. Perhaps, like an old fashioned girl, she'd offer to mend his proverbial socks (oh wow) and thus would begin a period of total happiness; he slipping into her room, she slipping into his room, and so on, but always very excited, you know, baptizing everything with abundant semen, you know. And then it turned out that it wasn't necessary to go to such lengths (to the third floor) because he found her in the lonely doorway and said four stumbling lovely things to her which made her blush and lower her long modest black lashes. But, who would have dreamt that the doorway would be occupied? For, by the elevator he saw the infallible shadow, the very Aleluya himself, severely friendly, he who pricks the evil consciences of many, then she oh fluttered upstairs delicate luxurious vision in the deplorable frame of the building. Modestly, chaste, Gerardo had become as red as his hair: beet red, his cheeks redly rouged, his purely pure blue eyes gazed at the floor full of grey and black sins, breathless, once more timid but always prepared to defend himself. A disgraceful comment occurred to him:

"I hope she doesn't tell Kress. I don't want any trouble."

"*She is Kress.*"

Gerardo with his mouth open. Not understanding a word.

"You don't believe me?" asks Aley. "The day you see Tom Kress and Anne Couvert together, you let me know. Then I'll believe in miracles. Kress has his high class beauty salon for dames on Fifth Avenue, of course. Even Jackie herself, the ineffable merry widow, entrusts him with her sweet face, her lovely hair. I don't understand why he lives here."

"Jackie?"

Aleluya disregarded the deplorable limitations of his compatriot's mind.

"You never know what to expect from an eccentric. Outside of his circle. Or because, in the final analysis, he's very marginal."

"But, I've even dreamed about her! I mean, about..."

The imperturbable Aley, looking through his things, his finger on the bridge of his horn-rimmed glasses, grave, ceremonious, but shaken by subterranean laughter (it could be, after all!).

"His last happening was two months ago. Fantastic open improvisation. Come what may, you know. Blame it on his split personality.

It had only been two days since he'd moved into the building. Thus, Calabrio and I believed faithfully in the little sign: a young married couple, the young married couple on the third floor. On the third day, they didn't ascend to heaven, forgive me, but we heard her terrifying shrieking. Mister Kress was beating Miss Couvert who, we thought, retained her maiden name because of her work. One of those things between man and wife, you know. But the thing went on too long. When Calabrio went up the stairs, I reacted. The shouting: "Help, help, this brute is gonna kill me!" It sounded as if he were breaking the furniture on her ribs. I thought about her fragility, about her wounded butterfly appearance. We were going to break down the door, but it wasn't necessary: the battered Anne managed to escape the ogre's claws and opened the door. Everything was turned upside down. The upholstered Louis the something furniture upside down, the purple crepe curtains torn, broken plates, windows, pictures at all angles, the records of Viennese waltzes scattered all over the floor. Anne cried tremblingly on Dino Calabrio's virile shoulder, without the beautiful black wig, revealing her thin adolescent chest, without the foam rubber supports. She had one green eye and one grey, a subtle point I noted immediately and which was due to the loss of one contact lens fallen in the course of the scuffle. Only the false eye lashes on her left eye remained. Her make-up had run from her bitter tears, a disaster, lad! In one corner was a rather primitive character, torn from a jungle novel in the style of Don Eustasio, half-drunk. He had recovered a certain lucidity after beating the fragile beauty. He seemed frightened, more than anything else, upset by the turn of events: a sweet daisy of the salon had been transformed into a virile thistle in his very hands. I realized that he was from Guatemala, with his imagination full of Miguelangelasturianoesque enigmas and other common features of the Third World. But he couldn't understand such a metamorphosis: that a winged quetzal could have become a slithering anaconda. Let them tell me about the magic-realism of the Latin American novelists! Dino Calabrio asked...her, him, he didn't know to what he was talking... He finally asked the creature who was crying on his shoulder: 'And Mr. Kress, where is Mr. Kress?' To which the creature responded: 'That's me.' Calabrio couldn't believe it and asked: 'And where is Miss Couvert?' To which the creature sobbingly responded: '*Mademoiselle Couvert c'est moi!*', in the manner appropriate to a high class Fifth Avenue stylist. The Pole said shit, he's one of them, leave him alone, and went to his room to continue smoking his pot. The Guatemalan went scurrying between the legs of the bystanders and went down the stairs in less than two seconds. Oh, of course, Gerry, you should know that this doesn't happen everyday. The beaus drawn magically to the attractive always lively Couvert's cubicle habitually leave after this tremendous surprise, their reality turns upside down, there's an argument, perhaps a slap, the door slams: the guest goes away perplexed, without yet believing in rainbow fishes, the simplest fact is placed in doubt and it may even be possible that two plus two do not equal four, so that, farewell, frustrated love. But don't think that it's always so dramatic. Most of the time, the beau goes along with it: if you can't get bread, take crackers. The beau will think that the street is hard, and the shortage of money and love, he just shuts his eyes or half-shuts them and, why not!, he takes what's given. Do you understand now, Gerald, that they're two people in one? Look at them play the role of Mr. Kress: youthful, limber, gracious. I don't know if it's a woman who wishes to be a man or a man who dreams of being a woman. But, does it make a difference? Does this story have any meaning? None, compared with death! Poor Mr. Blake, poor old man, after so much suffering!"

And Gerardo said that probably the whole world out there, the curious, would ask themselves why the ungainly Mr. Blake hung with tragic perpendicularity to the floor, above the overturned chair, his head leaning toward his shoulder, the rope attached to the ceiling.

This is why they were all there: the Pole, Aleluya, Anne Couvert-Tom Kress, Dino Calabrio, the family from the second floor who-never-pays-their-rent and other strange characters who only came to sleep in their rooms: old people, young, blacks, Boricuas, Dominicans. All squeezed together, looking at the photograph that seemed to gaze into the contorted face of the venerable dead man: a Blake overflowing with happiness beside his wife and two small children, behind a luxurious 1940 shiny black car. She, a little plump, her hair frizzed in the style of the times; he, with a jacket, hat pushed back but still with tremendous composure, a dignity that was maintained into the present moment which arose from those remote distant unnameable times. The girl held a doll as big as she was; the boy held up a small replica of his father's luxurious car. But, to the side, the reality of the recent years: the bed a shambles as though a horrible nightmare had prevented his sleep, a night table with two empty bottles of cheap whiskey, and massive piles of newspapers reaching to the ceiling.

"Did they inform his son?", asks Aleluya.

Calabrio looked at him, grunted. Then he says:

"He said he'd come when he had time."

"He'll wait till he rots," says the Pole. "Shit!"

"Death is always terrible," shuddered Anne Kress. "We are not prepared."

"No one's born to be a rock," philosophized the Boricuan Gerry. "That's the only thing we know for sure."

Then, like in an episode from Cannon or what's his name, the paraplegic in the wheelchair, a police siren wails. Action, excitement, here come the blue coats! Calabrio's Sicilian face showed signs of tremendous discomfort, some type of mysterious nausea, a certain hatred, he would vomit if the siren didn't stop. The Pole was now on the landing with his body leaning parallel to the rotting handrail, a runner waiting for the detonation zap! to run out shooting boom!

"Shit!" says his voice, now from the fourth floor, his blond invisible presence. "Let them take the scarecrow."

"He runs from him like the devil from the cross!" laughed Calabrio bitterly. "The poor Mr. Blake, who was a saint, dead, and this pervert alive and kicking."

"*Así es la vida*," pronounced the Puerto Rican philosopher with the huge worker's hands and the tanned salty skin, and he translated for the benefit of those who did not speak his beloved tongue: Such is life.

A black cop and a white cop contemplated the corpse from up close. The black cop spoke brilliantly.

"He's real dead," he said.

The white cop surpassed him in ingenuity:

"We have to call the coroner. Where's the superintendent?"

Calabrio doubled over and forcefully covered his mouth with his clenched Italian hand. He was going to vomit right there! Aleluya touched him gently, firmly, on one shoulder. Calabrio stood up. To Gerardo he resembled, at this critical moment, the detective Colombo, but only at this moment.

"That's me," Dino said.

"Who discovered the body?" the white cop asked him.

Quivering all over, unable to control a traitorous attack of nerves, Tom Couvert approached with inviting eyes, white teeth chewing on his (her?) long index finger, nibbling on it sensually.

"I, sir. I returned from a party and was surprised to see the door open. It was six in the morning. I put my head in and..."

"Saw him," said the black cop.

"Let him finish, Friday. Was there any light?"

"My God, it was macabre. Yes, the little lamp on the table."

The white cop turned to Dino Calabrio.

"What was the name of the deceased?"

"Blake. Seymour L. Blake."

The white cop and the black cop gazed confusedly at the contorted hanging face whose former line of sight led them to the photo on the wall: in effect, this was the celebrated Seymour L. Blake oh gosh gulp. Friday didn't recover from his astonishment and said with the whites of his eyes and his fat African lips:

"The same one who...?"

"Exactly" Calabrio affirmed, determined to appease his antipolicial nausea.

"Let Friday finish!" interrupted the white cop.

Friday completed the question in this manner:

"The Blake who worked in the Department of Traffic in the city?"

"Seymour L. Blake," said Calabrio proudly.

The white cop was left breathless also, his shamrock green Irish eyes looked perplexedly at the Sicilian. He stammered, he choked, he could hardly holy cow express Saintpatrickally what he felt. He only said:

"The prophet?"

"Anda whatta elsa?" Dino burst out. And he added words of the purest Tuscanese derivation: "Basttardo, fucka yourselfa, the cunt of the Madonna who bore you! Look at the pictures! He's the same man!"

"Call the coroner, Friday! This is going to hit the front page. Does he have any relatives?"

Dino Calabrio held onto the door, sweating like a dog; a wave of nausea knocked him over almost making him lose his balance squeezing his mouth his tanned Mediterranean anti-Duce head green with seasickness. He finally set aside the repugnance inspired by the blue uniform and said:

"A son. One, he has."

Which made Gerardo the Good think about human relations families fathers sons mommy the baby of the house and sum it all up with profound Puerto Rican wisdom:

"Raise crows..."

And he repeated the maxim two three four times and they'll pluck your eyes out wandering from one side of his room to the other while Aleluya observed him from his friendly perch on the bed, his legs stretched out, the light from the bulb shining on his gleaming patent leather shoes. Aleluya said to him:

"Impressed, hey, brother?"

"Poor old man. Calabrio's right, only the good ones die."

"Sometimes the bad die, too."

"But this guy upstairs," said Gerald passionately, "the Pole. Yelling, on drugs, did you see him? Like he was asleep. Until he heard the police. Where does he get the money? He doesn't work."

"His old man. An importer of German sausages and Polish ham. It's a wonderful world. The guy would stick the Empire State Building into his veins and feel great. He probably spends a hundred dollars a day."

"Wow!" grunted Gerry. "A week's salary. And another thing. I have a cabula..."

"Cabala. Of Hebrew origins. The cabala is..."

"...a feeling. Two deaths in one month. Mr. Blake and the one they killed in Dutch's bar."

"'Cucaracha'? He was an informer."

"You know everything, Aleluya."

"Two dead. One good, one bad. Manicheanism. Sorry, I don't mean to use bad words around you. It bothers you."

"When I don't understand. Like now. Who was Mr. Blake? Why such a fuss? The police were almost frightened. 'The prophet.' He drank a lot, but he didn't mess with anybody. He was a nice little old man, he was always laughing with the children."

"When he didn't have whiskey he locked himself up in his room and chewed on the curtains. Calabrio went up and gave him money or brought him a bottle because he didn't like to see him suffer. Sometimes he'd bring him pizza, manicotti, a variety of spaghettis, ricotta and all those victuals of well known provenance. Sensitive Sicilian heart, not completely hardened by the New York air. He went as far as to sing him a lovely and fiery Neapolitan song on the old man's birthday."

"One time when he met me on the stairs he said I was a good Latino and he let me by. He smelled like whiskey and piss."

"Calabrio?"

"Blake."

"Seymour Longfellow Blake became famous several years back," said Aley, well acquainted with the city's history. "There were many stories about this man, part of the bureaucratic folklore. He worked in the Traffic section of Public Works. His extraordinary job consisted of making estimates of the expected number of deaths produced by automobile accidents: drivers, pedestrians... Every month, he'd produce his gloomy calculations. He would also predict the deaths which would occur during the year. His divinations, achieved through scientific means, began to astonish people. I don't remember the exact figures but if, for example, he said that 273 people would die in one month, a hypothetical figure, Gerald, it was likely that a number close to the given figure would perish: 269...271...and so on. The incredible part occurred on the long weekends, when people usually leave the city in droves and the number of deaths can reach chilling proportions. Once he predicted, let's say, 184 deaths for the whole country on one weekend. There were 181... But it turned out that he had actually hit the mark exactly, because two days later three deaths were discovered which had not been properly recorded. Clearly, the Blake myth was being created. Television used him on various programs. A firm which manufactured canned soup had him appear on a television commercial where the announcer would ask: 'Tell us, Mr. Blake, which will be the soup preferred by millions of all-American families?' To which Blake would respond by roguishly winking one eye: 'The label says Fedder, you can't cook 'em better!' The best part of the commercial was that behind Blake appeared a film with a montage of fast moving cars which crashed grindingly, leapt off the road, the drivers flew out and were dashed against the street lights or remained hooked in tree limbs; in one case, two cars trapped an unfortunate old man between their front bumpers; meanwhile, below the images a stream of numbers flicked past, similar to those on a speedometer, which indicated the number of deaths in each of the past five years. And the commercial would end with a jingle which announced: 'The man to believe is Blake/ when he predicts there is no mistake/ the label says Fedder/ you can't make 'em better/ yeah yeah yeah oh yeah/ you can't make 'em better...' They published books of crossword puzzles where the words were the names of the streets and avenues where the worst accidents had occurred. People would say, for example: 'If Blake predicts 500 deaths, I won't go out in my car and there'll probably only be 499.' One also heard of aspiring suicides who, unable to execute the final act of their lives by their own hands, would throw themselves into their cars on certain special days in hope that they'd round out the projected figures; these shy suicides had an incredible loyalty to Blake and would pray that he wouldn't be off. Before I forget, our compatriots immediately created and clandestine lottery, the winning number of which was the number of deaths for the week in the whole nation. Bolo, the folkloric Bolo, was one of the founders. At first, Blake would be off by three or four accidents; he went out in his car, he studied the roads with the most traffic, the accesses into the city, the average speed, all of this, with maniacal precision. There even came the moment when he began to question his own good faith. The time he missed incomprehensibly by five, he got drunk and caused problems; he wagered that 'those dead men' had to be somewhere, they just hadn't been reported. Did he need them to continue to enjoy his macabre prestige? He was transformed into some sort of cabalistic murderer, if you can put it that way. With evident gratification, he listened on the radio as the numbers of deaths continued to increase implacably and he clenched and twisted his fingers and leapt and contorted himself like someone who sees the horse on which he has bet all of his money approaching the finish in a hard fought battle with the others, transformed into some sort of sinister 'horseman,' into a thanatotically sports fan, no offense. They even began to say that when his statistics went badly he would fix them by 'provoking' accidents by, for example, darting suddenly out into the most dangerous intersections in the city, which would force the drivers to brake suddenly and create the conditions necessary for an accident to take place. They also said that he took a lively interest in the injured and that he called the hospitals under an assumed name to ask about their progress; perhaps one nice little death to round out the statistics. On the other hand, when he guessed accurately, they said that he went out of his way to procure help for the injured and prayed that they would be saved: the predictions mustn't be too low. Obviously, there was no proof of this reputed behavior, but there were many rumors about a certain vanity in scientific prophecy, if such a thing exists. In general, he was known as a peaceful man who lived with his beloved wife and his beloved children in a two story house in Queens, a nice little family—bourgeois or petite bourgeois—who attended the Anglican services every Sunday without fail; who liked to tend the lawn, have a barbecue on the patio on Sunday afternoons, read the New York Times first thing with a breakfast of fried eggs and ham, toast, orange juice, butter and apple jelly and Nescafé coffee. He also liked to clear his mind by playing tennis, ping pong, golf once a year, filling up the tank with Exxon or Texaco; some Sundays he'd take his family to eat at Howard Johnson's or he'd simply go to Burger King, where they'd smilingly consume big hamburgers drenched in ketchup, french fries and drink strawberry milkshakes. In a word, he was one hundred percent American. When the press interviewed him he would seem surprised that they had attributed supernatural powers to him; merely a technician, he would demonstrate through calculations, computations and various analyses of an obviously scientific nature how he obtained his predictions. He liked to compare himself to old Ben Franklin: an ingenious and highly practical man with an inborn sense of scientific matters and an astonishing intuition which had taken him from being a politician to an inventor to being an investor with an extraordinary sense for earning. But when you rise high, you are bound to fall, and you don't have to be Aristotle, Galileo or Newton to know it. When Blake hit it on the nose seven weekends in a row without being off by one death, his secretary, the accountant and the messenger boy staunchly and forcefully quit their jobs and subjected themselves to long and arduous psychiatric treatment. On the eighth week he supposedly missed by three, but he alleged that actually a death had occurred in the Bronx, another in Brooklyn and another in Manhattan, only due to inexplicable carelessness, they hadn't appeared on the official list. And, in fact, he produced a newspaper clipping where it reported on the last page, in small print, the three unfortunate accidents. In passing, Blake let it be known that there was a plot on the part of the Democrats to discredit him now that he'd become one of the untouchables of the Republican Party and aspired to a high position in Washington. They said that the Republican Party used him as some sort of a political oracle, a type of human computer who could predict the number of votes a candidate would receive in the primaries, in the elections, and so on. Rocks were thrown at his house by the infuriated members of a religious sect, I believe it was the ineffable Anabaptists, who left huge signs on the fence calling him a son of Satan, a warlock, etc. and at the same time they perpetrated a strange act of repudiation: each member of the congregation defecated sacredly in front of the gate; you know, apostolic shit sanctified by these Calvinist Cretins, predestined shit. Other folk made references to the stake and the Inquisition, and one right wing scholar spoke on television about the witch problem in Salem, Massachusetts, expressing the opinion that Blake's success represented a new case of witchcraft. This fellow explained that now it wasn't necessary to use the old and reputable bonfire, whose flames could expand dangerously in all directions, but that one sitting (a single sitting) in the electric chair would be sufficient to exterminate the Devil's messengers. On the other hand, a southern governor accused Blake of being a red infiltrator sent by Havana, Moscow, Bucharest, Peking or Prague and said that he intended to confuse the public democratic US opinion, free enterprise free press. And there was a moment of genuine hilarity when the southern governor, wearing a wide hat and a pistol beneath his overcoat, was questioned on television about the imputations that he had made against Mr. Blake. When he said that Mr. Blake was a messenger from Moscow, Havana, Bucharest, mentioning all of the communist capitals but one, the commentator said that he had forgotten to mention Sofia; the governor turned red, became embarrassed and stammered that his flirtation with Sofia had ended three years ago, but that his adversaries threw his romance in his face for evil political purposes, that now Miss Sofia was happily married to a rancher friend of his and that his (the governor's) marriage was once more an oasis of peace. Clearly, the southern racist imbecile didn't know that the subject was Sofia, the capital of Bulgaria, growing confused and incriminating himself by mentioning his romance with one Sophia Berenson, a Las Vegas dance hall girl with a lasting reputation earned in politician's beds. But the whole scandal against Blake vanished overnight and several millionaires offered him grossly overpaid positions in their Wall Street offices so that he could take charge of predicting the rise and fall of the stockmarket, but he limited himself to responding that his social responsibility consisted of rendering an inestimable but modest public service, that he had no economic aspirations, that with his modest salary, his house in Queens and his children's future protected by the John Hancock House, he had enough to be happy for the rest of his days."

"Ah-hah," said a very interested Gerardo in consternation, not wanting to miss a word of Aleluya's marvelous tale. "And his children?"

"His son, an engineer... I'm going to sum it up, brother, because I see that I have overextended myself in recounting facts which probably don't interest you..."

"No, on the contrary, Aley."

"Rose Marie became a school teacher. His daughter. Blake had reached the zenith. He didn't miss. He was so involved with his work that on some weekends he would take his children to the office to help him. Also, as I said, because he wished to be 'properly accompanied'. One weekend, his predictions were fulfilling themselves monotonously and there was nothing he could do. It was nine at night and, feeling hungry, he asked his son to go downstairs to get him a sandwich and some coffee from the cafeteria on the first floor. The son obeyed and took Rose Marie to get something to eat, too. Blake kept on, submerged in his work, and only came to his feet with a start when he heard brakes squealing two blocks away. Blake wasn't concerned. But this is what had happened: a car had jumped the curb and fatally struck Rose Marie. It was inexplicable. She and her brother had gone to the first floor as they were told to do. Nonetheless, she died two blocks away. It turned out that the cafeteria had closed early because the owner had gotten sick. And Rose Marie paid for this infortuitous event with her life. Her death completed the total her father had predicted."

As was to be expected, Gerardo's blond hairs stood on end along his spine, his balls like olives, his throat dry not breathing without even a beer oh sweet Jesus. What came out was the pure Castillian pronunciation of his island.

"Listen, Aley, but ih thih fol real?"

"It was in the papers at the time."

"Oh swee' Jesuh oh daln oh wha' did the pool man do then swee' Jesuh gosh."

"First, he quit his job," stated Aleluya without paying attention to a certain sugarwater flowing from the other's lips, a recognizable molasses native to a specific parallel of the earth. Because of this, Aley was immediately convinced that he shouldn't pay too much attention to him or, better, he didn't need to tell himself anything because he only knew how to respond directly, without deviation. Then he added, with his customary narrative efficiency: "After resigning, he mourned his daughter and endured insults from all sorts of people. They began to spread rumors that, in his vanity, Blake had been glad that he hadn't been wrong on that weekend either. One group of his adversaries wanted to subject him to proceedings, but that was absurd. Then Blake fell into the hands of a long succession of psychiatrists and gave himself over to drink; in time, his wife and son came to blame him for his daughter's death. Drunk on the streets of Manhattan, Blake screamed, explained that he was simply a technician, not a warlock, that he had operated scientifically according to given laws of probability. The person who took over his job had a rough time, as you can imagine. He was off by the normal amount: forty, sixty, but this was intolerable to people who, under Blake, had come to love precision. They proposed reinstating Blake. But he rejected the idea. They said that the city needed him as a matter of life and death. His successor in the office quit after a month and became a chicken farmer. Blake's son changed his name from Seymour L. to John F.—which was in vogue at the time—not because he felt especially angry with his father but for very practical reasons: people distrusted him, were suspicious of him and didn't want to do business with him, which would be reason enough for any self- respecting Yankee to sever his family tree at the roots and replace it with another. Blake was divorced. His wife accused him before the high courts of having subjected her to an intolerable degree of mental cruelty, although in reality he was an inoffensive man, a petite bourgeois who mowed his lawn at his house in Queens, walked his dogs, went out of his way for his family and helped anyone who needed assistance. He lived for a while in São Paulo—haunted in Portuguese by his own name, and also in Haiti, Venezuela, Bolivia. They had accused him so often and so firmly and so minutely of being an evildoer, a truly scientific 'murderer', that he came to accept his guilt as a reality. Then, after several years, he returned, dressed always in strict mourning from his hat to his shoes. When he came to this building and had to give his name to Calabrio, he seemed ashamed and weak, completely vulnerable: not even alcoholism could make him forget the guilt which had been criminally cultivated by more than a few politicians, bureaucrats, and reporters of the written and spoken press. But, to the surprise of those present, including myself, Calabrio began to cry disconsolately, hugging the poor, disgraced old man and saying the most beautiful words to him in his sonorous Italian. Calabrio adored him. The ending is there, upstairs, the end of this story... Do you hear that noise? The television cameras. You'll see the story on the front page tomorrow and headlines like 'An entire era passes away with Seymour Longfellow Blake!' Perhaps they'll interview Anne Couvert and Tom Kress, which will cause a commotion within that two-in-one. Or Calabrio, who'll surely send them to hell in the most correct classical Italian. I shall hide myself, as the publicity does not suit my purposes."

Gerardo thought about the expression "does not suit my purposes", and watched his friend disappear down the fire escape outside his window; the very mysterious Aley, look at the way he goes down to the street, disregarding such comfortable indoor stairs. And the good-hearted Gerardo stood looking out of the window without noticing the lovely landscape composed of overflowing trash cans and abandoned cars rotting without wheels and drunks and leprous buildings and the unemployed who wandered there and the fellows who were shooting up inside a deep dark doorway, and so on, but he thought about Aley, this mysterious friend who disappeared, reappeared and was capable of talking to him as a friend for hours to then redisappear and return once more to the building without wanting to talk, sober, a prick like no one else, sometimes spoiled, and he was content to remember an expression that his grandmother had planted in his grey matter which summed up a world of wisdom gathered during who knows how many centuries:

"Brainh and pelsonality to the grave, brother."

On the floor above, the Pole listened to the Stylistics, full blast: "...you make me feel brand new..."

$$6.$$

EARING EVEN the sound of the sun break-
ing on the trees in Central Park, the ululations of the water that
circulates surreptitiously from arcane places and rears up like a
serpent responding to a dervish's flute all the way up to the most
controversial floor of the U.N.—to give an example—disgorging
itself into the mouth of the flames of the ghetto pouring burningly
between the leaping legs of the boys, the water also moans dripping
from the faucets, tamed in the East River and in the Hudson; everything hummed, the electric current supplied by Con Edison humming
in the motors, hundreds—what am I saying!—thousands and thousands of factories stuck like leeches to the power lines, everything
pulsing calmly with indifferent coolness, as things electric pulse, in
reality, the city crackles on this late August afternoon, crackling
monotonously sonorously, softly almost, while multitudes exhausted

by the interminable sun drag themselves out and wander about with
a bare minimum of functional apparel, the girls almost completely
revealing their exciting anatomies. A thick perfume comes from a tree
with martyred roots, swansong fragrance, the words of the dying
whore in which a whole life is expressed honestly, but also the thick
smell, an unbearable stench coming from the open-air fish markets on
the sidewalks where the dust shines, from the garbage cans, from the
fat garbage pails where the refuse ferments at the speed of sound—
that's a figure of speech—and in the cafeterias and restaurants and
cafes and bars and homemade fried food stands; the kitchens smell
strongly to such an extent that the smells stick to clothing like the
sharp and persistent smell of mustard on your fingers, coloring your
fingernails with the yellowish paste, the smell of onions frying on the
flaming grill and of the universal sweat that flows laboriously covering the globe; every street was an oven but he thinks of places with a
rubbery quality where the air conditioning and the muffling thickness
of the rugs make one forget the harshness of the climate, tall glasses
with rose-colored drinks uniformed waiters, padded silent bars dazzlingly bright like certain personal futures: a self-made man who ends
up as the president of Something, Inc., everything cushy, sophisticated, burnished legs crossing in the blue smoke of the cigars, perfect
gentlemen articulate ingenious phrases or close deals for a million
dollars or plan the extermination of a remote village down to the last
detail, bouquets of American Beauty roses release a tranquilizing
fragrance into the placid atmosphere, mixed with the scent of scotch,
sweet tropical mint cacao banana, ice creams in delicate colors for
ladies of good taste who are not afraid of gaining weight without
knowing, naturally, that nowadays there are certified non-fattening
ice creams which moisten perfect, delicately colored lips. Elegant
china dishes give off sparks of chilly electricity, silverware reveals its
elegant mineral heritage; where they agglutinate these delicacies the
incandescent air of la city does not offend, this remote world remains
cool a few blocks from the steaming hot dog which he had just gobbled
down in an unmistakable Nedick's; so that when he got up from the
eat-'n-go he felt a slight liberation, at least he knew that he could
choose the shady sidewalk or seek shelter beneath a leafy tree which,
to tell the truth, existed only in his humble mind, his own beloved tree,
his unforgettable illustrious flamboyan, his fatuous carob tree, his

delicate shadowed Anacagüita, he knew that in the summer it let a thick smothering heat fall from its foliage that would be the despair of the flies for example (not to mention the humans). It involved, then, an illusion, to face a waterfall that beats on slimy stones between the branches of a stream so densely umbrageous beneath the trees that to put one's aching feet in it would be to take a step towards the paradise of total well-being, but this was also not here, he thought confusedly. His whole being fell back upon a jumble of sensations, of mechanical responses, no way to think clearly. Nonetheless, he didn't lose his sense of humor, infinite relief, and he smiled when, on the corner of Third Avenue he bumped with a crash into who else would it be! but his best buddy Aleluya, undeniably a strange character who parades about the streets like a *gran señor* holding the leashes of half a dozen handsome fluffy little dogs with bows, carefully groomed and as gracious as ladies; they leap gracefully, sniff, bark crystalline barks. And he had to say something to him, that he didn't know he had so many little dogs and such lovely ones, he added to butter him up. Aleluya observed him seriously, restraining the retort which bloomed in his messianic soul. He said:

"Are you making fun of me, brother?"

This dry reply was out of place, he realized that it was inappropriate, as if he were to ask his friend about his sister and he'd responded that the Eskimos live in completely cozy igloos, for example. Gerry sensed that in every conversation there exist defective junctures, loose threads, currents that escape secretly and get lost in nothingness and charge the atmosphere with a tension that, even if it is not completely felt, still weighs upon each person, an indefinable contamination as when a fractured bone is badly set and never mends properly: there are hidden hurts due to this defective connection (it's really too bad, isn't it?). Or as when a perfect jet of water with clearly defined features, shaped by a tube, advances, releases a few filaments through a minute fissure: the tubularity awaited roundly at the connection is ruined, the rhythm breaks, a light trauma arises which is registrable in who knows what mysterious context. These snatches of painfully articulated thought registered in his mind the desire to answer that no, he was not making fun of anyone, and much less of him, his friend, but he simply didn't know that he had one dog, let alone half a dozen. And he added:

"I figured you were at work now."

Aleluya gazed at him, although in reality he hadn't stopped gazing at him, this time he gazed at him and looked into the depths of his being, wanting to decipher the labyrinth which possessed his compatriot, to contemplate his startlingly tropical blue eyes: the shore of ignorance on the one hand and that of mockery on the other. So that he gazed at him as-though-he-had-never-seen-him-before, doubting without allowing doubt to shine forth in the least gesture or in a shadow behind his glasses.

"This is my job," he says, shaking the leashes. "Do you think I am going to bury myself in a factory where they'll bleed me dry and won't leave me a minute of creative leisure to devote to my morning meditations and to the enjoyment of matters of the spirit?"

Aleluya's verbiage was always intimidatingly disheartening, there was no point in smashing your head or shoving against the fortress with your shoulder, a castle of words as impregnable as the vulgar castles which in other times who knows how many bastard nobles had ordered built. There was no termite which could even slightly tarnish the wordrock of Aley, nor romantic catapult that could efficiently hurl weighty boulders against the walls. His stony fortitude aside, the boiling oil would slide over him from the heights of the walls, intangible muskets would continue firing inescapable words. Therefore, he found himself obliged to abandon the dialectical wordy battlefield immediately and he shamelessly sought refuge on land which he supposed belonged to no one, appropriately a land of peace this no man's land where there are no arms of any sort. He said saying with each word, paving the path of evasion with words, throwing up a smokescreen amidst the heat. He said only that Dino Calabrio, the incredible Sicilian superintendent, appeared to be in a profound state of intoxication. He also added that Calabrio had openly conducted an argument with the vicious Pole on the top floor. Inconceivable, incredible! But during this inopportune evasion he recognized a fact which confirmed him in his status as a New Yorker: by now he had learned the necessary racial denominations to get by with relative ease: Pole, Jew, Italian. In his island neighborhood there were only men and women, a fact that was actually very boring, but here it was possible to blithely segregate humanity with the invocation of a few magical words.

He believed that the succinctly narrated fact—the Polish-Sicilian fight—would move Aley's speculative fibers, interesting him in occurrences closer to earth, to his building, that is, but Aley interrupts him with visible, unexpected impatience:

"It is none of my business what happens to the super. Furthermore, I'm not accustomed to chatting while I work. Good afternoon."

Gerardo felt the shudder of the city: cars, buses, traffic lights, impertinent honks, secret subways making crystals mysteriously chosen by fate (if you can say so) vibrate, imperceptible bottles dance confused sideboards, Bowery bums deteriorate in the shade of discredited old buildings, flocks of ragged bearded men Village bosom buddies chattering city birds darkened doorways the speculators what are they doing at this hour!, speculate, Wall Street secretaries drum their fingers boringly chewing chiclets awaiting the call from Johnny met at the Palisades Washington Square the New Yorker movie theater 88th and Broadway married divorced *Dios mío*, the bosses lean over the sewing machine operators rubbing them disturbingly with fat stomachs (thin stomachs, it's the same thing). And the only thing that occurred to Gerardo, involved in a disagreeable situation (take note) was to place a small charge of TNT before his compatriot's presumably unshaken verbal castle, saying with unaccustomed inexplicable irony:

"Well, bye-bye. Don't work too hard, you'll have a stroke."

Clearly, Aley did not register the slightly Freudian air of parricide which crossed his path. He simply bent over in a stiff bow and proceeded on his way driving his leaping handsome little dogs with bows. Soon afterward, Gerardo saw him cross Third Avenue, strictly obeying the pedestrian light, and slip down an alleyway where those eternal adolescents tossed their eternal ball shouting their eternal shouts (because these things are always to be seen in these surroundings, naturally). Gerardo laughed with dangerous complacency. Perhaps guiltily. At heart, fearful of having offended him, but not having been able to talk to him about the thing last week, Aleluya going into the

CHURCH OF GOD, INCORPORATED

for blacks, mainly, it flowed bubbled a steamroller
    *cumbachero* rhythm rock
    electric guitar

synthesizer
electric bass
a trumpet that not even Satchmo, brother
clarinet
tenor sax
drums
exciting chorus, the whole church, baby
electric organ
Yamaha conga
clapping
the metal section: cow bells, sleigh bells, etc.

nonetheless everything very well mixed everything gently latinized in the dilapidated temple where there wasn't room for even a pin (it's understood) Gerardo suffered an imbalance in his thoughts he hurled himself toward the past exhuming old things like any mortal given to recollection, he sees the Pentecostals dedicating the temple on the outskirts of his town

tambourines
maracas
guitars

primarily popular instruments of distinguished vegetable origins as is appropriate to an almost but not quite industrialized country. A minister who became unglued as an old man directs the service, closely aided by his wife, a dry little old lady expert in matters of divination who stands trembling beside the wall with the whites of her eyes showing, the faithful comment aloud that the sister wife of the minister is being visited by God, that she's in divine rapture but when the service ended the ministress continued to tremble, in a hurry to leave for home no one is interested in the event, the minister tells her it's okay now Marcela, tomorrow will be another day, let's go it's getting late but his wife continued to shiver her eyes turned inward then a proven materialist-lady said hold her it's a stroke and everyone else began to shout heresy at her, our beloved sister Marcela is in the rapture of the Lord and the minister said once more while he put on his hat

okay Marcela it's time for us to go enough is enough the body needs rest

But the ministress didn't say anything because it was not the divine rapture which had entered her but an ugly thing which came from the brain and which left her seated forever in a wheelchair, thought Gerardo while the trumpet that not even Satchmo shrieks and the tenor sax neighs and the blacks all throw themselves on the ground howling showing their big immaculate teeth in pleasure he noticed that Aleluya, dominated by a cold dry lucid comprehension of the Galilean reefs with which nature opposes nature, hesitated slightly before dripping, before joining the general free fall, he looked at the floor, exploring the possibility of an unoccupied space—one wouldn't want to hit a bench—and let himself fall on his side with the grace of a soccer player missing a goal, shrieking with a Spanish accent and opening his jacket so that it wouldn't get wrinkled. After this composition in black, Aley had disappeared for a few days (nothing unusual, actually) and Gerardo had happened to see him just today at his curious job! Gerardo laughed, shook, as they say, his head looking with anxiety at the door of the gloomy bar where three of his compatriots drank. Elbows on the counter. There are people who spend their lives this way, defeated from the beginning, he thought with concern, pushing out his chest which filled with sweaty contaminated air. From the door of the bar arose a song sung by three genuinely Puerto Rican drunks:

The ballads that sing youl histoly,

call you preshooos...

Gerardo simply bulst out laughing with an irritating bulning in his eyes.

# 7.

R<small>ADIO</small> WAYO always broadcasted one
of Gerardo's favorite programs
## HEART TO HEART
a thing which made Aley smile (better said, a preference which
made Aley smile) when they happened to speak about it and Gerardo
pointed out that if there were in fact lonely people who needed advice
there was no reason they shouldn't communicate with the person in
charge of that program. Aley agreed that consulting someone on
sentimental matters could be helpful, but only as long as the counselor
was properly counseled and not, he said, one of those fools full of
prehistoric prejudices who do nothing but confuse their thousands of
listeners with their subjective anarchical anti-scientific advice. And
he reminded him that once, a girl had written to this same program
about the red-hot event, the loss of her virginity, which was sufficient

excuse for the announcer to assume a serious, deep voice with which he urged the "fallen" girl not to allow herself to be dragged down again, just like that, by the indecorous appetites of the flesh and that, finally, she should not "sin" again, after which, he asked her for her phone number. Gerardo laughed and muttered something about the problem of virginity on his island, and then Aley changed the subject and talked about the first cool breezes of September, and Gerardo said yes, that he felt inexplicably happy, though the cold was snappy, and that it made him forget the woes of underemployment and helped him get by more cheerfully. Aleluya applauded the fact that his friend had unconsciously rhymed happy and snappy and after saying so openly, after admiring this ability which, according to what he said, was native to his culture and race (remember the lay singers of olden times, he said, that race now vanished in the thunderclaps of industrialization and the television era and rock and salsa) adding that, yes, it was true that many of the characteristics of the Puerto Rico of yesterday appeared to have disappeared but that they remained, in reality, beating beneath a cloak of apparent industrialization and worldliness, he said. Then Aley seated himself correctly on the bed, joined his knees tightly covered by black pants, clasped his hands and gazed at the ceiling in a pious manner. But there was only a clear sky, no evident source of inspiration. So Aley said:

"I will soon enjoy my vacation, brother."

"Uh-huh," offered a pensive Gerardo. And he added: "Tell me, Aley, how come you went out the window that day. You said that it didn't suit your purposes to be seen."

"In time you will know why I am an expert at walking on roofs and in tunnels, through entrance ways and among the bushes. But this is something else. I'm talking about my vacation."

Gerardo made a blank in his memory, dug a small emergency hole in his memory, not to record but to bury the memory of the beautiful leaping little dogs. He didn't really know what to say as Aley observed him with unaccustomed interest. But he said:

"Do you get vacations?"

"And Social Security."

"That's great, Aley. You looked like a cat going down the fire escape."

"I don't like the blue coats. The cops, you know. They bring back bad memories. I don't want to get burned again, understand? In addition, we're fighting to obtain a medical plan. The UDW is fighting a fierce battle on this front."

"The what?"

"And it's likely that we'll be affiliated with the Teamsters, although it's a bourgeois union. The Union of Dog Walkers."

Gerardo offered an ahhh, not in agreement, but as a lament before the incomprehensible, an ahhh of weariness or confusion or mental laziness. Once more, and eternally, he felt extremely disconcerted. He washed off the shaving cream which remained on his face, dried off with his bachelor's towel, stiff and thin like a huge cracker, and confronted his puzzled face in the mirror; his joined golden eyebrows reflected a certain stubbornness above the blue eyes, the firm chin of the twenty-six short years to his credit, the large mouth with excessively fine lips. This brief act of narcissism annulled the motionless and vibrant presence of his friend, made him temporarily forget the enormous variety of occupations which exist in the disconcerting city.

"Have you been to jail?"

"Why do you ask?"

"Because of this thing with the police. Saying you've been burned."

"I have my ideas. Well, Gerry, someone must take care of my little dogs."

Gerardo did not think this affected him. He said yes, sure.

"It's true," he said. "They can't take care of themselves!"

"You've said it," says Aley implacably. "And quite charmingly, too."

There was a not so brief pause in which Gerardo put on his shirt and tucked his tails into his pants. The light of the Septembrian Harlemnian morning flowed in above the building across the way, a blind opaque light like that reflected from a sheet of mica. Children played on the fire escape of the gloomy building at which he gazed in distraction. He picked out a little black girl with a blonde doll in her arms. He asked himself if, in other parts of the city, little blonde girls were permitted to play with black dolls. But the thought hardly grazed him, because at the heart of it was Aley's fixed gaze and the conviction that the indirect suggestion had become direct and simple and straightforward and downright barefaced for sure. And to dispel the special pressure of the air, he commented that his watch had stopped at three, but he didn't know if it were in the morning or at night. He said it with supreme seriousness, and Aley smiled at his compatriot's angelic detour. Without a doubt, Gerardo was grateful for the gift of his pure and shining smile and, thus encouraged, dared to tell him the old chestnut about the woman who asked the man if he had the time and he said that his was up.

"Not everything you say is charming," said Aley, disappointed. "Listen, brother, the money won't hurt you. Take care of them while I enjoy my vacation."

Gerardo began to cough. Better said: he simply coughed and squeezed his throat melodramatically to restrain the cough.

"I'm sorry," he says. "Absolutely not."

"Why?"

Gerardo shook his head. He couldn't think of any reason to say no. But there were reasons. He says blushingly that he'd rather starve than take care of the animals he most hated. Hateful dogs. Aley clasped his hands once more in a pious manner, but his thought did not delve the divine, but the obscure shadowy revisionist realm of the unconscious. It wasn't long before he'd come up with a more than acceptable corollary. He mentally reviewed various psychoanalytical theories including Freud, of course, Lacan, Laing, the ineffable orgonic Wilhelm Reich and he even though briefly of the self-assertive positive rationalist Ellis and of the battered Frankl, concluding—after discarding several of these—that the image of the dog's tearing teeth was the classic symbol of castration.

"Machismo," he said, getting up and pacing around the room. "That old ballast!"

Gerardo didn't understand why he was being accused of being macho, since he was thoroughly proud of being so, but he simply turned off the radio and looked a bit harshly at his friend. When he didn't get any response, he did something: the day that his ex-wife had asked him what he would do if he found her in bed with another, he'd squeezed his cup so hard that it had shattered in his hand like an egg. Aleluya understood as he said it that his approach had failed, his analysis of the situation had met with counterproductive results, so he sought shelter under the divine canopy and said incongruously:

"Blessed are those who suffer."

Gerardo picked up immediately on the discursive anomaly. Surely he wasn't referring to the dogs, so plump and spoiled and elegantly groomed. But Aley continued delving with his inconsistent strategy, groping about, hoping to hit him in a sensitive spot.

"The last shall be the first."

Once more, Gerardo feared a dialectical ambush, a certain manipulation contrived without obvious malice. They were setting him up. They were weaving him a web of words. They craftily constructed a pit covered with wordleaves. But he decided that this simple fact could not be converted by his simple mind into some sort of catastrophe—and this without having read the aforementioned Ellis—and thought positively of himself, of his power as a fearless and determined man—based on what he'd seen in the mirror—, and he said with forceful positive rational self-assertion:

"Yes, very good. Excuse me, I have to take a piss."

He felt strong, not only because he'd eaten well the preceding week and had regained the pounds he'd lost, but also because of his ability to respond decisively to the ambush. He'd been able to stand up to the all-knowing Aley! He felt, with an immense sense of liberation, the might of the stream falling into the center of the bowl, forming a white foam as it churned the unlyrical stagnant water. When he finished, he shook his organ with feeling and gazed at it objectively, attempting a mental description of its heavy utilitarian contours. Not so long, but quite wide, tubular and potent like a sawed-off shotgun, with blue veins branching out from the base to the neck, the rosy head swelling out from the skin and slightly enlarged in the shape of a Nazi helmet, aiming a natural, clear and simplistic thought at the floor that could be translated as "I go rat-a-tat-tat like machine gun fire." Gerardo came to the conclusion that he had a well-proportioned, massive, precise and indispensable piece which was, above all, very experienced in chicks from fifteen to fifty. He shook it once more to disperse the last drops and realized that the action released prodigious energy, solid concentrated machismo. He pulled up his zipper slowly, sure of his actions, completely in possession of all his demonstrable virility. Piss, he'd said, instead of the feminine urinate (although it weighed on him that he'd let out that "excuse me" which seemed to reveal a weakness in his being). But he bravely coughed hard to hear the sound of his own voice, the leonine roar of the king of the john, and pulled energetically on the door which he had closed with masculine modesty.

And at precisely the instant that the door made a sound like something being violently ripped apart, a lightning association of ideas made him remember a certain story from his childhood: the sky is falling! But there were no adorable petals falling upon his head but, instead, a shower of old sand, like the sun and plaster in truly inconvenient pieces. The cockroaches crawling on the nape of his neck made him retreat with a cry from the assertively chosen path of machismo. Aleluya came running fastidiously with clean strides and helped him brush off the debris. Gerardo suffered a lamentable moral collapse when he shouted frenetically:

"IT HAD TO HAPPEN TO ME!!"

But Aley said, it doesn't matter, this could have a bright side, while Gerardo dried the cut on his forehead with his deplorable handkerchief, watching the blood fall down in front of his eyes to form an insignificant puddle in front of his shoes. And he said that he ought to look for mercurochrome and some bandaids for the wound, but Aley appeared supremely surprised and, for the first time since they'd met in Dutch's bar, looked at him as though he were a completely unforgivable idiot. And this display of defective communication or lack of comprehension between men who spoke the same language taxed the victim cruelly and made him murmur:

"There's no splinter worse than one from the same branch." to which Aley replied, the absurdity of the expression and its obvious lack of application in today's world aside, the best thing would be to consult his personal friend, the lawyer David Lean and, shortly thereafter, a distinctly open-mouthed Gerardo stopped in front of a building six blocks further south—as gutted as the rest—with the fire escape zigzagging the length of its six stories and overflowing trash cans lining the stairs of the entrance

DAVID LEAN

ATTORNEY

**Aquí se Abla Español**

Aley pushed the glass door and they entered a dark waiting room. Through the window one could discern the brick wall of the next building and Gerardo felt suffocated, as though the heat were deep inside him. Better to entertain himself by gazing at the curious paintings, appropriate to a lawyer's office. In the first, a lion hunted a deer. In the second, one enormous fish devoured another. The third contained the brainy allegory of the Law: a blindfolded woman holding scales. This painting was at an angle so that, in the semidarkness, the scale tipped obviously to one side. Aley smiled acridly and asked:

"Guess to which side the capitalist scale tilts."

"To the side of the rich," said Gerald, in outmoded terminology.

"To that of the bourgeois capitalist exploiters," corrected Aley profusely. "Parasites who live off the sweat of the workers. But follow me, brother."

Behind the curtains was a schoolboy's desk and, surprise!, behind the desk, squeezed in there uncomfortably, with his knees up to his chest, a fifty year old man looked them over circumspectly. Red spongy pock-marked nose. Watery eyes of a lusterless blue, like diluted milk.

"Hi, Dave," said Aley. "I've brought you one of my country-men."

Dave-did-not-recover-from-his-surprise.

"He's blond," he exclaimed, gosh holy cow. "And he has blue eyes!"

"We have an extensive variety of colors," recited Aley in the manner of a tie salesman. "Go to the island and you'll see. We're not like all of you troglodytes. We mingle, we unite."

"How weird! Why did you bring him in?"

Aley began to explain the case in words that Gerardo had only heard from lawyers of all shades (grumbling sleazy public attorneys; judges—drowsing after gorging themselves on lunch—listening to a delicious case of rape; defenders of etcetera), spicing his presentation with occasional Latin phrases.

"What's your name?" asked Dave.

"Who, me?" responded Aley.

"No, him."

"My name is Gerardo," said Gerardo, and added extraneously, "At your service."

Aley did not remove his long and pointed finger—violet on the outside and cream within—from his compatriot's tortured forehead. It was a delicate motion, like that of a naturalist accustomed to studying butterflies. Dave, unsatisfied, shook his head.

"Insignificant," he said. "A mere scratch. Resolve it as you see fit. I have clients waiting."

Gerardo came to the conclusion that the guy was nuts—he'd be damned if he could see anyone in the waiting room! He noticed a half-bottle of bourbon sitting against the wall behind the lawyer: it was the only object in the room that was free of dust and cobwebs.

"By the way," said Aley, "How's the case going with that child who was eaten by rats?"

"Oh, go now," Dave protested weakly. "I don't have time now. You go, come back, alright."

The lawyer David Lean, recipient of a degree from the prestigious, time-honored without parallel University of Harvard, took a cigar butt, lit it, sucked on it twice with feverish anxiety, stubbed it out on the clear sole of his shoe and put it away again. He immediately shouted into the waiting room:

"Next, come in!"

"He's a little soft in the head," murmured Aley, "but, every once in a while, he comes through. And, furthermore, he's cheap. We're not in the market for Patty Hearst's lawyer or any guy named Barriga, which means stomach, gut, you know... significantly."

The Lexington landscape appeared heartwarmingly familiar with its dark wood bars, drugstores, advertisements for whiskey and Coca-Cola, dogs and crowds, children screaming playing, teenage rebels, afros, jeans, windbreakers; and, in the distance, overshadowing everything else, the new high rise apartment buildings, now complete and newly painted. Others were still framed by supports with machines attached to their structures like ticks, and he thought that, with time, Harlem would change its physiognomy with new and perhaps boring habitats; he thought, feeling the slow throb of the bruise on his heroic forehead, his eyes resisting the blinding white light of a cloud-covered Septembrian day, uncomfortable light in which he saw a fire engine pass, blasting its angry hair-raising siren, startled by a howl that stood his hairs on end, this subhuman amplified groan that awakened him every morning accompanied by the sound of bells; Aleluya didn't seem to be moved by the famous New York sounds, he definitely seemed to belong in this world, as he carried himself with complete ease, despite his pseudo-ecclesiastical rigidity;

not a dive in the Barrio was unfamiliar to Aley; nonetheless, to Gerardo's surprise, the learned Aleluya turned and said that, one day, the entire city would be shattered by the force of the accumulated piercing sounds, a monstrous weight of decibels, he said serenely, but he was glad that summer had passed now; its temperature and atmosphere perilously accentuated the sensations, he said; irritated the senses drove—yes!—even the children of God to betrayal and then Gerardo, who was concentrating on his friend's complicated words, sensed the familiar smell of his building, an aroma no longer so rank due to the drop in temperature, and he watched as Aleluya systematically pounded three times on the door, which creaked open to reveal the virile figure of Dino Calabrio wearing a leather jacket and corduroy pants, his broken shadow falling across the tumbled rubbish.

"What is it now?" he said.

Of this inhospitable antiwelcome, what most set Gerardo off was this "now" which suggested many previous interruptions, so that he folded his mighty arms behind his back and automatically reread the graffiti on the wall so as not to look the super in the eye.

FREE PANCHO CRUZ

BLACK POWER

I LOVE JANICE

NIXON'S A MURDERER

TONY AND THALIA

VIVA TUFINO THE GREATEST PAINTEL

The paint on the roof was pitted, a grey paint full of the strange city smog.

"Pardon us for interrupting you," said Aley seriously. "It's about Gerry here. The bathroom ceiling fell on his head."

"Ah, so it was him, heh?"

Gerardo immediately felt his redly red blood rush to his temples. In fury, almost hate. Almost violence. Dangerous.

"What do you mean it was me? It fell by itself!"

The super brought his bad-humored face close to the Gerardian lump and then began to sputter curses, telling off the owners of the building as he paced around and around the following objects:

chairs without legs

mirrors with rotten frames

sheets that had seen twenty years of service

balding armchairs
moth-eaten dresser drawers
artificial carnations
foam rubber mattresses

in sum, hundreds of kitsch articles; cursing in Italian, English and
Spanglish, but Aleluya, infinitely less emotional and more practical,
concrete and realistic than the southern Calabrio, went to a corner,
made a careful review of the stock (*existencias*) of objects that offered
themselves to him bristlingly, jumping from their silence and immo-
bility; he leaned forward, grasped the lone melancholy table leg that
had been repainted frequently, the gold leaf faded by the seasons, that
ended in the form of a claw and sported a curve in the style of Louis-
somebody of France. He walked around it, looking at it, tested its
weight and glanced at the super who paused, looked at the curious find
and nodded yes. Then the two of them directed themselves tenderly
toward Gerardo, who had remained adrift abandoned in the surrealis-
tic chaos of the rubbish. Gerardo vacillated to such a degree that his
feet became entangled in a fallen curtain, a slight loss of balance
which Calabrio observed as if mesmerized and the stubborn, uncom-
promising Aley took advantage of by moving himself rapidly toward
his compatriot and

CRAC!!!

they filled his head with a detonation, a flashing light, and the sound
of the gigantic CRAC receded so that it could be represented graphi-
cally as it decreased—soundless but intense

CRAC!!!
CRac!!
Crac!
crac
ac

a luminous mass which blotted out his mind, filled all the chinks in his
cranial cavity, blinding it, blinding spark, crac, and he could only say
oooohhhh fuuuuck they've killed me make the light brighter while his
two friends watched him, with genuine fascination this time: Aleluya
with a fragment of the leg of the French table in his delicate artisan's
had, Calabrio shaking his head approvingly and, in the room, the
objects began their wild dance

a sheet rolled coquettishly back on itself and moved snake-like

before his eyes
a table went by, dancing to a dislocated samba rhythm
the top of a casserole paused as it turned in the air in front of him
like an overly domesticated UFO
a rug fluttered languidly by his side like a
giant prehistoric bird
a floorlamp balanced having acquired by dint of
strange proximities, the characteristics of a pendulum
the strident detained pendulum of an archaic clock
turned on and went out, suffering from the complex of believing
it was a traffic light. Lexington extended and undulated like an
elaborate anaconda, the streetlights bent down before Gerardo's
confused steps, the garbage cans stuffed with refuse flattened themselves against the sidewalks like accordions between the sky and the
earth, cars passed that were no more than twelve inches high, long like
hot dogs, and short buses, flat with large humps, advanced in a climate
without temperature block after block and then, David Lean said that
it was a case of a truly notable compound lump on the head and added
that the lack of concern on the part of the landlord surprised him and
how was it possible that their properties buildings *posesiones* were so
decrepit and that they so unscrupulously exploited their poor tenants
of various ethnic backgrounds, that if the bathroom ceiling had fallen
so villainously and had produced such a bloody result (by which cause
the plaintiff could remain deprived of his mental faculties), the urgent
and appropriate action would be to make legal reparation, file a suit
against the owner(s) of the aforementioned building(s); the President
of the United States; the people of the United States; the Island of
Puerto Rico and her larger-than-life governor; Gerardo Sánchez vs.
Mr. Mordecai Levine, owner of the Assailant Property.

"How could they be so heartless and racist?," asked Dave Lean
with an empty bottle of bourbon at his back. "He could have died on
the spot, owing to the criminal negligence of these vendors of human
misery and poverty."

Dave Lean scribbled on embossed paper, put it into an embossed
envelope and gave it to Aley.

"Follow my legal recommendations," said Dave, and shouted in
the direction of the deserted waiting room: "Next, come in!"

Three blocks further on, Aley had his silent meditative friend enter a building which, surprisingly enough, smelled of fresh paint, an extraordinary phenomenon in this area.

## JEREMIAS GUZMANSKY
## DOCTOR

In the waiting room there were, naturally, plastic flowers and antediluvian magazines as in any other doctor's office. Gerardo saw four languid pregnant compatriots sitting next to him in the same waiting attitude. The perfectly black receptionist smiled revealing four solid gold teeth and Aley expressed warm greetings to her and to the comrade doctor Guzmansky, and, in passing, in a low and persistent and even slightly irritated voice Aley embarked on the tale of the curious history of Doctor Guzmansky, descendent of distant Spanish Jews expelled from the Iberian peninsula because of the jealousy of degenerate nobles incapable of any industry whatsoever, and he told of the western pilgrimage of this Diasporian who carried with him a language later impoverished by its isolation and lack of usage, said Aley the philologist, and that later, with the centuries, this mistreated race religion culture was forced to disperse once more when that furious fruit, Adolph—maximum concentration of the capitalist mentality—with his horde of fat Aryan pederasts aging dipsomaniacs bourgeoisie supermen decadent aesthetes established themselves as the new defenders of western Christianity and proclaimed themselves guardians against the red threat: and Aley, furious, said that Adolph's case should be studied from the perspective of his bourgeois pathology to establish if, in truth, what he'd most wanted at heart was not to suck the good Slavic penis of a Soviet proletarian worker, a formidable red piece that would reach to the sadomasochistic Teutonic tonsils and would make the Vandal Goth Visigoth pass out from sheer pleasure, that would stick, long as a streetcar, into a Nibelung so that he would be transformed into a weak floating fainting Valkyrie, said Aley, growing more enraged by the second, but he suddenly calmed himself and said that Jeremías Guzmansky had just finished his medical studies at the University of Varsovia when the Nazis entered Poland destroying everything. Jeremías managed to escape the concentration camp hidden, ironically, in a huge cylinder of metal which had contained the carbonic gas used to exterminate half his kin (and, after he had decapitated a disagreeable sergeant bulldog of the SS—his certain aSSasin—with a surgeon's precise blow—using his scalpel, he had donned his uniform reeking of German sausages and the beer of Munich without emotion, with a fugitive's obligatory decorum). Led by his astonishing intuition, Jeremías, disguised as a fisherman, had disembarked on the shores of Alexandria, where he had the strong impression that he'd been centuries before; established his office in exile in that city but in time he learned that an air of inverse plunder was coming from Palestine, a powerful coterie of the formerly pursued had become pursuers, and so Jeremías had rolled up his Varsovian diploma once more and become a sailor on a ship flying the Panamanian flag (probably one of Onassis', so un-Panamanian, commented Aley); as soon as he touched Colombian soil, Jeremías abandoned his new profession as a sailor and he began a long pilgrimage from Carthage which carried him across the Andes on the back of a mule until he reached Bolivia. But, as you already know, said Aleluya, at the end of the Second World War, many of the top Nazis took refuge in South America, so that for two months Jeremías dedicated himself to the innocent sale of bananas, plantains and *guineos* in an alleyway of La Paz—incredibly managing to amass a small fortune which allowed him to emigrate comfortably to the United States, establish himself in Harlem, then predominantly Italian and mafioso and black, and continue going about his business with all the calm in the world. And Aley added something that the whole city knew: Dr. Jeremías Guzmansky had unleashed an active energetic campaign in favor of the elimination of gas leaks in the threatening city pipe system; in fact, his office was pleasantly scented in order to remove any odor which might remind him of the cylinder of carbonic gas in which he had escaped from the concentration camp. With his Golden Age Spanish, Guzmansky knew how to treat, with a sense of sacrifice, these strange distant cultural relatives, the Boricuas. Aleluya only occasionally threw a certain dissembled tendency towards Trotskyism in his face, but, at the same time, he understood that old Pete Stalin had been no innocent babe in the woods.

It bothered Gerardo that, before he went in, his friend Aleluya entered the examining room. But, shortly afterwards, the receptionist took him by the arm and led him babystep by babystep, as though fearing a fall, towards the doctor's door. The pregnant women gazed at him with distant curiosity, touching themselves on their bellies because there's no pregnant woman in the world who's not more concerned with what's happening in her belly than what's happening outside.

Aleluya spoke with Jeremías in this fashion:

"Yande thi yachyvimenttes offe oure coleyctivye endevours."

"Verraily," said Jeremías, a chubby seventy year old large protruding forehead bald triangular parrot-like nose on the powerful pock-marked bridge of which rested thick glasses; on his crown sat a forcibly placed round black beret often seen in certain Newyorican circles; he laughed and laughed saying yes yes but his eyes like those of an old beaten dog, his smile a grimace. He adds: "Butte, thou fyndest onsormontable ubstaycles to thi stroggle; tis a devylisshe sloewe taskee; wel, thi peples musttE bey educaytid! Natheles, onne mayst nevere losye payssiounce or bycom angryd. Yan obvyous ensample offe souch enystroccioun is fynded in thi bestte poblicacioun offe youre contrie: Claridad Pravda. Grete valyoure is reykwyrd to reelice souch yan endevour. Evere onneward!"

"Yande whet offe al thi haselsye offe mey contriemen yin theyse emensye sitie?" asked Aley. "New Yourke is thi newe Babel, butte wey musttE ovrethrew thi establice soucial ordre."

"Inne theyse contrie, tis costumayrie to leev thynges as thei yare yande nevere to thincan offe makyng the reveloccioun; tis eyvideant thaet thi werk offe suposidlye avauncyd leedres, souch as Gus Hall, dede na evene responde to emperialissm's agresyve acciouns. Fur theyse reysoun, tis offe mexymum impurtaunce thaet thi peples' onnehapynesse yande desynchantmenttes bey yutlysed yande thaet wey gette doun reyt new to thi werkes bey wych wey mey bee eyble to brynge aboutte thi permaenentte yande trewe reveloccioun, yande sawn its fruyission. T'wolde bey wondrous to bey eyble to reycognyze thi froostracciouns offe thi peple yin detayl. T'wolde pleyce us yin a beytre posicioun; better, you know."

Aley shakes his head, doesn't seem to agree. He says:

"Yatte preysont, oure ysslonde is na thi bestte pleyce to eneshiyate theyse deeplie desyrd tronsfurmacciouns. It musttE bee bygun yin theyse sitie wher thi wourkren lyve mur likke brootes, beestees offe bordain, then likke thi sonnes offe thi Lorde, depryvid offe al richenesse. Wey musttE cunsidere thise detayls."

Jeremías laughed provocatively:

"Thy ysslande, dere ladde: whaet a sadde feyte!" and, lowering his voice, compassionately: "Youre lovyerely ysslonde lustte yin thi see yande forgetten bey thi men who cowde liberayte herr fromme thi ynfeymous yokke offe thi yatefulle opressioun! I wil yalweys lovye thy contrie, dere ladde! Butte tis issential to lekwidayte this treitors, sonnes offe byches, fellonyes, lakkyes yande evele-doers who wants to snoffe oute thi fleymes offe thi onneyvitable reveloccioun! Oute wythe thi fatte cattyes yande thi pympyes offe thi morthre contrie! Doun wythe emperialissm! Butte, I goen too farye, Aley," Jeremías points smilingly to Gerardo: "Is theyse thi ladde offe whom yow spake, dere Aley?"

"Theyse is he," responds Aley. "Esamun his hede wythe carefullness, iffe yow wolden plese, honourd sire."

"Dere Godde!," exclaims Jeremías, letting out a cackle. "Youre ladde hasse getten souch a forehede thaet hit reymyndeth mey of the verrie Calvarie hitselffen. Lette him prepayre himselffen in theyse smale roum fur a thurough esamynaccioun."

Jeremías Guzmansky had an attack of laughter, of coughing, he couldn't contain the peals of laughter that shook his chubby person seated behind the desk. Aleluya, that careful observer, gazed at him with curiosity and profound sympathy; at such moments, the Varsovian doctor felt peaceful, relaxed, rested from his previous tribulations; he had witnessed too many far from pleasant scenes in his childhood, in his adolescence and his examination room in New York, so that now he felt he had the right to laugh as much as he pleased. Nonetheless, Gerardo felt the anger rising within him; why the devil was this fellow laughing so much after talking in riddles with Aley? On top of everything else, he had to hold his peace while Guzmansky pressed the stethoscope against his back.

"It's on my forehead!" grunted Gerald.

"He knows what he's doing," Aley told him. "He's been our doctor for a quarter of a century. He also writes verses in Judeo-Spanish. Once he told me that his father was a direct descendant of one Nebrija."

"So why should I care, Aley? I'm not enjoying this."

And then, Doctor Jeremías Guzmansky of remote peninsular Spanish origins and Slavic conditioning wrote on a piece of paper which, naturally, bore the proper crest, that Gerardo had a contusion and wound, etc. on his forehead, caused by the collapse of the bathroom ceiling on the third floor. Jeremías firmly rejected the honorarium Aley proposed but accepted, in exchange, that Gerald would bring him a modest sandwich of scrupulously kosher liver from the nearby delicatessen.

The medico-legal pilgrimage ended when the lawyer David Lean read Guzmansky's note with genuine enthusiasm, agreeing as he sat squeezed into his schoolboy's desk with a new bottle of bourbon behind his legalistic back. He then asked them to excuse him, that is to say to beat it, that he had people waiting for him in the empty waiting room, that he would arrange a date for them at the hearing if the parties involved in the lamentable accident could not agree to a *peaceful* settlement.

# 8
·

So, NATURALLY, Aley went to see Mordecai Levine and protested energetically in his impressively correct English. On more than one occasion, confronted by Mordecai's evident torpor in pronouncing that language, he found himself forced to demand that Mordecai express himself in Yiddish, a belabored language which Aleluya pronounced carefully, so as to make himself understood beyond a shadow of a doubt.

Aley smiled when Mordecai told him that he was not disposed to negotiate with his tenants. He simply left with assurance, took an Uptown bus and told Gerardo from the window:

"Stay here."

Five minutes later, unknown Puerto Ricans, American Blacks, Chicanos and Asians began to arrive with signs and voices raised in protest. They began to circulate in front of the luxurious property from which Mordecai administered his decrepit inferno of one hundred and seventy-four apartment buildings. The shouts condemned the owner's indolence, his merciless exploitation of the tenants. Nonetheless, things got a little more complicated when the police arrived and, swinging clubs, threw themselves on two men and arrested ten others. Gerardo received a hard shove and restrained himself from squeezing the neck of a tall Irish policeman between his powerful fingers.

The next morning, the news was out: a bomb had exploded in Mr. Mordecai Levine's automobile. Reasons unknown. Mr. Levine explained to the press that he had no personal enemies, that he was a well-known and upstanding member of the community.

Shortly thereafter, Gerardo ran into Aleluya just as he was about to go into his room.

"Mordecai called me," said Aley. "He wants to settle."

"Did you see they planted a bomb?"

"I saw nothing," said Aley dryly. "A thousand or a thousand five hundred dollars. Give something to Calabrio. He provided the suitable instrument, the poetic table leg with which we improved your insignificant lump."

"I can send more money to my ex and the kid."

"How old?"

"Twenty-four."

"No, the kid."

"Oh. Three. Little Gerardo."

"Proud papa. See you later."

And then Aleluya opened the door just barely enough to squeeze in sideways as though he were afraid that Gerardo might see the inside of his room. Gerardo stepped forward and peered curiously inside and stood astonished. The walls were literally covered with a double row of books from the floor to the ceiling. Not even a window escaped, for Aleluya had left only a large horizontal rectangular space uncovered to let the light come in. Gerardo held the door forcibly, preventing his friend from closing it in his face, and saw that there were piles of books in the corners, beside an extraordinarily small bed; Aleluya had left pathways between the mountains of books which filled the center of the room and permitted minimal movement: a path began at the door, bordered by books which grew like mushrooms from the ground, a tiny road opened between thick volumes from the bed to the washstand and from the washstand to a comfortable armchair behind which was a floor lamp. Beside this, a small table with a pad, ballpoints, pencils, papers. Gerardo immediately voiced the obvious question which good and unsophisticated and simple people ask those strange characters who dedicate themselves to accumulating vast quantities of books:

"And, have you read all these books, Aley?"

"*The Bible* six times. *The Divine Comedy* six. *Ulysses*, four. *War and Peace*, five. *In Search of Lost Time*, seven. *L' etre et le neant*, four. The *Studien zur der Florentiner Wirtschaftsgesch* by Doren, seven. *L' oeuvre d' art a l' epoque de sa reproduction mécanisée* by Walter Benjamin, six times; I couldn't find this work in the original and was forced to read a mediocre translation; the same thing happened to me with several of Adorno's works and, specifically, with a small interesting essay by Broch, *Einige Bemerkungen zum Problem des Kitches* which was published in Zurich in 1955; it is actually a conference, and, though remotely revisionist, his work is interesting and I would recommend his essay *James Joyce und die Gegenwart*, which simply means *James Joyce and the Present Day* to anyone, and you needn't make such a catastrophic face, Gerardo, German is also 'Christian' as our Spanish jíbaros say. *Kunst und Kulture der Vorzeit* by Kunh, seven times; *Storia della letteratura italiana* by Gaspary, five times. *Das Kapital* eleven times. *The Sociology of Literary Taste* by Schucking, three times. *El Eroici furori, I, Opera italiana* by Giordano Bruno, seven times. *Prostestanimus und Literatur* by Schoffler, twice. *Spiks* by Soto, twenty-three times: it deals with our compatriots in the urban environment; *Zur Soziologie des Modern Dramas* by Lukacs, an article which I was obliged to remove from the City Library because I tried for six years to obtain it without success. *Der bourgeosis* by Sombart, seven times. *Factors in German History* by Barraclough, three times. *Art and Society* by Plekhanov, twice. *La Bourgeosie Francaise* by Aynard, six times. And, naturally, I have read and studied Hostos, Martí, Che, Fidel, all of our thinkers, many times. Also the last book by Maldonado-Denis on the Boricuas in the city, which, I might add, I'm translating into Arabic for a publisher in Cairo and into Quechua for a Bolivian press. Translation doesn't pay very well, but I enjoy the work and the fulfillment it gives me. Does that satisfy your curiosity, brother?"

"Wow, Aley!"

"Mordecai will fall and bite the dust!"

The door slammed in Gerardo's inquisitive face. Aleluya remained cloistered in his strange printed world—a room where the books prevented movement. Gerald hurried in the direction of La Placita, going along a street now somewhat cold, wearing his leather jacket and his corduroy pants. Along Second Avenue, he remembered his experience yesterday with Caty. Lorenzo—the owner, Caty's father—had gone out, so Gerardo decided to spend a reasonable period of time contemplating the horizontal possibilities of his solid twenty year old countrywoman, so that at one point, when they were arranging some cases of crackers in the storeroom, they had a confused scuffle in which he wasn't sure if she grabbed him to push him away from her or to keep him from leaving but, in any case, as he contemplated her smilingly he told her that, whenever she wished, she could drop by to give him a little help, you know, decently organize his lonely oppressive bachelor's room.

"Women know about these things," he concluded.

She smiled, said with her Harlemnian accent:

"Sexist."

"I don't know what that is," says Gerardo. "But if you visit me, you'll be welcome."

Gerardo hurried on his way.

And also on the way back. He hurried. Because he felt a strange urgency to close himself in, to be alone, to think about what he hadn't thought about in the past week: *la Isla* and, on it, specifically, his town, his ex and little Gerardo toddling on the patio. And he thought happily of the child once more when he took an envelope from the mailbox which bore the crest of

### MORDECAI LEVINE

He opened it. Whistled. A thousand bananas, wow, the wow had stuck to him there, wow, man. Bow-wow. The Capital of the buck. What dreams, oh! The counterboy in the pizzeria with his depressing news. A quarter of a million workers laid off. Cab driver, a sure bet. But now... He didn't need much to hold it together. So he'd send a good part of the thousand bucks to his ex and to the boy. Taking off the leather jacket by the window he gazed at the darkened heavily clouded street. People drinking in the poorly lit bars. Men, women, children in the doorways, wearing light jackets and sweaters. The Pole crossed the street surrounded by a group of long-haired bearded guys covered in multi-colored ponchos. A cat jumped out of a garbage can. From the fire escape a childish voice shouted "Hey, Mister!" Cars took off before the lights changed. The city began to shudder with moderation and distant noise, not as deafening as in the summer. First thing tomorrow he'd cash the check, he'd give Calabrio a tip and one to Aley. He could invite Caty to a Chinese restaurant. Or to the Village, where there was a weird atmosphere, really weird, but *bien chévere* (as Bigote had said on Third Avenue and 23rd Street). He felt a mild excitement as he thought about Caty. He shot a quick glance around his room, but his eyes rested for a disproportionately long time on the bed. To get into the mood he turned on the radio. Music for being with Caty, you know. Though they always ruined it. Halfway through the program they announced that a bomb had exploded in the central office of ITT, for example, or that tension was mounting in the Far East. Another bomb had exploded on Wall Street. The smooth music, from smooth rock, continued as though nothing had happened. Darn,

between cabbage or cabbage you'd take lettuce

music and bombs, music *bien chévere* and tensions and wars. And suddenly, he couldn't help himself, he felt an extreme extraordinary love for this uncontrolled city full of human wreckage and lights and innumerable dangers and blazing human successes, an enormous extension of cement and glass and brick and very little wood and lots and lots (how crazy!) of sidewalks. Almost grateful lots of people there all in the same boat Manhattan like a ship

floating quietly between the Hudson and the East River;

on the left side of the impossible island,

on the Upper East Side, the bleeding heart of Harlem

the Spanish Barrio, and he was there, *señor*, as if it were the center of the silent storm which day after day exhausted the multitudes squeezed into the old, it's been said already, Methusalistic buildings! Sweet Mordecai's 174th Street. Incredible, 174th! But that's the way it is, love. Dutch's bar is also in a building that belongs to the bald bewhiskered Mordecai, old parrot nose. And the building where La Placita is located, 174th. Caty paying Mordecai. He himself paying Mordecai. Aley, the Pole, Tom Kress and Anne Couvert and all the rest of them: paying their good money to Don Morde. Aleluya, serene, quiet, talking with Don Morde in a bizarre language. Hum. Where he'd fall, a goat would die, thought Gerry very Boricuanly. Shit, and what does the fellow do with all that money. He'd have an airplane, two yachts, a dozen blonde secretaries for his bed. What he must eat and drink. Yum. Kosher, that stuff Aley talked about. Those people. Aley says lots of them are shameless, exploiters, villains, heartless. He says. But there are others who are angels. The big men of the world. Inventors. People who make music. Science. This bearded man he showed me in a book: Mas or Max or Marx or something like that. Also. One of the good ones. And many teachers. And Aley says that they learn Spanish quickly and make friends with you. And because they're also persecuted, he says, like us, says Aley the joker. They're not a majority in the world, but they count for a lot. They make their presence known, you know. They control the city, it's said, but no. Aley says that Morgan, Rockefeller, you know, Rockefeller Center. Incredible, thinks Gerald. With their grave cuadrangular buildings raised enormous and paralleleptic one beside the other resounding with people, with business, with display cases, with show windows— luxury power integrity. The cathedrals of imperialism, Aley calls them. Wow. The cathedrals of capitalism. The Sacred Father Don Rocke. These fellows do as they please, *hombre*. Who'd rock the boat! Who'd bell the cat! Aley says the people, that the workers can do it. That the Rocke's were also, for example, in Cuba. And many others, outside and in. Multimillionaires. Preposterously powerful. And twelve started in the mountains. When Aleluya talks to him about this, he talks calmly, but Gerardo suspects a vibration behind his eyes, and his voice comes out more firmly and somehow more clearly. And the twelve men multiplied because the peasants from the mountains were drawn into the guerilla warfare. The army couldn't deal with them. Nor could the millionaires from outside, nor the millionaires from inside with their silk ties and their bombs manufactured in vestries. Aley knows, Aley's read like crazy. All those books! And the twelve bearded men became eight million militiamen who had made a revolution from the cunt of their mother, says Aley to sum it up when he speaks of these things which are so dear to him. The same thing happens in Borinquen he says, industrialized colony but. Almost half the population in the USA; because there's no, *tú sabes*, work. And now it turns out there's none here either. And, with all of that, Gerardo feels affection for the city, but he thinks that it's for people like him, with all their dreams like empty packages, shit, hombre, it's gotten to him, and that's why the city is pretty, Broadway is corroding, so wide, raised like a shining storefront against the breeze, on the verge of collapse; Broadway marked now forever; Aley tells him all this, serious and rigid like a prophet who predicts things, says things, like the very prophet himself thought Gerry modestly, thoughtful beside the guillotine windows that he'd lowered to escape the chilly September air still without heat, very thoughtful, watching how the people fidgeted on the street, the Boricuan girls passing with their boyfriends with huge afros faded jeans big jackets little jackets plastic jackets sweaters, now without any desire to go out remembering that he didn't have any reason to because a little later Caty would visit him. Again. The excitement. Mordecai must have women by the dozen. Money can do anything. Mordecai I came to tell you the revolution's begun. Ugh, what will become of free enterprise, of liberty, oh! Caty, look after me, just for a while. Yes, so that you can help me set up the room, this stuff. It's okay. But talk to me straight. Sexist. Mordecai Sánchez, alias Gerald Levine, will spend a delicious evening with his ladyfriend in his spacious apartments on Upper Lexington. Catalina. Caty. Or Cathy. Now he remembers. He should bring up some bottles of beer, so that she'd, you know, get hot. But never mind. Hot at room temperature when he had her there in front of him, with no way out. On the bed. Or standing up. Or in the chair. Or on the small green rug which still smells new. Today you put your arm around her waist, mmm... Lorenzo ringing up who knows what, when he shifted his gaze he nearly caught you. Caty decided to burst out laughing. Laughing so you'll laugh. And Lorenzo saying this girl's crazy in the head, look at how she laughs like a fool for no reason. Yes, at nothing, you go right on thinking that. And afterwards, she pulled away from him, Gerardo was daring, with his hand in her pocket to squeeze without being noticed, and Lorenzo told him that this way, like an amputee (Caty let out a yelp) he couldn't even ring up a book of matches. Gerardo let himself be carried away by the warmth of this thought and stretched out on the bed staring at the ceiling where the Pole and his hairy friends' footsteps resounded now making unimaginable noise, beating out a violent music of guitars, drums and bass.

He stared at the dark sky which seemed to rest on the rooftops, and found a rebellious and essential star close to a gadgety television antenna, but he realized that it wasn't, that the star was in a remote realm of his mind and that this light was the signal from an enigmatic inner beacon or perhaps, simply, the light of a tiny plane astonished above the millions of startling lights from the impassible, noisy city, as dizzyingly attractive as an abyss, that is to say, of the city as dizzyingly attractive as an abyss. Perhaps at this moment there was a similar light above, let's say, a coconut palm (just like it sounds, vulgar and Third World and everything), or let us be honest: no longer above a coconut palm or royal palm impregnated with other more secret lights inherited who knows when, but above one of so many similar multiple housing complexes on his Isla of cement, let us say Bayamón (the city of Bayamón) now treeless but with houses of cement cement cement all the same or similar, of course, above this present-day reality without *jíbaros* or huts that were necessarily huts as before but above all this infernal cement solid plague inescapable epidemic still shine, let us say, all the stars of the 18 1/2° latitude where you find in its designated meridian the aforementioned Borinquen, by all indications the homeland of Gerry the Pensive Nostalgic: perhaps close to tears despite the fact that real men don't cly, scold little Gerardo, ahem. Dialogues, snatches of conversation still vibrating in some tropical chink of his mind, words from years earlier received in an indelible manner (can you say: words said indelibly? not necessarily written, we'll say, with-indelible-ink?). There are words that wear out, faint, fall flat from weakness and breathe their last sigh, that is to say they even gasp and everything, you know, but you know there are others that prevail nonetheless like the marks of a branding iron: the time that the fellow called him a cuckold and he didn't say anything but went up to him and, with a left hook—Gerardo is a lefty, too!—he simply made him bite the cement: it was a dry crackling rapid violent powerful hook which those present couldn't see, like the lightning you don't see but whose effects you feel, and the bad-mouthed individual did not only fall onto his left flank without moving his feet from the ground—a perfect ninety degree angle from his original vertical position, as perpendicular to the terrestrial horizon as the line from a lead pencil, until he reached the dishonorable horizontality induced by the blow and the fall—, but rather the blow was of such an inexplicable quality that even when fallen the bad-mouthed adversary appeared to continue falling with a momentum as decided as it was frustrated, because the cement where he lay did not allow for further incursions toward the tormented center of the planet, and it seemed that the fellow maintained the genuinely linear inertia which wished to carry him to the aforementioned dark Newtonian center. Or more simply, without taking it any further, it simply had to do with the will to hide one's head and want to eat dirt. They had to empty several containers of water over his bad-mouthed face so that he would open his eyes and say the ritual words where am I what happened to me what Sealand trailer did I run into. But the bad word he'd said remained bloodily engraved although Gerardo knew that he wasn't, that his wife was poor but honorable, nonetheless the bad word made many things bleed in his tender very macho Antillian heart. So began certain misgivings, nocturnal quarrels, Gerardo packed his suitcase and went with amicable delicacy to Mommy's house, where he was received with overprotective happinesss, but his Mama didn't make him his guayabana drink the right way, and then he felt in his bones that he missed his own home, that would cover him with a genuinely familial roof, so he repacked his bags and returned trembling with emotion; that night he had a second honeymoon and left his little woman—as good as she is my goodness and as bad a life as I lead her, you know—breathless. But all of this is far from the TV antenna and the fleeting aforementioned light. Gerardo shrugged off his thoughts, which were growing gloomy beneath the insistent music from upstairs (not from the sky, because in NYC this word is rejected as one would not wish to think of the word water in the middle of the most harrowing desert) but from the Pollack's room, the Pole, you know. Nonetheless, the music didn't impede, but rather, stimulated, the thought that Caty, Harlemnian Newyorican, would arrive shortly and enjoy this fucking dislocated music that in actuality, to be completely honest, didn't bother him because he is young too, like the noisy young music, like his blood which pounds hot when he thinks of brief scuffles, of romantic surrenders, Caty open like a flower beneath his virile, insistent rhythmical push, so that he leaped to his feet to the beat of the music when he felt the two hard knocks on the door—not weak and timid, but hard, this is New York, not *la Isla*—and he opened it with a certain rhythm in his muscles, a rhythm that came from above—it doesn't have to be explained, right?—loud music which set his nerves on fire with a fascinating rhythm, nevertheless he was mentally mapping out a quick strategy, a plan of attack: the male would take the entrenched female by surprise. In a personal attack there are no shots: you whip out your bayonet and you enter with it pointing straight ahead, something sharp enters something that opens, thought General Gerald vaguely, four star strategist (but with only one in his head). Seeing her seated simply he sensed the perfume of the rice powder, her simple cologne, her gleaming skin, without makeup, seemed to smile at him and, in fact, she looked at him smilingly, joyous, defenseless, frank soft delicate when, without saying a word, he took her hands and made her stand up. In reality, Gerardo did the following:

1. He took her by the hands (to do so he had to lean over slightly, because he is almost six feet tall).

2. He made her stand up gently.

3. Without smiling, without haste, he reached out his left hand and unbuttoned the top button of her brown coat (a frankly loathsome color).

4. When he opened the third button from the top, he pushed it aside to uncover her chest. He found that she had fulfilled the agreement sealed with a kiss in the storeroom: she was wearing absolutely nothing between her coat and her skin. So he saw her bounteous (this is how they are usually described by poets who respect themselves) protruding breasts, full, the small hairs raised in expectant pleasure, the nipples hardened. Gerardo controlled himself to keep his cool, you know, do it right to the end, keep from leaning over immediately and touching the space between her breasts with his tongue, circle each resplendent nipple with the red flag of his tongue...

5. With a slightly trembling left hand, almost stiffly, he unbuttoned the three remaining buttons from top to bottom.

6. He proceeded to pull open her coat so that her solid brown body with disturbing roundnesses appeared before his blue eyes.

7. Without breathing, he pulled himself out of his shoes without tremblingly jumping out of them, pushing one against the other, without even leaning over, and extricated himself this time with a little more haste from his shirt and then unbuckled his belt and let his nice corduroy pants slide to the floor along with the boxer shorts wide like

panties, he lifted his legs one by one—if he did it at once, he'd kill himself! The old Botticelli couldn't have imagined such a birth of Venus: Caty on a lovely shell, a so humbly tropical Lorenzo di Medici seeing her to the depths, in reality gazing at the ineffable foxy Vespucci and then their two bodies came close until they grazed touching each other on their hot spots a sea of sensitivity: her breasts against his smooth hard breast, his penis—what do you expect!— perfectly erect touching her perfumed hair-covered fleshy triangle, then they come even closer and touch face to face in the center of the room, without having turned on the light of course but with enough light coming in from the street, two well-defined bodies in the middle of a late Harlem afternoon, solid, sturdy, burning itself in an advanced September of streets stiff with the most noisy and spoken and wordy silence ever experienced by any Boricua lover whatsoever, the words caught fire in their noble youthful minds and acquired a blinding density illuminated hidden interstices and then burned out as they fell like shooting stars while words continuously arose which repeated the preceding process and mixed with one another, they imposed themselves and competed in brilliance, it seemed that each one sustained a fiery contest of wits shadowy without sonorous words formed by luminous features

filaments of sunshine

a starry substance

the central nerve of a column of fire

wordfire in the perfumed Boricuan night

a luminous thread escaped from a furious bolt of lightning atop the peak of El Yunque

the heat arising from the raging heart of we'll say a Guatemalan volcano

Chichicastenango: the first two syllables of this indigenous name suggests unions similar to Gerardo and Caty's: they join further, their mouths seek each other, touch, connect, and Gerardo's tongue makes an excursion beneath her teeth, he makes it move with precision over her lower teeth rubbing her moist lip from one side to the other, he does the same with her upper lip, which he pulls a little, takes it between his, and then runs it over the area behind her teeth, including the palate, with his excellent boneless instrument—the tongue—at the same time Caty retreats slowly, united in a progressive dance that carries them inevitably, fatally, not to the door, naturally, but to the white bed which jumps for joy beside the half-lit window, and to the sheet that receives the girl's buttocks first, then her back, then her slightly bashful and separated legs in some miraculous way without there being a crash of both bodies because Gerardo, inconceivably conquering the force of gravity, remained attached the whole time to the descending body so that they both landed united on the bed in an almost floating violent manner, without striking it, but rather proceeding downward from the inevitable biped verticality in a progressively inclining manner until they achieved the horizontality dreamed of by souls moved by desire, and then he begged her to personally take his organ and place it where it belonged, and he felt Caty's fingers take it with a dexterity not excluding caution and place it there, in the burning moist cavity and then she gently moved her hips upward in such a manner that he responded with a swordlike thrust, penetrating her with a certain violence which made her retreat instinctively and moan, but Gerardo persisted with his assault until they reached a fundamental agreement: he would move downward and in a circular motion and she would move upward and in an inverse circular direction, so that the music of the dance did not wait for the music from upstairs, the music of the almost shouted rock with guitars that whined and drums that beat, and then the tempo picked up and the drums beat dryly making the room vibrate

the guitar humanly absorbed all of the accelerated rhythm without a definable melody

the rhythm was unsustainable the drums desperately sounded fired a long drum roll

The guitar vibrated to its most recondite string

wrapped in this inexpressible violent rhythm he she rhythm rock an ancient muscular knot released

a discharge of flowing burning electricity shakes the room loud low music escapes

he exhausted she exhausted they smile one on top of the other sweaty satisfied

because there's nothing like music to sedate the nerves and make people love happily into delirium

$$\frac{9}{\quad} \cdot$$

T HE LIGHT OF MORNING
the horns
the voices
the footsteps
the sounds of the city!
weigh upon your slow sleep flatten, sweetly torture your head
upon the pillow. Yawn ho-hum. Bitter sticky saliva as a remembrance
of the cheap wine that Caty brought. The perfume of rice powder on
the pillow sticks to your skin, has penetrated your pores, has become
part of the whiteness of the sheets, of the shattering clarity at the
window. You fall into the trap of a daydream, delicious recreation.
Her eyes are everywhere, like God, her indigenous skin, her soft
breathing, oh sweet sonorous substance, persist. Under the door? An
envelope with a message? Written before leaving you snoring plac-

idly full/empty? You get up heavily and open it. Aley has returned the twenty dollar bill that you had given him in gratitude for the luxuriant lump on the head.

*...and if you really want to help me, take care of my little animals for a few days, I'm taking a well deserved vacation...*

It's true that your joints function better, oiled with a certain honey that flows docilely in the center of your bones, but you must get dressed, wash your face, grudgingly brush your traditional teeth, prissily confront your solitude with every movement, above all, to answer Aley's note in a friendly way.

When you knock carefully on his door, silence. The only available image is that of Calabrio, the super.

"Do you know where Aley is?" you ask him charmingly. "I knocked on his door but he didn't answer."

Dino breathes deeply, makes a gesture with his hand. Itsa rough thing, sucha harda life, bitching world!

"Why do they make so many hassles, shit. I can't tell about the lives and miracles of the tenants. First, because I don't care, second because they don't pay me to do that. Do they want me to take Mr. Blake's path? No, grrr! I'm still going to set things on fire! They won't get me down so easily! Twenty years in this rat-trap, twenty! You were a little brat when I was fighting with as many *lumpen* as God created! Don't think that I'm going to give in. You know what I'm going to do now? Look, look at this!" Calabrio extracts a handsome, fat, heavy, very shiny crop made in Italy from his back pocket and shows it to you, Gerry. He shouts: "You know what I'm going to do? I'm going to collect the rent from the dirty Polack! If he doesn't pay me grrr I killa heem, I murder him grrr! Anyone who kills a fellow like that deserves a reward. And now, to top it all off, you come here asking stupid petty questions."

Dino should know better. He should know—for the sake of his health—that people suddenly shatter your peace when they come at you with anti-aesthetic shrieks, with a certain shoenbergian wave that doesn't interest you. You do the unspeakable to comprehend that he's going through a rough time, that you yourself would kill, singing out from pure joy, the aforementioned Pole, but your left arm tenses dangerously on the verge of a hook like the one mentioned earlier— about the fellow who after biting the cement seemed to obstinately obey newtonian momentum, a blind impulse in a direct line toward the center of the planet—but you control the muscular impulse that's blinding you.

"I only asked about Aleluya."

"Stress, stress!" shouts Dino.

"Three, four, five, it doesn't bother me," you say patiently, "but it would be a good idea to control yourself, Italian shit."

The word fires your desire to strike his Sicilian chin, but Dino is saved because he continues his anti-polack mission upstairs shouting hell stress I can notta putta uppa witha thissa shitta; just like in certain movies, you lean against the wall and you have to laugh like a Hollywood actor who conquers the situations in which the scriptwriter commercially embroils him, imagining Dino's silent nights in the general devastation of his objects of historical value. You can see that the dust of the city, intensely concentrated in his cave, has cracked his voice, drying out his throat like a centenarian grapevine, upsetting his originally clean meridional gaze, although it could not prevent him from being heard on quiet evenings bellowing *tarantelas*, *canzonetas* in a mellifluous sweet tongue. Short concerts which close, naturally, with the topical *O sole mio* or, surprisingly, with an uncommendable *Volare*. Afterwards, his room, which smells of rusting iron, of old urine, sinks into a scandalous silence, tense and dramatic, from which one could expect any sort of new development or, we'll say, the eruption of his vaguely vesuvian temperament. You think again about that song that was so much in fashion on your island years ago, the aforementioned *Volare* by Domenico Moduno, because the Pole did exactly that at this moment: he flew down the stairs shouting help, help this Sicilian monster wants to kill me, while Calabrio, celestially consecrated by love of the vendetta chases him, riding crop raised high shouting sonna offa the whore, as you hear it, thinking about this far from common ordinary city that's converted quantity into quality, with its stubborn face (NYC) but, you know, *hombre*, it's tremendously exciting. And you even smile like a fool without focusing on the crowd that jams the sidewalks along Lexington thinking of this tremendous Polack-Calabrio *maratón*, help help mediterranean monster *o sole mio*.

Nevertheless, there's no time to lose. You look at Aley's note. How you like to take refuge behind sayings and expression,

Gerry! To rest in the shade of the leafy tree of stereotype! Above all,
at moments when you have to make such bitching decisions. You bark
amiably:

If you don't want broth, they'll give you three cupfuls.

Guided by the directions that Aley had written in an elegant
hand, full of large and exquisite flourishes that you've only seen in the
fat volumes of the Demographic Register, you go from house to house
looking for the dogs. Apartment to apartment. Three of them live with
their fat owner in a luxurious, sumptuous apartment on lower Park
Avenue. You learn of the "dolce vita" led by some fortunate dogs. The
three little dogs live in their carpeted room—walls covered with
paintings of docile, amiable animals, little lacquered cribs, the atmosphere scientifically climatized against the rigors of cold/heat, they
eat from silver trays that have their names encrusted on them in golden
letters: each one gobbles down a healthy thick beef steak for Mrs.
Parker, she personally takes charge of cleaning their teeth with a gold
toothpick (*palillo*). Mrs. Parker takes them in her arms: a fat, loving
woman, double chin insured, in a room worth millions of dollars.
Arms jingling, neck burnishing jewels, silk on her ample bosom. She
says sweetly:

"Pete, Ruggiero, John, let me introduce you to your new friend."

You decide that you ought to say something. Just to make
yourself agreeable.

"They're cute."

"A delight, my dear. And so intelligent! Sometimes they won't
eat the least little tidbit for me, because they are my spoiled little
darlings and they can do as they please. But I threaten to take them to
the doctor and they shape up. Then they behave themselves very well,
like good little dogs. Oh, that featherbrained Daisy. Their little cousin.
I don't even want to think about it! You know what?"

"What?"

"She got away from me."

"Oh, gulp! A runaway, *sí*?"

"I called my friend the mayor, who stepped in immediately and
we found her after a week. She was a wreck!"

"I'm sorry to hear it, ma'am," you say with cutting irony. "It
makes me want to cry."

"Rolling in the mud with a dog twice her age!" The double chin restrained by a diamond necklace trembled, the formidable bosom rises and falls anxiously. "A vagabond without a pedigree, a filthy, drinking, stinking drunkard; oh, wow, such suffering."

"Wow, ma'am; oh yes, wow. Beer, whiskey?"

"The bums in Harlem gave him scotch and soda on a soup plate. He was called Mac. Afterwards, he'd walk up Third Avenue getting into fights with others of his breed. A brute, a common bully. Not everyone knows how to drink properly: one glass too many makes all the difference with his sort. To come to the point, I'll tell you what happened: Sergeant Patrick O'Casey broke it to me gently. He said to me—'Mrs. Parker, strengthen your soul to receive the bad news.' I knew immediately that it had to be about Daisy, it couldn't be anyone else! Had someone run over her with a truck? Had she fallen into the East River? Had she been kidnapped by some common criminals? Had she given herself over to alcohol? Had she decided to abandon her home forever? Was she suffering from one of those so-called Oedipal complexes? Had she taken refuge in a foreign embassy? Had she thrown herself off the Empire State Building? Had she joined the feminist movement? No. Worse yet! This wretched dog without a pedigree had dragged her obscenely the length of Second Avenue. The poor little creature couldn't stop herself in her forced march backwards. The unmannered bums shouted that instead of Second Avenue, they were going for the second coming, which made more than a few immoral neighbors laugh. Daisy, the laughingstock of the rabble! It was almost impossible to separate them, they were so united in their mad and desperate love! The same Sergeant Patrick O'Casey, the apostolic super-Catholic, took charge of the painful operation. Daisy, who was inexperienced and had not been properly counseled, surrendered herself passionately to someone who had lived four times as long as she. You know the sweet talk these bohemian streetrunners have, which so easily mocks the good faith of innocent souls. They spent the first week in a hole infested with cockroaches and rats; he came in late, she stayed at home, faithful and loving. She loved him blindly, as far as Patrick could tell, but the vagabond simply wanted her for reasons of convenience; I have no doubt that, despite his anti-social and anarchistic behavior, old Mac had reflected upon his long, disorganized life and had decided to settle down with a debutante. He was a 'status seeker' who aspired to improve his race and live with complete financial security for the rest of his days! When they tore Daisy from his clutches, he fought, bit, protested obstreperously and then, disappeared. They found him, hopelessly drunk, in the Bowery, that miserable slum that's overrun with drunkards and bums. Fortunately, his illiteracy prevented him from making out the street names because, otherwise, he might have shown up here with his buddies from Spanish Harlem to sing her sentimental and tearful serenades, you know. The doctor cured Daisy's mange and asked me to keep her under observation because the emotional shock had been tremendous. But what I most feared...was that she might have been made pregnant. And, when she missed her period, I nearly went mad. This presented me with a horrible moral dilemma which I discussed with Patrick: should we force her to abort? With children, no young dog of good family would come near her. We would have to wait until an old dog appeared who wished to take advantage of my little darling's youth and faux pas; a grey-haired widower obsessed with his dwindling years—what an alternative! Daisy was at the height of her youthful flowering. She died in childbirth, sob, uh, sniff sniff. The pups...two were stillborn. The father was syphilitic. Do you see why I insist that you take good care of these little animals, my friend? They must not consummate a horrible marriage like their little cousin!"

How much do you have to put up with? And all to return the ineffable friendship of your pal, buddy, brother, friend Aley. Elegant ladies and gentlemen admire the cute little animals, they look at you; you think that they judge you financially underendowed to be their owner (of the dogs, naturally). Oppressed by a consistently negative feeling of shame about your own immaculate person, you enter the marble vestibule, push the gilded bell, and when you pretentiously enter the inconceivably luxurious apartment of Mrs. James Woolworth Burroughs, you stand thoughtful, asking yourself if the woman might not regret placing her two little dogs in your calloused worker's hands, but this reflection, which places you on a par with the floor irritates you, you stand up straight, Gerald, firm, painfully majestic, while the slender woman with white hair pulled up into a high bun smiles amiably; teeth matching the necklace of pearls; flat-chested; sharp bones, shoulders, dry hips; her long dress caresses the rug where you sink in up to your knees. An older, very bald man remains seated in his armchair, reading the *New York Times*.

"It's a scandal, Cornelia," the man says suddenly. "How can they allow such outrages?"

"Jimmy, please. Don't pay attention to the bad news. Remember your ulcers, love. And your pressure."

The man throws the paper down and begins to pace, dragging his slippers across the plush, well-kept, snow-white carpet, bending over, profoundly preoccupied, he shakes his head.

"What the devil do the police do?", his voice like sandpaper over zinc. "Are they going to wait until those anarchists blow the city to pieces? They should have learned from the blackout! Now it's the bomb at ITT. Tomorrow it will be in our home, Cornelia, oh, Cornelia!"

Madame Cornelia pushes a button. Down the dazzling hallway: past gilded oil paintings, rugs, luxurious panelling, appears a decidedly black young lady with a tall glass on a gold tray. James Woolworth Burroughs takes a pill from the marble box decorated with applique and swallows it with the pink contents of the glass. He lets himself fall into the overstuffed chair, head reclined, eyes closed exhaustedly, tired. Cornelia neé Emerson pushes another button—or the same one, you don't know, Gerald—and in the long passageway appears a decidedly blonde vision, tall, blonde-haired, eyes so blue they don't seem to see. White head-piece, spotless white uniform that lets you see her legs above the knees. You observe her curly golden hair—clearly she's not from any part of the city. She carries a little dog in each arm, reclined against her long, thin body.

"Have they eaten their tea, miss?"

"In part. They accepted the canapes of caviar. They refused the ice cream cake."

The girl speaks with an accent you've only encountered recently, Gerry. The powerful are in the habit of importing Nordic maids. Crude snobbery, Aley had said. And you had replied harshly: Where the fuck do the rich come off...? Bourgeoisie, Aley had explained. You will meet a Scandinavian angel, Birke Andressen, torn from a Danish village. You watch her disappear subtly into one of the inner passageways. Mr. James Woolworth Burroughs has covered his face with the *Times* and snores stridently, making the stockmarket section tremble.

"You can take them out with Mrs. Parker's dogs," Mrs. Burroughs whispers to you, coming close enough to almost touch you with her leathery shoulders. "They're from a good family; the widow idolizes them as much as I do mine."

"*Sí*," you draw back from the whiskey breath. "They're cute, ma'am."

Mrs. Burroughs corrals you between two Chinese vases, beneath the illustrious portrait of a New England ancestor. You retreat, wishing it were the black girl or Birke Andressen who was so bold.

"But they can be disorderly and they put naughty ideas into my innocents' heads. They suffered a serious emotional shock when their little cousin Daisy died in such an unseemly manner. Ruggiero has transcended his shame and has gone over to the left, to imply that class differences should be abolished. It's known that he even went to look for the miserable bum who abused Daisy's maidenhead, intending to form a cross-class friendship. The young are idealists, that is why you have to watch them. Sons of good families, but rebels while their fathers maintain them generously. They preach things that run counter to the security of this country. The *gauche divine* wolves in sheep clothing, what in Federal Germany they called *Wolffendesguizzenlambenn*. Be energetic, love, and avoid all types of agitation and cohabitation. They've gone so far as to plant a bomb in the central office of ITT! Are you responsible for collecting Mr. Olivio Jones' dog?"

"Yes," you say dryly, like a professional dog walker and, in passing, with a brusque gesture, you push away the sinister hand that has alighted tentatively on your crotch. "Hey, leave it alone...!"

"Mr. James is asleep."

You manage to escape the senile entrapment, get into the elevator, push the button to the 69th floor, as though it were merely to your third floor in Harlem. Marvelous ascent. One second and there you are. Ding dong. Residence of the constructivist artist, Olivio Jones. Had Aley said that Jones was an artist, in one of his rare moments of expansiveness? A loft. Glass-enclosed, as befits his profession. But you experience a fleeting confusion at the hammers, nails, saws, pieces of wood: a carpenter couldn't live in such a pretty place, with the walls lined with posters, a giant painting by one Andy and another of a fat man named Capote.

Legalize pot.

Gay Liberation Front.

You're attracted to the poster where the signs of the zodiac are represented by couples fornicating. Soul music emanates from the four track stereo, slow and wild, you know. A girl lies on the vast white sofa in skin tight white jeans, her dazzling white breasts exposed. She looks at you with curiosity, smiling. You shift your gaze toward Mr. Jones, fifty years old, red shorts, hairy bare chest. Beneath the thin hair, a bald scalp burned by a recent trip to the south. Twisted tree trunks, scrap metal ashtrays, spilled cans of paint. If the truth were told, Gerry, apart from the bounties of the reclining girl smiling at you, you feel a certain repulsion and rage, while the dog with the red hide barks, jumps and growls at the animals that you hold on their leashes. Olivio Jones gives the finishing touches to a construction on his vast worktable, that is to say, he nails a triangle of aluminum to the board which he has filled with spirals of iron, screws, springs. To this, he's glued pieces of pictures of camp actors. Finally, he attaches the construction to the wall, steps back and contemplates it with half-closed eyes, sighs deeply with satisfaction. No, with triumph. You take it all in, Gerry, standing firm in the hallway, defiant; a cold smile surveying everything, shaking your head. The girl jumps up.

"The area in the upper left represents the frustration of youth in search of itself," she says.

Olivio Jones looks circumspectly at his work. He responds in the manner of a master of ceremonies:

"I appreciate your observation, Moira, my guiding star. Naturally, in the other areas I also wished to dramatize this search for identity which tortures you, not unusual in girls of Greek descent, my dear. You seem reserved to me, enigmatic, bequeathed with the mysterious ancient smile appropriate to a considerably pre-Hellenic period."

"Kretta," says the girl in perfect ancient Greek. "Knossos. Tirinto."

"The crisis of our epoch. The galloping industrialization, aeronautics, cybernetics, McLuhan, you know."

"'Who am I?', the central area to the left seems to shout. But, where does that leave you, my dear? How do you project yourself into my existence? This is the question that the work suggests to me."

Olivio Jones goes gravely to the work, encompasses the upper part with a sweeping gesture of his extended arm, his palm upward. He indicates a large fat vertical screw, at the base of which are attached two circular bolts, one on either side; the base of the screw and the bolts almost disappear below a smooth entanglement of dark, metallic thread. The tip of the screw points ominously toward the triangle of aluminum which shines in the middle of the work. Moira assents.

"You have achieved it. You and I amidst the anti-erotic repression that asphyxiates this decadent society. The utilization of the means of the mass media and the manipulation of Eros by big business."

"Marcuse."

"Anyone of them. Adorno, Benjamin, etc."

"Agreed. Anything more with respect to the work, my dear?"

"It is symptomatic of the mechanization of the aggregate of values," she explains, her flaming red hair plastered to her ears, her frankly violet eyes surveying the painting. "But, how will you express the symbiosis between what was formerly called the spirit and the concrete, immediate, on-going struggle of the workers?"

"I see what you're driving at."

"What means can you use to make the great industrial and financial capital disposed to negate, in circumstances that could even appear optimal for the total liberation of man, the real, efficient and undeniable participation of the workers in the economic means which have been systematically denied to them?"

"Look at this," Jones indicates four parallel nails in the upper right-hand corner of the construction.

"Bah!" Moira places her hands on her hips. "Metaphysics."

"Oh, no, please!"

"Apart from the fact that it in no way reflects my reading of Bakunin."

"Moira, my dear, I can't lower myself further. Figuratism is limited. I try to be as true as possible to perceptible reality. Especially to your reality, within the neo-revolutionary context."

Moira draws her green-fingernailed hand over Olivio's head, her white serpent body undulates and you, Gerardo Sánchez, ahem, contemplate her, you savor her in silence: who knows how far these people will go?

"Don't get mad, love," the serpent Moira pleads. "Oh, the

sensibility of the creative spirit explodes so easily."

Olivio Jones, the constructivist, is off-balance, beside himself, nervous, choked up, misunderstood, miserable.

"I don't know how the devil to understand you!"

He pulls open a drawer, takes out a small, burnt pipe, empties a brick-colored powder into it, tamps it down and waits while Moira applies the lighter flame. They both suck with tranquil fervor. Moira closes her marvelous, slightly Cretan eyes. You remain standing in the middle of the livingroom.

"Listen," you say brutally, "I came to get the dog!"

Jones gives you a vacant look.

"Oh, certainly. Yes, this rogue."

Moira captures the dog, she rubs it between her breasts, she caresses it, oh, caressingly, while Olivio Jones affixes the leash to his collar. The dog shows his teeth, shakes himself, barks.

"Son of a bitching rascal," smiles Moira, pulling his ears, eyes lost in a peaceful cloud. "Doubly a dog. We don't even know what breed he is. If he bothers you, hit him. If he follows behind a bitch, let them fuck; we humans suffer enough repression! Child, this hash is delicious, has Andy tried it?"

"He's in the Far East."

"What? Gone without a word to us? And Norman?"

Olivio Jones growls. "Don't worry about it, love. That thing with Norman won't happen again. A moment of weakness. Solitude...oh, my dear, this material makes me sentimental."

Naked, Moira dances, slowly raising her arms, oscillating her hips Greekly. Fascinated, you can't take your eyes off the body that seriously threatens to keep you anchored in the studio.

"What's the name?" you ask, lost.

"Moira," says Olivio, an ephemeral presence, who raises his gaze to the glass ceiling, ascends in a paradisiacal cloud.

"No, the dog."

"Oh, Allen, in honor of my poet friend."

When Olivio Jones begins to unbutton his shorts, you scoop Allen up and leave precipitously, indignant with traditional modesty. You are highly impressed, Gerry, but content. The night before you slept with—that's a figure of speech—Caty, after long months of strict monastical abstinence. Today, everything seems to have conspired: sex and more sex. The impact of the Scandinavian Birke Andressen upon your intensely earthy brain, the old Cornelia neé Emerson with her hand thrust into your crotch like a fishhook, Moira dancing placidly naked. It is as if people live on an astral cycle, too, and in one particular month there is an unbridling that no one can escape. You conclude that

Misery loves company

but that has nothing to do with economic conditions, but with the solitude denied immediately by angelic feminine visions, by surprising unions.

Distracted, you arrive on Fifth Avenue, you walk several blocks Uptown to Central Park, and enter through a path of trees that have just shed their leaves. You think about the zoo where an exemplary elephant feeds on tiny peanuts, that is to say, only on peanuts; the heavy mass of a rhinoceros launches itself with a giant splash into its private swimming pool, artistic giraffes look over their shoulders at the rest of the unhappy living creatures; the amorous llamas from the Peruvian-Bolivian tableland of Titicaca look with languid eyes, sensually blinking at the multitude that says justly, what a delicate loving primal structure from the tableland, a delicately erotic spectacle which provokes furious masturbation from an impeccable, very New York young man. Seated on a cold iron bench between trees deteriorated by the season's advance, you meditate while the animals jump, bark at the butterflies, make bigger smaller puddles...Just the thought that the fortunate Burroughs' dogs sleep in the same room with Birke Andressen fills you with a humiliating envy of an irritatingly doglike quality. Cold doggie tongues like boiled ham lick the opaline bodies of desperate maidens. Moira, Jones and their dog— undreamed of positions on the red rug, on the vast white sofa. Oh, Catalina!

Englishwomen
American girls
Polish girls
Irish
Boricuas
Cubans
Greeks
Swedes          IN SUM, THE UN

Jews
Mexicans
Chinese
Italians
Argentines
etcetera

open like flowers awaiting the luminous arrival of the bee, his ex-wife fallen below him like ripe fruit in the obstinate summer without respite of his island, oh. The semen runs frenetically through the sewers of New York. But semen isn't the only thing that runs. Raising your eyes, you see the Pole leaping obstacles with exemplary grace and agility, closely followed by a Calabrio transfigured by the joy of a Greco-Roman marathon. You watch them disappear at high speed among the tangled bushes. A vitriolic word tears the cold air of that hour, warlike shouts ring out once more, "you whore" in Italian, and you smile, you laugh, truly happy with your dogs leaping, barking with maximum grace, assuring dozens of curious bystanders that yes, they're yours, you adore them, conscious that you've begun to dominate the art of lovingly deceiving your audience; because the sense of ownership is strong, deeply rooted, and its negation—non-canine ownership—will disappoint the masses. The Olympic image: Calabrio-Polack arises, still sliding in your memory, you laugh, what can you do? You find yourself talking to yourself, growling affectionately at the dogs. You also recognize their individual quirks; you hate them fiendishly, murderously; you acknowledge the solicitous loving approach of the brown-haired brat who plays with them, throws himself on the ground and talks to them, hold them side by side in his nine year old hands, six years older than little Gerardo; the memory catches you at a good time, Gerry, you need direct sunshine, perennially leaf-covered trees, green shade contrasting with the blue white violence of the light, little Gerardo plays with his mangy dog, okay, as much a dog as any other! And, paradoxically, to further underline your decision to leave, the dry old woman with an extravagant hat interrupts. She comes leaning over lovingly, flaking the regrettable powder on her face with her dentured smile. You see her stoop in the direction of the boy, blind grandmotherly instinct in search of her grandchild; the child smiles at her and opens his arms. The grandmother swoops down on Ruggiero and hugs him warmly—darling, honey, precious little creature, my child. The boy is left out, Gerry and, overcome by bestial fury, you give the leashes a forceful tug. The startled dogs leap. The old woman falls on her ass, her spindly legs spread wide. You get up, are about to leave, but find yourself staring directly at a policeman's solid chest.

"I could send you to jail," says this character.

"I'm leaving," you say shortly, eying the Irishman. "She got tangled in the leashes. The woman."

""What woman?" says the guard, while the old woman howls at his feet. "I could send you to the shade for mistreating the poor little animals."

# 10

.

NATURALLY, EVERYTHING WORKED OUT according-to-plan: Aley didn't argue when his compatriot told him—with a firmness he hadn't shown till now—that no and no and no, I'm not going to take care of them anymore. Aley shrugged his shoulders, clasped his bicolored hands and, once again, gazed piously at the empty sky as though he were saying forgive him he knows not what he does. Nonetheless, he laughed, he didn't think about his usual esoterically manufactured gods, reinterpreted by his small African-look cranium.

"I thought that Birke and Moira were going to convince you to continue for at least two weeks."

"Listen, this Moira...she's rich, right?"

"It isn't a question of where you're from, but where you're going, Gerry. The filthy rich Engels like a comet straight for communism. And poor exploited John Doe like a comet straight for the capitalist dream. What did you think of Birke, authentic Nordic angel, vulgarly imported Valkyrie?"

"The most interesting part of your job."

"That's your opinion. Which I respect, but don't share. Bigote tells me you have been to see him."

"I wanted to talk to someone. I had to."

"That you want to go back to *la Isla*."

"I wanted to go back that day. He's forming a band. Bolo's in it, too. Bolo doesn't play anything. He's running numbers."

"Strange fauna, right? This is where you come in."

"What?"

"Into the everyday circus."

"Give me a break, Aley. His wife doesn't want him to be a musician. He bought a second-hand drum. He told me that he'd played with Eddie Palmieri himself. And with Puente. Is that possible?"

"If he says so..."

"A musician lives the good life. They work at enjoying themselves. And they have tons of women."

Aley gazed at him, smiling.

"Well," he said, "I suppose that isn't everything."

"They make good money."

"What do you think of the Parker dame?"

"It's ridiculous, the way she takes care of those dogs! As if they were people."

"And the Burroughs?"

"Dangerous. If it had been Birke, I wouldn't have done it. Or Moira. Wow, Aley, she's great! She smoked hash and then danced naked. They say he's a painter."

"You've seen it. He makes a fortune. How'd it be if you became a constructivist painter?"

"That's it!," laughed Gerald. "I can do a bit of carpentry!"

In Gerry's very cold room at nine in the morning on a cloudy, grey, threatening day, at the end of September, Gerry and Aley doubled over with laughter, clutching their delicate stomachs aching with a fit of laughter.

"Go for it," said Aley crying, wiping daintily at his nose, laughing convulsively. "But I mean it. It's fine art. Don't think that you can conceive today's world with yesterday's tools. The only thing that seems to me to be truly disastrous in today's art is the *Ladies in Waiting* by the brilliant Picasso. Brother, he should never have even come near Velásquez' painting, much less disturbed it in such a fashion!"

"That's what's wrong with you, Aley. You start talking about things that not even God understands."

"I know that, on the surface, Calder's mobiles have no relationship to the delicious sensation of damp delicate wool, nor to the immense Policleto and his bestial unforgettable Canon where he astutely seeks the secret of beauty, that is to say, with regard to the human figure he seeks the exact proportions so as to understand at which point beauty is to be found. The ideal perfect man has set proportions where the following proportions come into play: head, one eighth of the body; trunk, the last lumbar vertebrae as the point which divides the statue exactly in half; from the waist on down, knees, legs. He outlined the formula necessary for creating the sculpturally perfect body. You must see his celebrated Doryphorus, it illustrates what he was trying to say. And, as far as the illustrious Praxiteles, he creates beautiful feminine sculptures with interesting results. Sensual and simple human figures. You must see his *Venus of Egnido*, Gerry. And also, his humanized *Apollo*, the 'lizard hunter', and his *Hermes*, messenger of the gods. They deal with the celebrated praxitelesian curve, where the figures appear, resting on one foot, with rounded forms and they're perfectly amazing. We could also speak of the aged Escopas in his desire to represent the inner being, the expression of the human face. And then, rebellious Lisipo with his discredited, beaten athletes, who clean the mud and dust from their dirty, non-classical bodies. Common everyday people: us! And he was able to create a space between the observer and the piece when he had his figures bend an arm in front of their bodies. And, Belvedere? This incredible torso that influenced the aging Michelangelo, Gerry, and is a landmark in the Greco-Roman iconography, I mean, that's how it seems to me. Of course, we won't get into the Paleo-Christian art, nor the Romantic, nor the Gothic, nor the Byzantine, because I suspect that it would take us some time and the morning isn't for that. But you could see reproductions, pictures of *La Pieta* by the illustrious Michelangelo, and then leaping jumping ahead we will come to Rodin and then to Brancussi, Chillida, Calder and a flood of contemporaries who're on top of it. Art, dear friend, has had much to offer in the course of its history. Enough for now, do you think that you're sufficiently educated to begin a career as a constructivist? In the style of Olivio Jones? It would be interesting," smiles Aley prissily, eyes sparkling behind horn-rimmed glasses. "Rousseau, the customs official Rousseau 'didn't know how to paint', and produced marvels. Grandma Moses, the centenarian, didn't know how to paint, but she produced Fra Angelican marvels. Think about Birke Andressen. 'Paint' her with the instruments you have at hand, as Olivio Jones does with his Moira, a word which, you might not know, means something like 'destiny' or 'limit' in Greek. Furthermore, beauty is not achieved only by creating it, but by putting it in order, by organizing it with already existent elements. In dealing with the Scandinavian Birke, it wouldn't be necessary for you to make, as the ancients did, some new version of the charming Swedish Virgin Viklau, because time has not passed in vain and Danes and Swedes are not the same. In regard to your plump Caty, perhaps you could follow the highly idealistic but figurative model of the celebrated and immaculate Venus by Willemdorf, Gerry, because both tend to be somewhat on the heavy side, with pronounced breasts and abundant hips of supreme reproductive value."

"Lay off Caty, Aley. Your black babe isn't anything out of this world, either."

"What?" Aley appeared surprised, but also very concerned. "You've seen her?"

"A black American, long like bamboo. With an afro so big that she looks like a pencil with an eraser."

"Don't let me hear you criticize her, Gerry."

"Or you Caty. What's her name?"

"Sister in the faith, Iremita Johnson. She sings in the temple. And she's a soul singer."

"You had her in your room."

Aley seems supremely worried, serious, gazes at him gravely. At his friend and compatriot and neighbor. He lowers his voice. He says:

"Listen, Gerardo, you haven't seen her here, okay? She's a highly valuable comrade. I didn't think that anyone..."

"One night, I couldn't sleep because of the Pole's music. I was sitting on the stairs. Three in the morning... There wasn't any light, you didn't see me. The two of you were carrying a really big package."

Aley gazes at him thunderously. Worried, exceedingly concerned, he paces around the room, steps on Gerardo's green rug several times. Circles, meditating, really very meditative. His friend had never seen him so, thoughtful, but very..., you know. His footsteps don't stop. He says:

"An error which I can't afford the luxury of repeating. Okay, not a word."

"Okay. And don't you say a word about Caty."

"All right, comrade."

The word comrade fills him with pride, it's the first time that his friend has used it, he puffs with pride and smiles, pushes out his chest, his muscles stronger than ever, a certain clarity also penetrates his brain, shines from his now radiant blue eyes. Aley knows, he understands.

"Do you have anything to do?" Aley asks.

"Not until twelve."

"So you might as well get to know Manolo, who can give you work until you're established as a constructivist."

"That's great."

DELICATESSEN
BOTANICA
DRUGSTORE
LIQUOR STORE
COMIDAS CRIOLLAS

The subterranean rumble of the subway rattles the thin glass of a furniture store. Strange fellows with sleepless faces drinking cheap wine in a doorway. Strange fellows who spend their whole lives there, without leaving the Barrio, seeing the same faces. Like staying in the little village in the center of his Caribbean island, nothing more nor less! He remembered that in Brooklyn the elevated train passes an enormous expanse of white crosses in a cemetery. The dead of the whole world. The German who fled Munich after the coup of the hitlerian brewery; the tiny Yugoslav, whose eyebrows formed a single line, who began by cleaning shoes and ended up as the owner of a butchershop; the Russian who swam out of the Crimea in 1917; the Greek who cried as he left the Pireo, vowing to return, surprised, thirty years later, by a thunderous heart attack; a young Dutchman came to familiarize himself with the personal history of the Knickerbocker's Manhattan and spent forty years running a dairy on Long Island: the rest of eternity (that's a saying) beneath the serene soil of Brooklyn; the dead of the world, united beneath the imperishable shell of the earth. People move, they travel. But he hadn't seen, in that sea of crosses, 'Latino' names that weren't Italian: evidently, his compatriots preferred to be buried on *la Isla*. Eastern, Pan Am, American tranquilly provided commercial transport for their sentimental coffins. Oh, live Boricuas for hire, dead Boricuas for hire ay, leaving behind a river of sweet nostalgia, an 'astonishing' sea of righteously excreted sweat. Is this the way it is? he wonders doubtfully. Toward the Bronx, the elevated train passes over rickety roofs, streets full of human, motorized transit, windows raised on walls of old brick where disheveled old women—clearly his compatriots—come to hang out their clothes, clothespins, *sí*. Yes, people move, not like those fellows who drink their cheap wine. They move from one side to another, which is why he'd seen veritable train congresses in the tortured underground of Times Square, of Penn Station from whence the trains depart meteorically toward the outskirts of the incomprehensible city. Hard-worked tireless metallic serpents whistle sinisterly in certain areas, cackle in the hair-raising tunnels, changing lights in the darkness of the caverns.

They walk down Lexington, past 116th. Buses, cars, a number of trucks discharge merchandise on the sidewalk children toddle among the beloved barkings like certain unforgettable memories, suddenly surprised by a frozen current of city wind, unknown to the distant Rocky Mountains which incubate strong doses of snow for the not-so-distant winter, today's cold autumn. Ashen men, with rat faces, blacks with pronounced jawbones, yellowing Boricua women without makeup, with weak watery turbulent secret eyes. Enormous billboards, walls of brick. Trash cans now not so malodorous, the intensity of the smells softened thanks to the mildness which the season imposes on every perceptible thing. Coca-Cola, Fanta, of course. Old Grand Dad Whiskey. Schaeffer. Goya. The sidewalks persist in their obstinate grey color against the darkening brick of the buildings, the darkened facades, the black mouths of the entrances; the pavement that seems to extend over a ground as hard as granite.

Manhattan is an island, but an island supported by the rocky immovable solidarity of a continent. What will happen in the winter?, he asked himself lazily, an inconceivable question without rhyme or reason. He immediately remembers that his ex had always been against the idea of flying to the city. Oh, this business of winter, you know. The snow, ay! Because she considered it an abnormality, a sickness, nature's gelid grippe, frozen fever, chronic cycle, God's punishment on Man, inconceivable plague, an extended lustrous white ulcer that crammed the houses with ridiculous objects, useless in his parallel: thick pullovers, monstrous sweaters like skinned animals, variegated jerseys, knit tops, thick gloves, scarves, ear muffs, human-canine muzzles; the thought of winter had given his poor ex the chills. Is it possible that—just as the Christmas stamps say—the white waves deposit themselves on the sidewalks, on the aggressive roofs, on the vilely neglected handball courts, on the visors of the vigilantes? That a snow with questionable intentions disfigures statues, erases the sometimes shining profile of the equestrian statues, murders certain birds surprised in their preparations for immigration to warmer climes? Gerardo dug his exceedingly tropical hands into his plastic pockets, instinctively pulled his decided chin to his chest, exhaled an unparalleled smoke ring, smoker of the cold, almost pleasurable, adapted—*sí*—to the environment, experienced in the life of the capital of the world, uf. But this isn't so bad. It isn't winter yet. He was pleased to see that he could still do without his heavy coat, that his imagination had simply played a trick on him (is that how you say it?), freed his hands from their confinement but, nevertheless, rubbed them together, smiled at the father of the family who-never-pays-their-rent (who tended a complex kiosk with handkerchiefs, sheets, highly unaesthetic scarves, votive candles, used magazines, plants with designated spiritualistic powers) on the corner of 113th; he walked spiritedly, recognizing himself in his compatriots' faces, hearing his language sadly dominate the halls, the bars, the doorways, the stands with hot dogs and coffee, the wretched little shops, the *botánicas* which disseminate plants with an unexpectedly universal power against the evil eye, herbs that reunite separated lovers through strange emanations, hot leaves which placidly dynamite tranquil family gatherings, shoots of forcefully designated power against envy and loss of love and forgetfulness and other non-manufactured products. All of the foregoing—with the exception of the snow, the autumn cold, etc.—gives a falsely Boricuan, Caribbean flavor to the sector, as though a flotilla of mad sailors had dragged their native island to the 42nd parallel, pulling it with fantastic cables of reinforced nylon until they deposited it in this recognizably cold belt. You don't have to talk too much, he said in absolute silence, to tell where you're from. He thought about this while Aley walked erectly at his side, greeted by hundreds of people who approached to inquire about his health, to wish him the best of luck, to demonstrate their friendship: men, women, children, an envied Gerardo, proud of such good company.

"Look," Aley points out a sign. "There it is."

EL MESON DEL CORDERO

They were received by a stout, hawk-nosed man with penetrating eyes that were as light as his folk songs from Avila. His abundant and attractive salt-and-pepper ash-grey hair, greying with age, seventy winters, *joder*. Standing between the small tables covered by immaculately white woven tablecloths.

"Is this the man you told me about, Aley?"

"Yes. Gerardo."

"Oh-ho, they'd call the lad a Scandinavian."

"Meet Manolo," says Aley. "He's as stubborn as the famous mule of Toledo, but he's one of us."

The two hands gripped, let's see who'll win. Real hard, between men, whitening their fingers. Manolo withdraws his hand and wipes it on his apron, which smells of onions from Granada, of pimentos from Cadiz, of garlic from Castile. Gerardo understands that this reaction arises from a purely professional compulsion: to wash one's hands before making the soup, dry them, wash them after touching dangerously unfamiliar objects like, for example, his hands. He spoke firmly or, rather, with unnecessary brusqueness, unable to avoid the inheritance of the thousands of priests and conquistadors of the great anti-indigenous campaign of centuries before in his tender comrade's soul, a temperament which weighed upon his being against his will, as he carried it like a huge national wart which could not be uprooted, furiously visible, identifiable: *Español, sí*, you know, as they say.

"This is your great opportunity to learn a trade, by God." Manolo tells him with indescribable tenderness. "Unless you'd rather do something else."

"This is the delicacy which I have observed in so many Spaniards," smiles a not-so-smiling Aleluya. "Harsh on the outside but
with a certain very warm inner wine. This is rare these days."

"You tread on dangerous ground, braggart," Manolo, seriously,
it's a joke after all, but he is very serious, immovable in appearance.
"You open your mouth and, by God..."

"You're not responsible for your roots, Manny. You've fought
hard to rid yourself of a certain obscurantist heritage..."

"Well, it's best not to talk about obscurities, you. By the way,
what's up with *la iremita*?"

Aleluya remains frozen, pales. Gerardo notices something's up,
even a blink is enough to show him that his friend has lost ground. But
Aley bounces back immediately, upright, stiff. He says:

"Don't say *la*. Her name is Iremita, with a capital I. Johnson."

"But, man, that's a typical Spanish expression. *La Lola went to
the port*, if you know what I mean."

"Well, Manolo, here's your man," says Aley gazing penetratingly into his eyes, into those clear eyes accustomed to centuries old
walls. "You don't need to say that I recommended him to you. You
don't need to say *anything*."

"Okay, Aley." Manolo gazes at him intelligently, agrees. "You
know me well, comrade, friend."

"Thank the Lord you don't have to pay for my services. As an
employment agent, I'm the best, right?"

"When can you start?" Manolo asks Gerardo.

"Tomorrow."

"Well, I'll expect you bright and early. Hey, go with God!"

"Regards to the *doña*, Manny."

"You'll both be welcome, lad."

"Until tomorrow," says Gerardo dryly, to bring things to a close.
With Aley, he begins the trip back to his building.

# 11

.

DOING WHAT? Oh, a little of everything!
He brings in the trash, cleans, peels plantains, denudes tender potatoes
of who knows what patriotic precedence. He becomes emotional
before the tear-jerking-smile of the onion, cold as the sap of a summer
in his land; it's sad to hear him cry so loudly, weeping, appropriately,
because the onion is an extremely sentimental bulb and lends an air of
melancholy, of tragedy to anyone who comes in contact with its fine
skin, a certain restrained desperation, a resignation which is tradition-
ally ascribed to mothers: abnegation before all else. He also takes
messages, because his future trade has not yet inundated him with its
paralyzing pride, tomorrow's professionalism obtained with great
effort has not yet penetrated his heart to create an arrogant public
image for him, wrenching him from the masses.

Gerardo realized that he was flooded with happiness like warm broth every time he thought of the clear egg white of his future. Aided by his personal, ruminant, modestly reflective philosophy, he thought, without turning his ideas over too much:

The way the world spins, mistel!

He summed it up in this way—without daring to sum anything up in depth—his experiences, the things he had lived through from recordable childhood up to his newyorican present. He also arranged them in order to incubate a few dreams to which, because of his vigorously tranquil youth, he had full right. He saw himself returning like an anti-Indian to his town in the Boricuan hinterland, establishing not, we'll say, a *mesón del cordero*—the lamb, a four-legged animal whose only island representative is deeply engraved on the official seal like a sad admission—but, let's say, a *mesón de* pig, *de* cow, *de* hen, *de* goat, *de* guinea pig, *de* hog pudding, *de* rennet, *de* tripes, *de* famous fried food, not very European things admittedly—at least, in style—but, finally, things with which one could make do while killing what kills us. And, then, he could deal exclusively in all kinds of vegetables, because Manolo taught him that the Spanish—regarding that which grows from the earth—devour, or are capable of devouring, without caution or prejudice, the most humble shrub, in the same way that there was not, according to Manolo

> a terrestrial insect
> an underground insect
> a freshwater insect
> a marine insect
> a flying insect

that was unlikely to be baked, in garlic, in the imaginative heterodox paella, in a stew, in a broth, gnaw-gnaw. Plants, minerals, every imaginable animal must be minutely bitten, sucked, demolished, masticated, exterminated, digested with a delightful peninsular hatred, subjecting the romantic jawbones (*quijadas*) to quixotic adventures of the appetite, somewhat Christian termites, the world is a bloody banquet.

Clearly, the stupendous Gerry was not alone even during the least hungry hours following dinner. He was accompanied, in the most momentous moments, by the waiter Kenneth Rivera—long-legged, black-haired, beard-less—who took advantage of these moments of relative peace to extricate himself from the thick confused

Spanish accent which Manolo (Manny to the Barrio) had made him acquire to give ambience to the *mesón*. His compatriot's excessive release of z's and c's and shameless j's had grated upon Gerardo, but he came to understand that this was nothing more than a colorful costume which Kenneth donned and discarded with the same ease as his little red jacket, his black bow tie and the black pants with black silk ribbon down the side. It was clear, nonetheless, that Kenneth didn't always find the proper angle in which to situate his motley stock of z's, c's and j's of noble descent, for which reason, he was accustomed to expending them extravagantly in an exercise as fruitless as it was draining, endowing the narrow intimate atmosphere of the small lounge with a zort of zonorouz monotonouz mezmorizing buzz, zubmitting Gerardo'z zenzative peazantz eardrumz to a deafening buzzing zound from which a rezonation of mmmmmmmmmm that reached a high pitch on the zyzenthezizer ztayed vibrating in zee air. In the same way, it was clear that the Avilian Manolo, a man of an absolutely folkloric mentality, flamenco dancers and dark singers, was not opposed to his employee's linguistic excesses, since they plainly added a lively and flashy glitter to the atmosphere, for which he didn't have to pay a dollar, forget the dollar!...not even the thinnest copper coin. Kenneth was not only the picturesque waiter, but also the vaguely unsolicited show of the *mesón*, a spectacle which Manny's compatriots enjoyed with typical sweet sadism, as they were by now accustomed to the peculiar Spanish which greeted them at lunchtime. Naturally, Kenneth was not disturbed by the peninsular whistles and digs to which he was gently subjected, given that it was enough to hear them speak among themselves—if the miracle of communication were to be achieved one day—to cheerfully conclude that he was dealing with citizens of various countries who were not accustomed to one another, were incapable of speaking directly to one another, for which reason they should easily comprehend the Kennethian deficiencies with regard to spoken language.

Every one of the peninsulars embellished his words so that his companions would not be able to understand him, so that the *mesón* contained a babelesque concentration of strange accents and languages. The ineffable Manolo remained untouched, gazing at them from the heights of his Avilian Castilian Spanish—although he also detested certain syntactical twists of the also Castilian José María de

Rivera—criticizing his compatriots' mania for entangling themselves at any hour in a dispute *(garata* in Basque) longer than the Tajo River. There arose moments of such agitation—when the misunderstandings circulated as thickly as the cars on Lexington—that Gerardo feared that the blood would flow. Kenneth, for his part, dismantled his personal show and avidly enjoyed the peninsular spectacle par excellence. The dialectical quarrel (if that's possible) escalated, acquired the most unheard of, the most unexpected twists. In general, everyone was agreed that the Andalusians were little more than a peninsular disgrace, third worlders who were difficult to tolerate as neighbors, wine and guitars and *nécoras* and *chistorro* and *olé sangría* and *tacos*, inconsistent, changeable, Moors. The Andalusian defended himself principally by assailing the Basques and Catalans, adducing that the main *industry* of both regions ( a word spoken slowly to infuriate those referred to) sailed along with such ease thanks to the hands of the crudely exploited cheap labor from half of Andalusia. He added that the Catalans, for example, spend their lives talking about the duty and honor of work, but never work, not even when forced to, and that there's nothing to be said about the Basques, because it's only natural for beasts of burden to work until they drop. The divisions within the group were highly notably scandalizing. With one exception: there came a moment of agreement when everyone united to proclaim that the Gallicians weren't even worth discussing.

Gerardo contemplated the furious assembly where there were dissidents in excess and where the dove of peace seldom flew, full of wonder that, in spite of it all, a riot had not broken out on a representatively provincial scale—one champion per province, although there were many who were absent from this bitter discussion—, the blood flooding the tiny Spanish embassy in Harlem. On the other hand, he had to admire the demeanor of these gentlemen who, after perpetrating such questionably friendly epithets upon on another as

    imbecile
    fool
    loudmouth
    lunatic
    idiot
    swine

pig
son-of-a-bitch
dirty old man

and others, remained around the table without passing up one single dish of the tantalizing culinary display, reddened only with rage, cursing with a fluidity only slightly less than astonishing, but erecting a wall of romantic width which impeded any assault on their personal, physical position; corporal aggression—not a finger on anyone, for goodness sake!

Gerardo congratulated himself on his luck in having obtained a job which not only permitted him to place himself in contact with men of diverse latitudes, but also, and more importantly, assured his future, because people are always going to eat, people work to eat, steal to eat, immigrate to eat, make revolutions to eat. In contrast with other trades hard hit by trends—barbers who went hungry after the hippie wave, violinists displaced by synthesizers, traditional orthodox brothels closed by the disloyal competition of the gay bordellos—one could not identify a tendency in mankind to renounce the pleasures of the table, it was different before!; it's been shown that if in other epochs a good part of humanity supposedly gave tearful thanks for the crumbs tossed by their masters, it's clear that today the large majority has decided definitively to seat itself at the table and eat, eat, eat; crumbs are for the birds and the former owners who created the vulgar counterrevolution from the hunger of the masses (Gerardo more or less remembers Aley's words of the role of the cook in decadent societies). On the other hand, Manolo turned out to be, as they say, an exceedingly curious fellow. At times, while the *cocido madrileño* gurgled in the stew pot, Manolo became inspired amidst the suffocating heat of the ovens:

> *Here is contentment*
> *here peace is king, seated*
> *on his high and mighty throne*
> *love is sacred*
> *surrounded by pleasures and glories*

And he explained modestly: "Fray Luis de León, Castilian poet of the Golden Age." While they puttered in the kitchen, the conversation arose:

"Are there many Gallicians in your country, Gerardo?"

"In my town, there were two brothers. They had a clothing shop called 'El Narcea'. It must have been the name of their town."

"The name of a river. Did they have *guita*?"

"What?"

"Money."

"When I was born they already had the shop. They sold toys, too. I think so.

"They were Asturians."

"How do you know?"

"The questions you ask, by Christ. The Narcea is an Asturian river!"

"I don't know the first thing about it."

"You talk like the Andalusians. Did they marry locals?"

"Who?"

"Come on, who do you think! The Asturians!"

"One married an old maid schoolteacher who had a house outside of town. She helped him. She had cash stashed away."

"Naturally. People emigrate to move up in the world. If you know what I mean."

"I know. Why do you always ask me that? The other one married a rich widow. They said she was rich but she was flat busted."

"What did you say?"

"That she didn't have a cent."

"What a drag, to blow it all on one hand."

"Afterward, the two brothers started a theater and showed a film with a boy who sang."

"Oh-ho! Joselito. Even to the 'J'."

"A real smart kid. And a good-looking woman who sang in a theater and sold violets."

"*La violetera*, by Jove! The pride of the national film industry. Sarita Montiel."

"The two brothers stayed in town. I don't think they've changed much. They don't seem to get any older. They're real little, with square heads, and they're always telling people to save their money and not waste it. All the priests are their friends. Haven't you been to *la Isla*?"

"Naturally. They're addle-pated, what a way to drive. But the heights of Baranquilla are exquisite."

"Baranquitas."

"'*What a restful life/far from the bustle of daily life*' Fray Luis. The people are hospitable."

"Too much so. Over there it's a *mogolla*."

"A what?"

"A lot of people from all over the place."

"Ya. Do you know what I've often thought, Gerry? That we Spaniards are the Puerto Ricans of Europe. We emigrate to France, Germany, Holland, Sweden, England, in search of work. The Andalusians are the Puerto Ricans of Spain, they've invaded the factories of Barcelona and the Basque cities. Like your people here. They speak of the 'puertoricanization' of Barcelona by the Andalusians."

"They don't treat them as badly as they treat us."

"I'm not so sure, lad. There are Spaniards even in Australia. Can you imagine how far away that is? Ho! '*Traveler there is no road/ the road is made by walking*'."

"Serrat sings that."

"It's by Machado."

"Aley says that lots of Boricuas went to live in Hawaii early in the century. To the pineapple plantations. They stayed there, so far away. They say their kids speak English like Americans, but they speak Spanish like *jíbaros*, you know, from the countryside. They had to stay there; they didn't have enough to eat right, much less to pay such expensive airfare."

"And how could they go there in the first place?"

"They tricked them into it."

"Ya. They took them there with pure *camelos*."

"What?"

"Tricks."

"There're even Boricuas in Japan. They went to the Korean War, they fell in love there and they stayed. A country as small as ours and look how spread out we are. Should I peel more spuds?"

"Three more kilos. Potatoes. It's a slow day."

"Look. They've ripped us off with these spuds."

"They've gone to seed. I'm out on ten."

"What?"

"Rotten."

"Antulio wanted to join the Merchant Marine to see places. But they didn't take him. I think he was off the wall, that's what it was. If he gets lost here where there are so many Boricuas, just imagine what would happen if they let him loose in a Chinese port."

"He couldn't make it here, *chaval*."

"He wanted to go to Brazil."

"Ya. That's not so hard. The same hemisphere."

"But now I don't believe a word of it. He gave me a fake address. I searched for him like a detective and no luck. Should I turn off the garbanzos?"

"Maybe you won't find him for years. Turn down the heat. Not so much."

"And anyway, I don't know what the devil he's going to do there. The Brazilians come *here* to find work. João Braga da Cunha told me so. That's it's really poor. He was looking for work in a shoe factory."

"Man, this da Cunt business, ho!"

"I don't know what's become of him. I understand almost everything he says."

"Of course. Since Portuguese is nothing more than an underdeveloped Spanish."

"Antulio said the same. But João said it's not worth it. Here you can cover yourself better. When I was married, I wanted my wife to come with me. But she didn't want to. She's afraid of the snow."

"In any case, this isn't the North Pole, by God."

"There's no snow on *la Isla*."

"With a good coat and enough heat, you're just fine."

"Shouldn't I put the mussels on to boil?"

"Look at these tomatoes, aren't they marvelous? Wash them first. Yes. We have to raise the price of the tossed salad, everything's sky-high. And mix the olive oil with the soybean, our customers aren't gourmets who'll know the difference."

"Now you can't buy it, even *en la marqueta*."

"It's rampant, eh? Everything goes up with inflation. Even in Spain, which was poor tourists' paradise, the cost of living increases. Don't throw out the water from the mussels, it's got all the flavor. Strain it and pour it in till it covers the rice."

"In Puerto Rico, everything's expensive too."

"You don't have to beat it when it starts to harden, because then it will...get gummy, as you'd say."

"I know."

"It's just in case, Gerry. If you compare it, the cost of living in this city isn't as high as it is in Berlin, Paris or Stockholm. Yugoslavia, Greece and Turkey are countries where the prices are still reasonable for tourists. In Tokoyo, you pay a thousand a month for an apartment that isn't so big, how's that grab you, lad?"

"They gave me short grain rice."

"It doesn't matter. Today isn't the best day we've had."

"Have you traveled a lot, Manny?"

"I was a cook in Frankfurt, Germany. In Belgium, I had problems because I couldn't learn that accursed Flemish, which is the language they speak in the north."

"Will you go back to your country?"

"Then I was in Mexico. Well, yes, but not to stay. I've been away for a long time and I'd have to think about it. My children were born here. And I'm not so young anymore. And they don't speak a word of Spanish! Avila calls, it calls loud, and if you let yourself get carried away by your sentiments, pst, you tell everything to go straight to the devil. I hardly know anyone in the village now. My friends have all emigrated or are dead and buried. I know more people here than there."

"Look, there's no more vinegar."

"I'll have to go out for a few things. You know what? They nearly shot me on 115th Street."

"What happened?"

"I go in to buy some onions and what do I find: two blacks had the whole place there with their hands up. They pushed me against the wall and they threatened to shoot me if I didn't obey."

"I can see that you did."

"Haven't you been held up?"

"No. The soup's ready, Manny."

"Turn off the burner. You've been lucky, then. They've stolen my wallet seven times. I took the pistol from the last one and I held him until the police came."

"Good work, Frank Cannon!"

"He was one of your compatriots."

"You look like a capitalist. And so he was one of my compatriots..."

"It's just for your information. They held up the poor old Jew
who sells suitcases at 110th Street."

"The one who's always in the door and calls to you?"

"He resisted the guy and was shot six times. He lost his life to
protect a few lousy dollars. Yes, that's the one."

"I don't know what Antulio lives on. He said he had a lot of
connections. And when I get here, nothing."

"He's off in some other state. You worry about your cousin, eh?
The garbanzos are soft, very good. Hand me the sausage, Gerry."

"Is this going to be enough?"

"I think that's more than enough. I hope my compatriots don't
show up here. They drive the customers away with their arguments,
what a racket!"

"Why so much *garata*, Manny?"

"They're stuck on their *paella*, their shrimp in garlic sauce, the
*cocido madrileño*, the beans and bacon, the *pote gallego*, the *piperrada*,
the *gazpacho*, the red wine, the white wine, the claret, the riviera,
anchovies, bacon, cheese from La Mancha, cognac, tortillas, braised
spinach, Moorish seafood, which we cook for the Latin American
taste and betray our Spanish cooking. Basque style hake is really Latin
American *soncocha*. And the Andalusian saying that our sweetbreads
are more like a tropical *mondongo*, that the tripe is impossibly
expensive. The Gallician wants the real *pote* from Coruña and ham
with turnip greens. Pere Puig wants us to serve him the same sausages
with potatoes that they serve him in Esplugues de Llobregat... They
don't dare to say much about the house specialty, the lamb. They
grumble, but I swear to you that they won't get any better *cordero* in
Sepúlveda than in this house, ho! They always ask for what's not on
the menu. Gallician tripe, not *a la madrileña*, *joder*, I toss them a few
garbanzos and that's that. One time they took it into their heads that
they wanted piglet, it was the only time I saw them reach an agreement
on anything. But, where can you get live piglets in this city? For these
people, to kill a little pig is to commit a crime. They're accustomed to
people killing one another and to wars and to throwing napalm on
entire countries, but a piglet is one of God's creatures and must not be
sacrificed. Well, they told me that you could eat the best piglet in the

world in Botín. So I told them: 'Well, all right, get yourselves off to Madrid if you want to eat in Botín.' It's just that they get carried away, ho."

"Yes, they get really upset."

"What a ruckus, man, what a pain."

"What are they doing in New York?"

"Well, the same as you. Working. The Andalusian is a teacher of something they call strestruralism, something like that, in New York University. The Basque teaches the Basque language to a group of private students. When he talks you have to turn on the light to see what he's saying. The Catalan, Pere Puig, is a television technician. The Castellan, I think he teaches Spanish poetry... The Gallician has a vegetable stand in *la marqueta*."

"They don't do badly."

"No. The Andalusian has even bought a small summer place on the Costa Brava. He works all year here and the summers in his cabana. Isn't life a wonder, lad?"

"Hum. Why don't you do the same thing?"

"Who could do that? Someone would have to take charge of the business... No, no. No one can do it like I can."

"The Spaniards in my town are real suspicious."

"Go on. It's not suspicion, lad. What do you think, that all Spaniards are the same?"

"I didn't say that."

"Just imagine if I thought that all of you were cut from the same cloth."

"Yeah, and what of it?"

"Oh-ho, well, almost nothing!"

"Now I know where you're going with that. We have a bad reputation."

"Yeah. It happens to all the minorities. It happened with the Italians and the Asians. But, in addition, many of you are blacks and mulattos, and by now you know how racist these people are."

"The people in lots of countries are racist. The whites."

"You're perfectly white, Gerry. You look as if you were from the north of Spain, I swear."

"But I, it doesn't even affect me, you know, it doesn't matter to me. We're all the same. You know, I don't even notice if people are white or black. What I really notice are people's names. You're Manolo, this brother is Kenneth, the other is Aleluya, the girl is Moira, you know."

"You know her?"

"Who?"

"Christ! Moira. You just mentioned her. Take this, clean the stove. Let me peel these plantains."

"There're aren't many, we're going to be caught short. Yes. Don't tell me that you know her, Manolo."

"Well, yes."

"Why?"

"What do you mean, 'why?'. Well, because, that's why! She's come here with Aley. Well, I shouldn't have said anything, so mum's the word."

"So they're friends then."

"They've had lunch together. That's all I can tell you."

"There's nothing wrong with you telling me. Why all the mystery?"

"You know Aley, man. Super-reserved. If you understand me."

"Yes, of course I understand you."

"Ya."

"Why are you always asking me if I understand you, Manny? We're talking about the same thing."

"It's an expression. I'm not asking you, it's an expression, understand?"

"Yes. Aley's lucky if he's a friend of hers. I met her when I went to get her dog. It seems that she lives with some guy. With Jones."

"I know that she's a professional model. Nothing else. She's been on the front of magazines. Look, the garbanzos are ready. Empty them out carefully. And wash the lettuce."

"Now. She's really pretty, isn't she?"

"Are you trying to get information out of me, lad?"

"You'd do almost anything for a woman like that. She must be expensive."

"I doubt that it's that..."

"Why do you say it that way, as if you knew...?"

"She wouldn't have come here if she were that kind of a woman. And not with Aley. I don't think he's rich. Jones, yes. He earns good money with those things he makes. He's come here more than once. Okay, Gerry, take the trash can out. I'll call the plumber: the dishwasher is dripping again. It'll cost me an arm and a leg, by God."

"That same day I also saw this fantastic girl. From Europe. A gorgeous blonde. Speaks with an accent. Birke Andressen. And to think that Aley sees them almost every day. If I were in his shoes, I wouldn't even take vacations."

"He's not a womanizer. Have you seen Iremita?"

"Yes. With Aley."

"She sings like an angel. Haven't you seen her on the T.V., Gerry?"

"No."

"Music they call soul. Outrageous. She sings with soul, she stands your hair on end. My children have all her records. It's strange that you've seen her with him."

"So mysterious! They're seeing each other and it's strange to see them together."

"Yeah. That's the way it is. How are the beans doing, Gerry?"

"They're getting thick."

"Your compatriots hassle me if they aren't ready. I even like her music, and by now you know that I detest this modern racket. Kenneth hasn't arrived, so we two will have to clean the dining room."

"*Chévere.*"

"I like the way you work, lad. Always willing to help out and cheerfully."

"Some day I'll have my own business. Or, even better, I'll buy this one off you. Everything free for Moira. Have you seen Aley's room, Manny?"

"Well, no."

"There isn't room for one more book. He even reads in German. And I heard him talking real strange with a Jew. With two. With Guzmansky, he talks one way, and with Mordecai Levine, another."

"Ya, you must be proud of him."

"I am proud," without even peeling onions, without provocation, Gerry's eyes grew damp with emotion. "How can I help it? He's my brother. If anyone does anything to him, I'll break their necks."

"You don't need to protect him, I've seen him toss a giant into the air! He's an expert at all kinds of judo, Korean, Japanese and

Chinese karate. Look, one day he was picketing outside the U.N. when they were discussing Puerto Rico's status. He carried a huge poster that said: 'Support the Boricuan battle for national liberation', something like that. Suddenly, this enormous guy came up to him, a provocateur and wanted to pull the poster away from him. No one knows how or where Aley touched him, but I swear to you that the guy flew into the air like a top and fell down three yards away twisting with pain and squealing like a pig. The best part is that no one saw what Aley did, something like poking the guy lightly on the chest with a finger and nothing more, and the guy flew into the air, as big as he was... I think that if he'd touched him with a little more force, he'd have killed him. Everyone was amazed, as you'd expect... When I asked him where he'd learned means of self-defense like that, he got mad and changed the subject. The fantastic thing is that, although Aley's tall, he doesn't weigh a hundred and fifty pounds. And this guy weighed over three hundred. It's amazing. Another time, a guy working for the police threw himself at Aley's back with a blade. Ale hadn't seen him. But with a simple movement he slipped out of danger, reached out a hand to the guy and the guy fell loudly to the ground, the wind knocked out of him. It was as if Aley had seen him, but that's impossible because he'd had his back turned. Aley is very sensitive, he perceives even the slightest vibrations in the air and how much sound, I can only guess. Don't open your mouth like that, I'm telling you the truth."

"Wow, Manny!"

"Why don't you lay off this stupid 'wow' business, you bark every time you say it."

"And so young. Twenty-five and he knows so much. That's far out: wow wow wow! You're a nag, Manny."

"Respect the mother tongue."

"Mother? *Shit*, I'm going to ask Aley to teach me karate."

"He doesn't want anyone to even talk to him about it. It's his humility. He gets upset when he's praised."

As was to be expected, Gerardo enjoyed the chat while he did his work. Sometimes it was nearly impossible for him to follow the thread of the conversation, because Manolo spoke with such speed and passion that it was extremely difficult for him to distinguish the subtle change of topic fast enough, in the entangled bustle of words.

Furthermore, he noticed the surprising changes in Manolo's personality. Manolo could be supremely depressed suddenly and his sixty years became eighty; then you saw him walk with difficulty, leaning against the walls, complaining about his lumbago, sickly. For those unhappy moments, he was invaded by a disheartening nostalgia and he proclaimed that it was time to return to the harsh sweet Avilian air where, he said, one could still breathe the reassuring presence of Teresa de Jesús in the atmosphere and even hear her precise verses of classical clarity, carried on an ancient wind. Gerardo ached in silence for the elderly Manolo, wishing from the heart that his moment of restoration would arrive, the recuperation of his subtly diminished energy, which would occur after several hours had elapsed. Then he commented to Kenneth:

"Did you see how he looked?"

"Like he was gonna die."

"What happened to him?"

"It hurts him to think about Avila."

"It's like he's a hundred years old, hombre. In his shoes, I'd go back to Avila."

"Will you go back to Puerto Rico?"

"Not now. When I can. This city doesn't bother me, but you miss your country, you know."

"I'll go home if I become a millionaire," says Kenneth. "There're no beaches like ours. But you can't eat them."

"There're a lot of people who tell you that shit. They say that the mountains and the beaches and the flamboyan trees are pretty, but you can't eat them. I don't deal with those people."

"What people?"

"The ones who talk like that."

"I talk that way."

"I'm telling you, too. The Statue of Liberty and the Empire State are very pretty, but you still can't eat them."

"Shit, Gerry. Where are you now? What are you doing here? Looking for a way to eat! There're a million of our compatriots in the city."

"There're unemployed here by the millions. I went four months doing odd jobs. What pisses me off is that they put *la Isla* down. 'You can't eat.' There are other things, brother."

"The beaches are pretty, Gerry."

"The name's Gerardo! Don't fuck with me too much."

After these brief confused arguments, Gerardo felt as though huge fissures opened in his brain, where an uncontrollable wind resounded. He went to bed thinking how he could rebut his comrade Kenneth, who so vulgarly exalted the food of here and now. You can't deny, he told himself, that's he's a waiter in a restaurant. Therefore, the dishes served and heated must be, for him, as a worker in his environment, his most authentic horizon. Then he remembered the furious assemblies of Manolo's compatriots who tormented the limited atmosphere of the *mesón* with their shouts and he concluded that, when all was said and done, in some way or another,

Every cloud has a silver lining.

In bed, he dreamt of Caty, of her sweet and solid body nourished on all the Newyorkian essences, her aromatic Boricuan body of markedly horizontal tendencies. Catalina, Aley, Calabrio, Kenneth and many others met in the last month formed a cherished diverting beat of hope in his brain while sleep inundated him slowly placidly like a warm ocean swell, tired and happy and smelling, despite his shower, of trans-oceanic condiments.

# 12

$\dfrac{}{}\bullet$

**W**HEN HE WENT OUT EARLY
  when he had time
  when he had the afternoon off, for example
  he went to walk around with his hands sunk into his pockets,
wearing a dark green jersey grey velvet pants, a red scarf, because the
autumn was now ending and he felt the harsh, howling, cold wind
whipping him—it was uncomfortable at first, but consolingly reviv-
ing once he got used to it. The blood flows with renewed impetus,
stings his resistantly warm veins, burns on his lips which he covers
with Chapstick (leaves flying still, gliding in the always harsher air,
could it bring him a miracle?). On these afternoons, Aley's tall thin
silhouette could appear, covered by strange solemn overcoats, slightly
inclined in a reverential air which remained fixed, especially in these
times of chilly gusts of wind. They could talk, moving their hands

covered with thin gloves, greet people they knew, stare penetratingly at Calabrio's cheeks, suddenly adorned with red caps, contemplate, between comments, the Pole's increasing pallor, for he had acquired a distracted somnambulistic gaze and wandered about the neighborhood looking at the ground as though searching for a long lost coin; they even heard him talk to himself in a strange language which Aley identified as being from the north of Poland, certainly learned from his father, since the young Witold was born in NYC (That's his name, says Aley, nothing more than Witold, he only needed to use the name Gombrowic to be recognized world-wide and be able to leave this sad drugged-out anonymity).

That afternoon when the friends embraced under Calabrio's smiling gaze, Aley didn't hesitate before asking:

"Are you happy with your job?"

"Yes," he answered. "But I want to save up money so I can go back to *la Isla.*"

Aley simply gazes at the stained cement of the Lexington sidewalk in this prematurely dark hour, walks slowly.

"If you think that's what's best for you..."

"Don't you want to go back?"

Aley looks at him. As if with a certain sadness. Sadly, actually. Gerald realizes it, hears his voice:

"My place is here."

Gerry notices it, something strange is happening to him. More than ten days without seeing him. Recently, this had been happening: Aley disappeared and reappeared somehow thinner...or something, you know, but, somehow, also tougher as well as distracted, tall and thick and tough and dark, very mulatto, with his small proud African cranium full of wisdom. He, the all-knowing, sage, wise man. The air of the end of the season had somewhat yellowed his hands and cheeks.

"I'm enjoying New York," says Gerry. "It's a trap. You live here a few months and if you get ahead, you stay."

"Now you aren't so scared."

"You learn. This is a shitty city."

"Tell me about work."

"I already told you."

"How are the customers?"

"I hardly have anything to do with them, but when a lot of people come in I help Kenneth. I'm almost a waiter, you know."

"One should learn a little of everything."

"I had a weird family. They don't eat meat—they say it's because they don't eat corpses. What people! It wouldn't have occurred to me. They drive me crazy with these ideas."

"What ingrates!" laughs Aley.

"Why ingrates? You and your stories!"

"This story is millions of years old."

"Manolo fixed them a super salad. Lettuce, tomatoes...even celery, man! He gave it a name: '*Manolo's Vegetarian Salad*'."

"Just think what would have happened if our remote ancestors had not decided...under duress, to eat meat."

"Don't get heavy with me, Aley!"

"We wouldn't have developed our beloved crowns. We wouldn't be here. It will interest you to know that millions of years ago a great drought brought down a good part of the African jungles, turning them into great plains... Our first cousins, the anthropoid monkeys, found themselves compelled to deal with this radical change in the ecological system, you know, the surrounding environment."

"Obviously!"

"The pressure forced them to seek new nutritional sources. They no longer wandered through the jungle looking for delicious tree bark to ingest...there wasn't any! Zero roots, leaves, tender savory branches. They began to hunt small animals without expending too much effort: young birds, newborn animals, and by attacking nests they turned into colossuses; a change in conduct, the first step toward humanity, Dryopithecus, *mon amour*! By eating everything, they turned into simian men."

"You were talking about vegetarians, about the ones who..."

"The new diet allowed them to survive in any surroundings... If there weren't any birds, they hunted for their grasses here, their roots there, their little fish further on... They could scratch and find delicious worms, for example. As an adaptation for survival, it was fabulous. When they were herbivores, they were limited to collecting fruit, gnaw-gnawing on bark and grasses... They had a monkey's jaw, superdeveloped molars and canines to rend their good woodsteaks when they had them..."

"A beam," smiles Gerry. "A *sapodilla* sill, man, that you can't even stick a hatchet into. Well done. Baked."

"To hunt his prey, your ancestor needed tools. A rock served the purpose, but when he saw it splinter, he used the stone like a knife, *bien chévere*, you know. The venerable Montague says that this was the birth of the first industrial revolution."

A surprised Gerry, wow, in the jungle, afterwards on a plain as dry as the devil. He gazes at Aley for a moment, surprised because he, Aley, knows a lot and is a good man, you know, and he's his compatriot and isn't going to deceive him. He says:

"Cutting meat with a rock. Like the Indians..."

Aley doesn't want to argue with what his friend says about the Indians. He gazes at him for an instant, afraid of losing the thread.

"Use a tool *ad hoc* and discard it? *Nein!* If they turned out to be so useful, Gerry, the best thing would be to manufacture them. This was the moment when these creatures became human. As if you would throw a machete away, or a saw, or a hammer, or a crane, if you could! The tools were a *bien chévere* response to the environment and increased their chances for survival a thousand miles an hour. To manufacture them, they had to think it out well, they made them first in their minds, and then concretely..."

"Ave María, Aley, it's not such a big deal."

"An enormous leap of the intelligence; more alternatives for solving problems."

"Today's lesson is very strange, Aley. All of this is really neat."

"Hunting improved with the tools. They decided to get down to the hunt in a big way, enormous animals, you know..."

"Dinosaurs, Brontesaurus..."

"We appeared millions of years after the disappearance of such sublime beasts... The big hunt required an adequate social organization and determined the separate economic activities of the sexes. Maternity and child-rearing prevent the woman from becoming a huntress, in addition to the weakness of her muscles... The female invented agriculture and contributed stupendous mixed salads, greens for savory stews, and the male brought meat for the barbecue, the grill, the oven. The need to share foodstuff brought about a situation where boy X associated with girl X, with all this resultant business of paternity and pampers, bibs, etc. Hunting necessitated an upright posture for seeing into the distance and the use of the front paws as hands. And the result is your face, Gerry, this Greco-Roman profile.."

"What does one thing have to do with the other?"

"Your orthogonathism. And mine, of course. Everyone's. The straight profile with the reduced jawbone."

"Ah...how's all this fit together?"

"Like a ring on your finger. So we didn't have to rend tree bark, with these good beef steaks. Therefore, we lost those mammoth mandibles: a T-bone steak doesn't require so much effort and then we could rely on our delicate stone knives. Hunting made us pretty and freed our tongues.."

"Arrea, as Manolo would say!"

"Is it rubbing off on you, Gerry?"

"What?"

"Manolo's Avilian speech. The big hunt is a group effort. And every group effort requires a system of signals. The first grunts grew more complicated until they became what we do here in New York City, USA, right now. The first words would have been ugh, urk, and they would have meant: 'Don't let this beast escape, shoot him hard with an arrow, strike him a blow on the forehead', among other utilitarian expressions..."

"Wow!"

"Your dog-like wow is part of that. What would have happened if we'd followed the diet of the jungles? Raw bark without vinegar, roots disgustingly covered with more or less virgin soil, branch-steaks dripping succulent, very cold vegetable blood, raw leaves, without salt or pepper. To sum it up, Gerry, so that you'll shut your mouth before the flies get in: the vulgar hunt developed from the need to survive, from which came language, the family, the social structure, the upright posture of the featherless biped, our lovely faces, the sewing industry, electric trains, *The Brothers Karamazov*, the pans in your kitchen, postage stamps, the theory of relativity, the Beatles, Antonioni, Pier Paolo Passolini, the honorable underpants of a Latin American dictator, rifles and bandages, the Chase Manhattan Bank, Kleenex, coconut ices, Givenchi perfume, the French language, German and Swedish, Kant, dimes, César Vallejo, Chu Carazo, José B. Díaz Asencio, the Hermes typewriter, the vaccine against malaria, toilet paper, Chablis wine, Don Q rum, Juan Luis Márquez, Adams gum, pencils, ballpoint pens, looking glasses and umbrellas, chimneys and handkerchiefs, shoes and syringes, windows and mirrors, rugs and flamethrowers, telephones and contraceptives, clarinets and bongos..."

"I thought you were going to tell me about vegetarians!"

"I've told you everything. Or almost everything, Gerry. Any questions?"

"Where were you last week?"

Aley examines him. To the depths. With some suspicion. He reads something in the open book of his friend's perfectly orthogonatic (is that how you'd say it?) face, he nearly detains him beneath the conical luminous stream of a streetlight to peer into his eyes, deep within, until he comes to what hides in the ex-peasant brain of this new newyorkino. They were surrounded by closed windows, by curtains pulled down behind the panes, which gives a supremely somber air to Lexington. The cold advances, they feel it more intensely all the time, every minute, better said, every half hour.

"Here and there, Gerry."

"So mysterious!"

"You've learned a lot," says Aley, withdrawing to the shadows of a corner, raising his coat up to his chin, pulling his small hat down all the way, "but you still have some naive little ideas, brother. Look at those fellows..."

Gerry sees two subjects straight off the assembly line pass beneath the streetlight enveloped in their capes, each one with a rolled up newspaper in his pocket, an identical hat cocked over his right eyebrow, advancing with symmetrical identical elastically uniform strides, the same little protuberance on the right side of his waist, leaning forward somnambulistically Dicktracyian profile they dart glances right left without moving their heads to either side, mechanically manufactured on the assembly line, identical fellows with the corner of their eyes to the right left, they disappear up the street with an unbroken rhythm, and when the good guy Gerardo says what's happening Aley, who are those fellows, he says it to the wind, because Aley has already disappeared up an alleyway off 117th going East, deserting the desolate Lexington beneath the clodhoppers of a truly surprised, open-mouthed Gerardo. Dick Tracy shadowing his brother Aley? He keeps walking automatically Downtown, without seeing anything, but he noticed that the temperature felt like a prolonged shiver, and the Caribbean arises with Aley's sudden absence among the shadows, the painfully lost tropics, painfully missed, thinking suddenly about little Gerardo, about his ex-wife and her anti-snow phobias, about a snow which she had never seen and which could cause infernal colds...

It's been said that Gerardo had acquired the habit of wandering through various parts of the city in his free time—well, naturally!— walking among leaves which he stepped on, causing a slight, almost frozen crackling on the roads of Central Park where he went in search of visions of more than likely vanished trees, encircling the lake where rowboats ventured, stalking up Park Avenue with the secret hope that one fine day he'd run into Moira or Birke Andressen on her day off, walks to forget his continual melancholy solitude because he can't always be with Caty, lovable and angry and contradictory and anti-sexist, sweet as sugar when she wanted to be, Gerry wants to escape from his solitude as from a dark cellar where the frothy wine of Tedium ferments, to perish from pure pleasure contemplating the children kids boys young lads playing, cheerfully protect himself from the thin piercing wind, cross Fifth Avenue and 23rd going toward Chelsea, now heading up Eighth Avenue

EL MESON DEL QUIJOTE

he could work there too, sliding in beside the YMCA where they'd told him certain gentlemen room who follow you when you enter the common shower they come close to you full of emotion like delicate lilies, so said Bigote, Bolo or Dutch, someone, Broadway now purple red blue neon flashing on and off shit these people are a curse, the pavement shining from an early rainfall, headed toward Times Square heart center capital of universal pornography boys sold to grave pederasts in enormous limousines (the grave pederasts, you understand, in enormous anti-economic pro-Arab limousines), Gerardo's hands enpocketed while he gazes without interest at the well-stocked windows electric appliances all sizes, clothes, umbrellas, heavy coats for the future months, Avenue of the Americas not far from where the Empire State Building raises its head among the heavy clouds, dotted with thousands of identical lights placed symmetrically, of course, but how super-symmetrically placed within, seated in a square—its base surrounded by luxurious store windows—oh delicate women's clothing glorious leather sports clothes for men, walking until he finds

himself exhaustedly in
### ROCKEFELLER CENTER!!!
an overwhelming cascade of dizzying lights dazzling the night solid
rectangular quadrangular skyscrapers shine like gold over the vast
extensive area of several elevated blocks—frighteningly dizzyingly
solid awe-inspiring okay gigantic okay—but the best's when, thinks
Gerardo putting it in other words, the best is when you find this man
in the foreground with his wife and son in front of the walls that block
their path, the gigantic walls of the Center, the woman now completely dwarfed with her hands dried out Fab ALL Ariel her face
disfigured Ponds Cold Cream her small sweat in her autumnal armpits
Aura Gillette Right Guard the man with $15.99 + tax shoes jacket
from a nameless store pants unknown origin old Arrow shirt second-
hand coat discretely acquired trying to maintain his shaken virility his
authority as father affectionate husband before her and the lad who
looks at him as though Papa were guilty of some indefinable monstrous act, Papa is only omnipotent when he sits on the General
Electric collection pot in the humid bathroom of his small house
mortgaged to the family who put up these walls, Papa revealed
immediately as nothing more than a human being solely and exclusively, that is to say: the big imbecile for whom it's enough to be only
a man husband father while glorified free-enterprise balls weigh upon
the magnificently solid roofs of the luxurious skyscrapers, neotemple
of neopharohs at a careful distance from the South Bronx Bowers
ghetto, oh it's nothing but an itsy-bitsy little oh so very banal contrast!
But he didn't have to stay there gazing upwards nor try to plant an
inconceivably small kernel or corn beneath the omnipresent name-
plate of cement to verify whether the ground had really been murdered
or whether it were still able to produce even if it were only a single
weakly yellow shoot—but dangerous by its persistence!; he should
move among the autumnally dressed throngs, cross avenues obedi-
ently obeying the winks of the traffic lights, take the subway once
more; then, immediately, the walls of the tunnel blend fervently,
undulated separating violently closing in close to torture the escaping
cars pulling away at spots where there appeared unexpected points of
lights humble bulbs forgotten in the extravagance above the play of
the lights of the express little windows deformed like a pack of cards
shuffled at luminous velocity trac traccata obsession repercussion in

his chestbone trac catrac remembering that he should have bought the paper to hide his face from the curious multitude, strangely distant and curious at heart, that gazes, crosses looks, exchanges rapid uncomfortable glances inlaid in their multicolored varied suits surprising for their many forms: jackets, fur coats, knits, green gabardines, black plastic jackets, short gloves and even one or two surgical masks in prudent expectation of the hibernal air (infernal, he though surprised, remembering his ex). Everyone expected to be completely swallowed by the city, he thought talking briefly to himself, move your lips, let it swallow you and digest you, darling, honey, my love, the capital of the world, shit, you don't have to make a fuss about it, more amazing than Tokoyo with its ten million and other largely millionaire cities, with the U.N. building like a box above the East River, when he gets off at Bleeker street he realizes that it's pleasant to penetrate the shadowy streets of the falsely, vaguely amorous Village (the Village, Greenwich, it goes without saying), transformed into the center of tourism where

> the artists pose with their handsome unruly manes
> poets who don't poetize
> lively life in the cafes
> languid long-haired girls
> male painters talk with female painters about copulations
> forgotten in the dim dust of time
> sculptors pile cardboard boxes on top of cardboard boxes
> untilthey reach, if not the stars, then stardom.

They look at him, they take him for a Belgian, for a hard-working and honorable and all that crap Czech, mister give me the time, shit, with that accent you're going to go far in an unknown direction, how can a city so aware of itself exist, which is everywhere like God, calamitously oppressing the foreigners who, having barely landed on its brutal cement pavement beaches, send expressions of historic value to relatives on the other side of the ocean so that they'll be consumed with jealousy like:

> I saw the beloved thrilling Statue of Liberty
> I drank Coca-Cola in front of St. Patrick's Cathedral
> I shat on the 87th floor of the Empire State Building
> Even the five year old kids speak English
> Many kosher shops

Too many people speaking Spanish
The Museum of Natural History—tremendous
Ugly, painted up subways blacks Puerto Ricans Chinese
horror beloved graffiti
There's too much competition and you can't get by
Everyone does it
Dear Papá. ghettos. horror. kisses. Gretten.
Pregnant woman threw herself under subway intestines
brains
Smoking grass under policeman's nose
Lots of people Madison Square Garden
Lights trains cars theaters stores windows
Eat-'n-Go Nedicks Donuts Full O'Nuts Island Fried
Foods
Waldorf Plaza Hilton Chelsea
People act like they don't know you
He suddenly saw the fallen leaves of a secret personal persistent
autobiographical tree gliding in the lonely street, they weren't bats, a
few leaves at this point in the dying autumn hardly survive sensitively
sensed, bat leaves struck down by the subterranean erosion of the
atmosphere and the malleability of the air, monstrously punished
daily because it can be proven: the smoke from the chimneys is a
thousand times more rentable than the antiquated oxygen.

"It's okay now," he said to himself out loud. "My feet hurt. I'm
going to my room."

And the image of Aleluya pursued by vampires with Dick Tracy
faces accompanied him to his room.

# 13

I F SHE CALLED at the *mesón*, if she told you I'm going to visit you tonight, honey, how can you tell her not to come? How do you tell her stay and watch, for example, any one of the dozens of shows on TV where police detectives charming spies freely dispense irreproachable justice?

| Cannon | McMillan | Ironside |
|--------|----------|----------|
| Colombo | Area 12 | Mission Impossible |
| Swat | Hawaii 5-O | Nakia |
| Kojak | Policewoman | Switch |
| Starkie | Christie | Six Million Dollar Man |
| Hutch | | The Bionic Woman |

Newscasters with polished voices objectively announce the latest coup d'etat provoked by secret ambassadors a la Terry and the pirates, Mandrake the magician, and others.

Or to smilingly contemplate fabricated dances among the stars, elevated choreography for dreaming ladies laddies.

Subterraneanly Aryan elegant blacks comportment cultivated smiles, ebony hair frizzed to the point of desperation working with winning whites to keep the peace.

Programs with set up fraudulent plots the bad guys escape justice toss a cultivated Carnegie smile into the foreground toward the millions of enthusiastic anonymous televiewers. Because if you call me, if you tempt me, he tells her, you'll find me. So he says, laughing, smoking, seated face to face naked on the bed listening to what the radio provides: Bob Dylan, *Also Sprach Zarathustra*, pop, soul, country, rock, ballads, lots of ballads.

Gerry smokes the minute, diminutive roach, the almost invisible spark lost between his thick fingers, and Caty threads it on a pin so she can place it like a grain of rice between her massive lips, she tokes with concentration, serious, concentrative on the strict ceremony of dominated fire, the room smells of burnt grass, of a specific perfume of the Colombian countryside where the cannabis—this line of merchandise for export that is a thousand times more productive than the boring coffee that kills sleep or than the monotonous diabetizing sugar—grows between shadows of future fantasies. A certain incense to conjure up certain enchantments. Facing one another, legs crossed, elbows on their thighs, the pinched roach lit in one almost invisible point of red encircled by grey ash passes in a secret exchange of solidarity. Minutes before, when Gerardo took the first toke he felt as if his body ascended a foot, half a meter, then the bed began a slow movement toward the ceiling pausing at a more than acceptable altitude. The sad colors of the room smiled, better said, they brightened like a somber face when it suddenly smiles, and then he talked for a while about how pretty the city is, what *chévere* people his friends are and Lorenzo has his quirks but he's all right, contemplating Caty's dark beauty, plump, her body leaning forward with her breasts falling gently of their own weight, her belly button buried in a sea of flesh, and barely lowering his gaze he finds the concentration of entangled hairs in the triangular patch, her strong thighs end in overly pointy knees, her thin legs disproportionate to her abundant body, which doesn't bother Gerardo now, happy with all humanity, perfectly integrated into the world, lacking even the most minimal drop of rebellion. Dominated by a sudden flame of overpowering native happiness, Gerardo leans over gently and embraces her uncomfortably, effusive, their foreheads meet hotly and support one another, the girl's square hands with bitten nails caress the recently shaved chin of the passionate Boricuan lover, his cheeks lashed by the cold and inclemency. Caty recovers her relaxed position and gazes at him smiling, showing her uneven row of teeth like kernels in a poor harvest of corn.

"You're making me hungry, Caty."

"It's the grass."

"Does Lorenzo know you smoke?"

"*La primera vez*, he screamed at me, when he saw the bowl with the pot in it. But *entonces* he got used to it; *yo le dije que* it's not as bad as the Camels he smokes, that alcohol destroys brain cells. Now he don't say anything to me. *Yo* his right hand. I help him in the store, I cook, wash the dishes, he can't mess with me. This isn't *la Isla* where the old man *de viejos costumbres* can hit his daughters women because they have a boyfriend. Papa's still got this idea, he says you can't teach an old dog, *tú sabes*. He listens to old Mayarí music, Marcano, Daniel Santo, *todas estas cosas*, and Ramito, *hombre*, the cat's from the country. *Pero* who'll tell him no. I took off one of his records, a folk song, he asked me *por qué*, I told him this old music doesn't make it in New York, and he started to cry *muy emocionado*, he didn't tell me why he was crying for maybe fifteen *minutos*, but two days *después* he tells me that he's lost me as his daughter, that he's strange to me, que *éramos tan diferentes* that he isn't like my father and I'm not like a daughter of his."

"Was he listening to the record?"

"Yes."

"And you took it off?"

"I wanted to hear rock. He hates *esa música*, he lives here twenty three years and zero English, no nothing. He only thinks about *la Isla*. A good guy, but we're different *generaciones*."

"Newyorican."

"They don't have to put names on us like that, the ones from *la Isla*. They don't know how it is. They think they know everything, they come to teach us. You have to be here *para saber* how to make it. Papá's just like them, think you must be sick because not talk like him and *la Isla*. He knows *todo* and he's old. I respect him because he's Papá you know but I have my ideas, he should respect me and I'll be *bien chévere* with him. Now he say he wants to go to *la Isla*, to the countryside to have a store. Then I stay here."

"When did you go to *la Isla*?"

Caty's eyes fill, mascara streaks her face, the two dark rivers of her hair on her breasts.

"To bury Mamá. Three years ago. We lived on Flatbush then. She said bury her on *la Isla*, she always said it before she got sick."

Gerry is moved in excess. Tears spurt from him in unexpected torrents, fall on his hairy hard-muscled legs. A powerful feeling of super-Boricuan piety ohblessedbe-ness makes him caress the sweet long-suffering Caty, sentimental soul. Caty raises her head.

"That's why *la Isla* makes me mad. *He estado bien deprimida después de eso*. I can't forget and it makes me sad."

"I had a dog that I loved a lot and it waited for me when I came home from school, it jumped and barked because it loved me so much..."

"She was *una santa*, a woman like in the old days, stupid *Latina* woman who took whatever the *macho* dished out."

"One day I came home from school and the dog wasn't there. I asked and the old man showed me a..." Gerardo swallows, his Magdalene face soaked with easy potted tears. "He showed me a bottle of rum. He said he'd traded the dog for the bottle, drunkard who couldn't help himself. I never understood how he could do business with something like that..."

"I kissed the clods of dirt and *entonces* I threw them on the coffin. Pop says that Puerto Rican dust for him *también* when he dies."

"Mamá had to break her back washing and ironing to raise us. I left school in eighth grade. I was a *machetero* in the cane fields, after that I got my taxi license, I also worked in the plastic factories. Everything, *hombre*. Now nothing can throw me."

"I don't like *la Isla* because of that bad memory."

"Want to light another...?"

Caty dries her tears and shakes her head. She looks at him seriously. Very seriously, the tears still flowing one by one, slowly, from her eyes.

"Gerry...don't you want to know some things about me?"

Oh! The moment of revelation. The eight o'clock soap. Yes, Caty, anything you want to tell me.

"*Está bien.* I want to tell it to you straight. I was sixteen, *una adolescente inocente*, very well protected by my *Papá de la Isla, tú sabes* what I mean. The guy had a show on Radio Wayo, he saw into the future, *dijo.* I had a good Jewish boy, he wanted to marry me, and I wanted to know if the marriage would be *bien chévere. Entonces,* I wrote a letter telling the show everything, with the picture in a bathing suit that the guy wanted. *El hombre* calls me on the phone and we go out."

This brings Gerardo's herbivore mood down somewhat, darkens a certain internal sun.

"I was sixteen!" Caty cries bitterly, furious. "The man was older, married, from Puerto Rico. I was like a fool in love, he like a god, whatever he wanted, he did it with me. Papa was going to sue him, or force him to marry me, he disappeared. He shows up in a year, *yo le dije que no. Me cago en su madre! Hijo de la gran puta!* He wanted to get married, I told him no way, *cabrón!*"

Gerardo with an attitude of repossession, his hands cold, his arm muscles tense.

"And the boy?" he says delicately. "Your boyfriend."

"His parents fought with him because I wasn't a Jew. *Pobre* David Solomon! He said I'd fallen but he said he'd raise me from the ground, something from the Bible. *Yo estaba tan avergonzada* that I couldn't even look him in the face. And Pop locked me in a room, *Latin honol, coño!* David Solomon wanted to marry me, he'd forgive me, *le dijo a* Pop, *pero* Pop said no, I had dishonored him and David Solomon too. I didn't do anything else with anybody, *yo me quedé bien impresionada con mi primera experiencia...*"

"No one else? Really and truly?"

"With you, but nobody else, I swear."

Gerardo moved, gratified by the privilege of having been selected love object of the year, but he's every inch the man.

"It doesn't matter to me...if you had something with some fellow."

Caty focuses her suffering sweetness in one tender look, in a vegetative smile and lifts her legs up together, turns to the night table where the jar of pot and the little rectangles of spotlessly white paper repose happily. The ruminant Gerry sees her pass her tongue over the edge of a little paper into which she's emptied marijuana; then Caty the tobacconist rolls it carefully making it roll over the glass of the table, takes the little cylinder and twists the ends.

"They found a plantation of marijuana near Ponce, Caty, and the police burned it. Bigote says that the insects, the cows, the birds, the police, all the animals who breathed the smoke got *bien chéveres.*"

Caty laughs now lying on her back, her hair spilling over her shoulders.

"That's crazy!"

"They had burned the best of the Boricuan agriculture, says Bigote. He says that the cane is wiped out, that the coffee went down, that tobacco is worse. And there are a lot of people who live off grass, people who work in offices to control drugs, detectives and their families, judges, lawyers, doctors, you know, lots of people," Gerardo tokes off the joint, holds his breath so the smoke will fill his lungs. "They caught a fellow. No, not the fellow. They caught a yacht full of grass off the coast of Fajardo. They didn't do anything to this fellow because he had connections in the government and big bucks. Mister Gerardo Sánchez will spend five years in jail at White Bear for having pot in his pocket," Gerry laughs with his eyes full of rebellious tears. "*Coño!* Fuck them all, Caty! The fellow was bringing the grass in from Colombia! Which way does the capitalist scale tilt, Caty?"

"Not your way!"

Gerry laughs, leaps upright onto the bed, vulgarly grabbing his balls shouting displaying them to the door, to the distinguished absent public:

"I pass your laws right through here. And I want to lay your women with this."

Caty falls down with laughter, raises her hands, totally entertained, mooring herself to the two hairy legs of her subhusband.

"No, Gerry, you nut! That's what those women want, *carajo!*"

"My proletarian peepee," sings the crazy Gerardo, "for your proletarian thing, *amada.*"

Seated against the wall, Caty doubles over with laughter, claps her hands, they amuse themselves in the little room—property of Mordecai Levine, outside the night dissolves, exterminates itself or simply does not exist, Gerry suddenly surprised by his unexpected testicular activity.

"It doesn't suit them to fight heroin, which is killing the people, because they live off that!"

"Hypocrites!"

Gerardo lets himself fall on top of Caty, who slides backwards laughing holding herself up with her elbows, her head fallen, they go up through an empty resonant space of slow exceedingly rapid duration the secret tender indomitable dizzy blood hurricaned lightning, freed from all irritation, beating like the Atlantic waves, outside the late November night fades away immaterial foreign full of velvety sounds, but the walls imprisoned them again, once more they formed part of this insignificant portion of the world. Concrete and necessary, triumphant, the objects proclaim their presence emerging illuminated from the ancient momentary fog, negating their negation:

The red curtain that Caty put in the window

The night table, jar, pot

The washstand with the small mirror

The rocking chair for reading the paper, the books Aley lends you and the porno magazines

The green rug

The door of the closet where he keeps his vast extensive wardrobe

The radio on the low table

"It's true, Caty. Mama serves some nice grass for lunch to the kids who aren't hungry!"

"*Yo necesito algo de comer, también.* Let's go eat and we'll see the Christmas lights...right now."

They jump out of bed. It seems to both of them that it takes them less than five minutes to get dressed; she, covered with her brown coat; he, with his leather jacket and wool pants.

On the second floor landing they meet Anne Couvert, wearing her hibiscus saihri, a topaz diadem holds back her black fringe, her big feline eyes smile at them, enveloped in an exquisite perfume. Catalina clings to the gerardian arm; they laugh at the silliest things, above all, when they hear the threatening snores emanating from Calabrio's room. They cross beneath the luminous cones of the streetlights, they advance between a very few bundled up passerbys who move stiffly in the cold air. Sad and gloomy, Lexington stretches toward the lower part of Manhattan. They both lean forward, raising their coats up to their ears.

"*Un* sandwich with coffee *bien caliente*, okay?"

"Okay," says Gerardo in a shaky voice.

"*Entonces tomamos* el Seventh Avenue subway and then we'll go to the Village."

"To lound out the ploglam."

A huge dark bus with little lit windows—where meditative heads hang—hurled a blast of its smelly exhaust into their faces.

# 14

$\bullet$

T
O DISTINGUISH HIMSELF from just any bour-
geois, so that he wouldn't be taken for one of them, so that his
proletarian affiliation will be recognized: the Prof wears a carefully
designed denim suit. Dark blue porous material, a jacket with side
lapels, metal buttons, a pale blue shirt, long bell-bottomed pants over
shiny patent leather shoes. He smells of a cologne recommended on
television: his tie with a huge knot, wide as a baby's bib, contributed
a dark, severe note to his outfit. Since scarcely a hair grew on his rosy
baby face, he has given up trying to cultivate a beard; instead, he
achieved a mustache whose Victorian luxuriance and texture attracted
attention. Surrounded by disciples and admirers, standing in the
center of the livingroom, the Prof consumes his scotch and soda
elegantly, commenting in a measured tone on the Janice Joplin record
playing on the four track stereo, the young singer's tragic death—an

overdose of tranquilizers. In the livingroom decorated with posters of erotic content—Babylonian Newyorkian obsession—the guests move from one spot to another: pale youths with huge afros, girls in slacks, an occasional skirt. They chat, laugh, slap five. The majority speak English but, occasionally, someone utters an entire phrase in a Spanish tortured by the isolation of the ghetto. Four young men of medium height, with afros of the same size, and blue jean jackets, attentively surround the Prof, besieging him with questions. The Prof doesn't really look at them, but at their bulging heads, like those of imported termites, as though he were searching for something beyond the tight circle.

"Take advantage of the circumstances," he says. "The historic juncture of our times. The city is willing to float the money as long as we apply pressure. You know. These people don't do anything unless you act aggressively. Right now I am preparing a proposal for the Department of Education with a group of comrades. An educational center for Boricuan students, with a small museum. Nothing political or they'll kill the proposal! This project will be multi-faceted and will consist of—among other things—a center for research into the history and culture of our country. We will also venture into the problem of bilingual education. There we have an open field. We estimate that, for starters, two million dollars would be sufficient. We have also considered developing bilingual television shows, now that Spanish has ceased to be the Puerto Ricans' only language. One third of the island's population lives here, so that this Spanish business is past history. Today we have among our numbers poets who write Puerto Rican literature in English, proletarian poets, you know, from the ghettos. In fact, we're thinking of pressuring them to intensify English instruction on *la Isla*, so that we would be homogeneous, culturally speaking: the Boricuas here and over there. Our literature in English is our most important contribution to the great contemporary movement of Latin America literature.

The four young men applaud:

"Yeah, man."

"Dig it."

"Fucking whites."

"Bastards."

"Later on, at the proper moment," says the Prof calmly, "we will be in a position to liquidate the outdated Spanish language in our country and clear the way for the conversion of *la Isla* to a state in the American Union. With this status, we would be in the ideal position to help the North American workers make the revolution. For now, though, the objective is to make sure that the city floats the money for programs on Puerto Rican culture—whatever that means. Another thing is that we can develop programs on the culture of the Taíno Indians, which greatly interests the young people, and on the African contribution to our culture. Our culture was created by the Taínos, savagely massacred by the white conquistadors, and by the blacks, enslaved by the whites. What did we inherit from the white Spanish imperialists?"

The four African look fellows applaud: clap, clap, clap.

"Bastards."

"Fucking whites."

"Dig it."

"Yeah, man."

A disconcerting black girl says to the Prof:

"You're white, Prof."

The Prof is offended. The quartet of afros is offended.

"What am I, comrades?"

The quartet choruses a capella:

"Black."

The Prof raises his hands, directing the chamber quartet:

"What am I?"

"Black!"

The Prof raises his hands once more, like the conductor of an orchestra:

"What the fucking hell am I?"

The glee club responds:

"A fucking nigger, yeah!"

The Prof extends his open palm and receives a slap of recognition from four brown hands. Gerardo, who has been watching the final part of this scene—having just arrived—goes to serve himself a whiskey and soda. Confused, confusing. They're Boricuas? They're not Boricuas? Then he sees a tall figure entering, hat dampened by the frozen rain of the Decembrian evening. Upon removing the muffler, Aley's severe countenance appears; he sheds the coat with the aid of a neat and amenable Bigote. Gerry soon approaches him: cordial greetings, what have you been doing, you were lost from...

"Want a shot?" demands Bigote. "To celebrate the marriage of Carmen Dionisia of Paraguay and Tommy!"

"I'll pass," says Aley.

"I'll take another one," responds Gerry. "It's good in the cold."

You hear the sound of applause, exclamations. A girl comes out of a room, wearing bridal white, her small native forehead encircled by a crown of orange blossoms. She carries a bouquet of flowers in her hand. She is accompanied by Bolo, in black, with a twisted red tie, smiling with his barren gums. Beside Bolo and the fiancée appears Kenneth, dressed in black for the occasion, and the tall, thin, leggy Tommy with his black hair slicked back and his long sideburns. The short fiancée, Carmen Dionisia, eyes bright with pre-matrimonial joy, smiles timidly.

"Hum," says Gerry. "What have you been up to, Aley? Ten days, wow, without a sign of you!"

"Watch this."

The Prof, standing gigantic in the middle of the living room, applauds Carmen Dionisia.

"Come along," he says, "exquisite damsel. Today we have the opportunity of celebrating the felicitous loving union of two worthy representatives of two Latin American countries: Paraguay, from whence comes the delicate and genteel fiancée, and Puerto Rico, homeland of the fortunate groom, Tommy Rivera. How do you feel at this moment of surpassing importance for you and Tommy?"

Carmen Dionisia says that she feels fine, just fine, and adds a long sentence in a strange obscure language that leaves the Prof in the dark and that no one understands. Except, of course...

"It's the purest Guaraní," smiles Aley, the super-polyglot complacently, deeply moved. "She says that it makes her very happy to know that she has so many friends and she hopes that everyone will enjoy the ceremony, that her home will be open to all men and women of good will, and that she will raise her children in the faith and Christian customs. Her parents had wanted to be present on this glorious occasion, but they had problems crossing the Argentine border. She didn't say what sort of problems..."

Nonetheless, everyone noticed Carmen Dionisia's humility.

Aleluya immediately deduces that it is the result of the tortured geography of her country, compressed into the shape of a gland between brutally immense Brazil, suffering militarized Bolivia, and shining silverplated Argentina, victim of uncounted right-wing convulsions; all the vast and complex and Cain-like tragedy of the Chaco war, so typically Latin American, is reflected distantly in her oblique eyes, clouded by the turbulent blood from the mighty currents of the Paraguay and Pilcomayo rivers; the winds arising in the Amambay and Mbacarayú mountains had ruffled her stiff dark hair of the purest pre-Colombian most American bloodline. Her once tribal heart throbs when remembering the sound of the Paraná where it flows impetuously together to form the Guayrú Falls or Sete Quedas. The songfully romantic Lake Ipacaraí contributes, contradictorily, a dialectic as fresh as the sap of the Andes, a profound peace to her spirit formed by ancient philosophies not recorded by the Western know-it-alls of all time. In the Eastern *mesetas*—swept by the broad harsh wind of the Brazilian Matto Grosso—she would have listened to the wails of an ancestral voice that locates her in the exact center of a resistant, indestructible culture; the crash of thunder amidst the leaves would have developed her now nearly domesticated imagination; domestication that had attenuated her aboriginal customs to the point of separating her—across time and the straightjacket of civilization— from the days when the Spanish adventurer Juan Díaz de Solís, from the distant Sanlúcar, discovered what is known today as the Río de la Plata and which, in an attack of peninsular lyricism, he'd called Sweet Sea, when he should have called it the Most Bitter of Rivers, given that it was on one of its banks that the natives, motivated by a ferocious patriotism, had devoured him without pausing to consider whether his tough white flesh deserved to be marinated in garlic and roasted on a spit. But how to speak to her now about this distant history? Tell her about the unforgettable Triple Alliance of Brazil, Argentina and Uruguay when they fell upon the heroic and then prosperous Paraguayan people and, in the course of a slaughter that lasted five years, reduced the country to ashes and its population by half? How to tell the tale of this disaster which transcended the five year period, which was survived only by the old, the women and the children; the young men having been decimated in the fraternal battles of liberation between the oh so brotherly countries of this part of the continent? No.

Better to contemplate the fiancée, Carmen Dionisia, melting before the lanky, handsome Tommy; hair as black as, it would be known later, were his intentions. Aley senses it. The Cuñataí brain melts before the tropically sexy Tommy, tall and thin and dark, unctuous and smiling, certainly twisted in his head. Sweet melodies in Guaraní. Carmen Dionisia smiles, greets three stumpy women with straight black hair from her country. Absurdly, the Prof proposes that they sing the national anthems of the countries which, in minimal and romantic form, are to be united by the tender bond of love: Borinquén, gem of the Caribbean, and Paraguay, agonized continental kidney, subcontinental braggart. But his suggestion was defeated by the majority of those present who alleged that this act doesn't approach the solemnity of the Munich jousts or, if you will, Sapporo. Then, the voice of one Lavoe, Hector Lavoe, emanates from the stereo, backed by the dubiously musical mark of the infallible Colón (Willie) singing the coarse words:

> Drive her away, piranha,
> this woman who destroys it all.

The inappropriateness of the theme aside, which might seem to insult the fiancée, mentioning the voracious fish nature native to the regions full of huge forests and waters of Amazonic darkness gives a certain flavor to the atmosphere. Aleluya, for his part, captures the fiancée's attention for a good while as he interrogates her with poorly dissimulated anxiety about the life expectancy of her honorable president, controlling himself just enough so that he doesn't reveal his impatience at this man's interminable persistence on the face of the earth, and he even manages to ask, in careful classical Guaraní, if it's true that this incumbent suffers from an unknown virus that will inevitably lead him to bite, though tardily, the sweet tortured Paraguayan dust. The resplendent international fiancée says that her General is still strong and that, without a doubt, the imported divinities, as well as the aboriginal ones, protect him from the common, hard-to-swallow disease of death which lamentably lays you flat. Serenely, amiably, Aleluya deduces that the General already has to his credit in the vicinity of ten long decades of existence, that is to say, twenty lustrous lustrums: from which he goes on to judge, in his own style, that it's probable that the weight of the saber, of the epaulettes, stripes, decorations, leather straps, armoured vest, cap, boots, pistol, twisted silken cord, lassos, sideburns and scapulars will tend to incline him closer and closer to the earth, in a perfectly comprehensible and explicable gravitational movement until his martial head meets with the neat burnished snares of his prisidential palace. Carmen Dionisia laughs at the pun which, if it's difficult to imagine in the Spanish language and hard to translate into English, is even more difficult to conceive and express in a surprisingly alive and open Guaraní (like Aley's). At this moment, the smiling, red-faced big man Prof approaches and says harshly that if he could manage to gather together a half a dozen Paraguayans interested in propagating their national culture in the city, he would immediately draw up a proposal for the Board of Education suggesting the creation of a center of Paraguayan culture. The Prof, in person, would explore the objectives of said plan carefully, he would structure the plan—an activity in which he is highly gifted owing to his long experience—and, right now, he says, you can calculate an initial allocation of some seventy-five thousand bucks—yes, indeed—and they could erect the economic bases that will make this culturally pluralistic project a reality. Immediately following this, the Prof launches himself with evident fury against the prestige of a descontructuralist Parisian professor who'd had the gall to offer to teach, in exchange for a juicy salary, "the Boricuan Spanish of the urban environment". With a great concentration of knowledge, the Prof asks:

"Who knows what the 'Boricuan Spanish of the urban environment' is? And, what do you do with it? And, if it in fact exists, with what purpose do you pursue its teaching, gentlemen?"

And he says that this Parisian infant, incapable of distinguishing a Boricuan from an Indonesian, has had the inconceivable audacity to present his plan to the big brass of the senior staff of Hispanic Studies at NYU, without consulting him, Doctor of Philosophy and Lettels, *nom plus ultra* of *tú sabes*. But, this furious digression aside, the possibility remains in his mind of effecting, in the company of the proper Paraguayans, the initial steps necessary for establishing the aforementioned center of investigation and teaching of Paraguayan culture. The Prof extends his hand, its upturned palm is slapped by the four disciples who surround him like Neptune's ring. Aleluya silently resists the Prof's crude interruption and then questions Carmen Dionisia about the Theater of the Absurd, kinetic art and electronic

music in her country; to which the girl replies that she isn't really up
to date on these things. Standing beside Aleluya, Gerardo is surprised
by the saccharin sound of this very strange language, which accepts
Castilian terms embellished by unfamiliar sounds and which end in a
brief sonorous addition or, as the Prof determines, with a scandalously
pre-Colombian suffix. But Tommy, who, standing beside Kenneth,
distrustfully watches the way that Aleluya holds his fiancée's attention, fearful that his evil intentions will be spelled out in the clandestine language, calls everyone's attention by proclaiming, with a glass
of whiskey in his hand, that the time has come for the ceremony. The
fiancée, trembling with virginal emotion—as described by the lyrical
Prof—stands still beside Tommy. Imagine Gerry's surprise when he
realizes that, standing tall, a bound booklet in his hand, Bolo is to act
as judge—a role which he can play marvelously given the many
occasions on which he has visited the courts! Everyone lines up.
Solemn. Bolo proceeds to open the booklet. As Carmen Dionisia will
acquire North American citizenship when she marries a US citizen,
Bolo has been inspired to show how, when and why he and all his
compatriots have such a brilliant legacy. So it is that he begins by
stumblingly reading a paragraph on the Spanish-American War; with
painful problems in pronouncing such fearsome sibilants, stopping
emphatically, revealing his true vocation as a numbers runner as he
reads the dates and numbers with professional pleasure. Every number contains, for the distinguished but marred judge *ad hoc sui
generis*, the pleasure of savoring the experience of the numbers game
once more: his life and work, in short, the bread for his six kids. In this
manner, those present who were uninformed, came to the clear
conclusion that the Beautiful Borinquen, Borikén in the Taíno language, had been invaded by the North American troops around the
middle of 1898, that is to say, at the end of the aforementioned war.
The judge, Bolo, stutters, loses his footing. He gives a brief pseudo-
historical recapitulation in which he mentions the Foraker Law; upon
realizing that this isn't where the key to his participation lies, he skips
pages sweetened by a vague colonial romanticism and comes upon a
cold, irreversible crudely expressed fact: in 1917, the Congress of the
USA imposed North American citizenship on all Boricuas. Then,
disoriented and out of legal perspective, the judge slobberingly—
remember his martyred front teeth, the disaster of his phonic instru-

ment—says a few words on the duty of women to follow their husbands, in sickness and in health, words which he graciously attributes to St. Peter, adding that life has its rough moments but that one has to "get down" (so he said) in all situations and have a way of looking at the world (*Weltanschauung*, thought Aleluya). Drying the excess saliva from his lips, Bolo says to Tommy:

"Do you take Carmen Dionisia to be your wife, Tommy?"

"Yes, I do."

"Carmen Dionisia, do you take Tommy to be your husband?"

"Yes, I do."

"Very well, my children," says Bolo—confusing his role as judge with that of a priest, "join hands and give each other a decent kiss. Now, sign the paper, the fiancée and the best man. Who has a pen?"

The Prof proffers his gleaming Parker.

After the ceremony of stamping the signatures, the dance commences. Comments, laughter, drinks. Gerardo notices it when Carmen Dionisia goes through the passage to her room and opens her spangled purse. The gallant groom waits with outstretched hand. Gerardo realizes that the girl is taking out an impressive roll of bills and giving them to the groom who begins to count them, wetting his index finger; serious, circumspect, like a merchant when the time comes to total the day's sales. Then Gerardo shifts his gaze and finds the document in the hands of his buddy-buddy Aleluya; the pieces fall, twirling gracefully to the floor. Aley shows no emotion, rather he seems distracted, even when he crosses the floor between the dancing young people and plants himself in front of the couple. You sense, within his calm, an extreme turbulence: a slow movement produced by violent internal movement (as in slow motion cinematography: the pressure chamber produces the floating motion; in this case, it is almost that). Without altering his expression, without looking at the couple who smile at him, Aley stretches out his arm and, with a gentle gesture which in no way resembles a seizure, takes the roll of bills. He doesn't even notice the startled faces. He simply introduces the roll into the spangled purse with a rapid, firm movement of his delicate wrist. Approaching him, Gerardo notices that Aley is talking to the girl in her strange clandestine language again. Carmen Dionisia's eyes widen, a cry issues from her throat. Just then, the groom launches a formidable right at the illuminated forehead of the disagreeable visitor. Gerardo sees it. And, before he can move against the agressor, Tommy lies flat on his back in the hallway. Aley looks at the fallen one with a certain controlled pity: he'd simply executed an innocent dodge that had gone practically unnoticed; he'd straightened out his right in the direction of the aggressor's neck with the speed of certain snakes of the Amazon who hurl their mortal dart as though it were a mere peck. He has not even changed the position of his body, which still hotly faces that of the girl, his left hand resting on her shoulder in a gesture of consolation; he doesn't appear fatigued: only his right hand seems to vibrate distantly from the violent imperceptible shaking, from the volcanic commotion of a second's duration, now motionless at his side, as though it were recharging its energies: Aley's knowing bicolor hand.

"We were going to get married for real," says the prone one, "but we couldn't find a judge."

"I love him," sniffs Carmen Dionisia. "In spite of everything, I love him!"

"That's your business," Aley tells her softly. "But you're not going to get the Yankee citizenship you want so much this way. Bolo isn't a judge. He's a numbers runner."

"You shouldn't have done it," Kenneth protests weakly, from a safe distance. "Tommy really wanted to get married. You don't do things this way, brother."

"It's done now," says the immutable, decided, very decided Aley.

"And he saved your cousin from prison," intervenes the Prof. "But the fiancée is melting for you, Tommy. Give her a real honeymoon night without the technicalities of marriage."

Sitting in the hallway, his back against the wall, Tommy caresses his suddenly tortured neck.

"This isn't the first time that something like this has happened," says the Prof, surrounded by the four identical Afros, rescuing his Parker from Bolo's pocket. "People have always married for convenience, but as far as I know, they've always been authentic marriages. A friend married a Dominican woman for a thousand dollars. She wanted to obtain US citizenship for this, ahem, modest fee. It was an authentic marriage, with a real judge, except for one insignificant little detail: when the bridegroom wanted to carry her to the nuptial bed, she refused; claiming that she was a virgin—how incongruous! He explained to her that girls get married to lose their hateful, unhealthy virginity as quickly as possible, but she responded that in her case, this was a mere business transaction in which there was no question of love and 'business is business', she said; if he had demanded a thousand dollars from her to help her obtain citizenship, she had every right to demand his respect for her obstinate hymen which she wished to keep immaculate until her cousin Cibao and her knight in shining armor, Patterson Piña, should arrive whom she would not only present with her pristine virginal maidenhead in a marriage ceremony with full benefit of the law, but with the citizenship which he, her hated pseudo-husband, had sold her for a miserable handful of bills. My friend had no appreciation for the girl, undoubtedly named Dulce Piña, which seemed like an ad for Libby's Sweet Pineapple, and she'd even seemed extremely ugly to him, but it took only her brief stubborn refusal for him to fall madly in love with her. What? His wife didn't want him in her bed? He begged, he pleaded, he threatened to have them stop processing her application for citizenship, a thing he wouldn't really have done because he was so crazy about her... Within the year, she had obtained the good she had so anxiously desired; Dulce divorced her bitter trampoline, alleging cruel treatment, mental cruelty, incompatibility, etc. A few days later, she sent for her tremulous suitor, Patterson Piña, who came folklorically accompanied by a noisy multicolored retinue: his widowed mother smoking a foot-long cigar, his fascinating cousins—eight men and six women, a grandfather rescued from the most distant of the Cibao mountains, four brothers-in-law, two municipal assemblymen and a personal representative of the mayor of his town. They've all remained in New York with or without permission, it's the same thing. The wedding was characterized by noise and music, a typical band played with the following decorations: four tambourines, two alto saxophones, two accordians, two *güiros*, maracas, sticks and other musical vegetables, without counting the hardware store of sleigh bells, cymbals, etc. In sum, a truly Antillian spectrum, a sweet Cibao contamination of the city. My friend, the mortified husband, suffered. He ended up listening to sentimental records in the small bars of Harlem, accusing even the children least contaminated by the Dominican Republic of being

Trujillo sympathizers. He's still in Bellevue, periodically receiving his electric shock treatment after his marital shock, which was, as I said, characterized by a forcefully imposed monastic purity."

In a few words, Aleluya eulogizes the Prof's indisputable ability to give a risque narration of such events. He smiles and admits that he would like to possess similar storytelling gifts. During the dialogue and succession of questions and answers, everyone was agreed that yes, marriage for love is not the norm; certainly, the multitude of beautiful, ethereal but poor nymphets who think only about money when they marry sickly old men with rotten prostates spring to mind, and the Prof puts forth the example of the conspicuous Greek privateers who do not hesitate to embark on the deepest of matrimonial seas thanks to their incalculable funds; chubby, ugly, repulsive characters similar to the slippery-est of toads from the shores of the Aegean (to mention a lesser evil among many), who contract elegant marriages with internationally known jet set widows whose husbands, as is common knowledge, have bitten the political dust, assassinated without the least compassion, says the Prof, blonde bankrupt princesses a la Anderson at your service; or, on the other hand, lusterless young men with some professional title or another who remain, oh, gulp, infatuated with aging princesses—victims of ugly genetic flaws—blind, frankly deaf, stupid but, you know, with a long bloodline of ruling rogues, aristocratic sons of bitches, the ineffable Prof recites without agitation; in this decadent society money is the grease that frees the most important screws, he says; and adds that only in a socialistic, classless society, when the means of production pass into the hands of their logical masters—the workers—will this pseudo-amorous aberration which is nothing, he says, but high class prostitution, be abolished. Aleluya assents heartily, agrees, in complete agreement; the group agrees; the four afro satellites agree, okay man, shit, fucking whites; the most tenacious screws, insists the Prof with incomparable metaphoric abilities as he slowly approaches Carmen Dionisia; inclining his large, rosy baby face, he kisses her on her worried forehead—abysmal little woman, in disgrace—whose presence reminds the Prof of the need to implement the new, culturally pluralistic project, so that right then and there, without transition, despite the quasi-bride's tears, the Prof begins to interrogate her about her Paraguayan countrymen in the city;

their favorite meeting places; intellectual capacity; formal education; financial status, and lets his decision be known, standing tall amidst the four fascinated afros, of his decision to visit the Paraguayan Embassy to propose his high culture educational projects to their excellencies. He adduces that it is necessary to stimulate the folklore of that country in this marvelous center of cultural diffusion—New York, and that, in the same way that the Boricuas had managed to baptise all of their noisy danceable music under the name *salsa*, the Paraguayans can, similarly, classify their own music which, naturally, will be known generically as Paraguayan *salsa*.

"I will take personal charge of the endeavor," he emphasizes, with a broad wave of his arm over the attentive heads. "I have high level connections on the Board of Education in this city. Seven hundred thousand dollars would be a reasonable allocation to enable us to take the first steps. Right now, I am engaged in a proposal for the study of the Taíno language of the Antilles. One of the members of the Board, Mr. Berenson, was impressed when I told him that the three words: 'hammock, enagua and barbecue', are of Taíno origin. 'Hammock, petticoats and barbecue!' he said to me enthusiastically, 'are the three things that I like best in the whole world.' So, one could say that the three hundred thousand bucks are in the mail or, better said, laundered."

Carmen Dionisia agrees, looking with supreme melancholy at her humiliated fiancé. She feels the bird of pain (*chowi*), sweet and slightly turbulent like the waters of the Paraná, has taken roost in her heart, that its beautiful plumage is making her chest palpitate to the beat of an indigenous percussion. Gerardo realizes that the girl, although offended in her marriageable dignity is, nonetheless, prepared to settle her differences lovingly with her mal-intentioned anti-bridegroom.

"Therefore, we will have to study the present-day Puerto Rican situation in depth," says the Prof, "without neglecting the fact that nearly half its population resides in this country. We will need to organize a symposium where the variables and constants of our culture will be, ahem, studied. We will invite sociologists like Maldonado-Denis, anthropologists like Seda Bonilla, writers in general and, why not?, paleontologists. As far as the organization of the symposium is concerned, leave that to me. Writers from *la Isla* who write about *la Isla* in, ahem, Spanish, and Newyorican writers who write about their experiences in this city, in English. Which is the language of the Puerto Ricans? Naturally, this is not a purely abstract question, as some friends would have it, but a serious problem. Thanks to our Newyorican poets, Hispanic American literature is now also written in English, friends and comrades! In the debate, we could have René Marqués, from *la Isla*, face off with Pedro Pietri, from New York. How does that grab you? A symposium of this sort wouldn't cost more than, let's say, twenty-five thousand dollars. And it could be recorded. Or, better yet, filmed by Channel 13. Along that line, the idea of filming reminds me that there is a need to establish a center of Boricuan cinematography. It would begin with purely educational intentions, but then it would evolve as a self-sufficient film enterprise, dedicated to great films of artistic and cultural merit. Already, a friend of mine has made an adaptation of *La charca*, Zeno Gandía's excellent novel, and he's considering filming it in Harlem. That is to say, rather than taking place in the Boricuan coffee plantations of the last century, it would be set in the streets, bars, fried food stands and apartments of Spanish Harlem. Man, and here we have the person who will take charge of the costumes...Ana, please."

The thirty year-old woman, long pale face, buck teeth, skinny, long sparse auburn hair, smiles broadly. Her eyes are very black and intense, contracted by several whiskeys. She smiles and says:

"Look, Prof, cut the shit. How long have you been on this *La charca* project? To tell you the truth, when this little director shows up, I'm going to make him pay through the nose for all the designs and costumes I've had ready for two years now. That one disappeared and left me in the street, without paying me a cent! The costumes are all there, rotting away!"

"You're such a character, Annie," smiles the Prof shame-facedly. "Nonetheless, this has always happened among artists. Temperamental people. Nevertheless, that shouldn't present an obstacle to our looking for a way to implement the project. I refer to the establishment of a genuinely Boricuan cinematographic industry. You may be sure that I will put a proposal before the Department that will have them between a rock and a hard place. We can exercise certain pressures: pickets, marches, strikes, in case the petition is denied us. We'll shout at them: 'Discrimination, racism, prejudice!'

and things will fall into place. Joe, brother, get me another drink. Yes. With soda. We'll fight the Jews who try to block our plans in the Department on their own ground. The establishment of a movie production center is, of course, an ambitious project, and would cost who knows how many millions... We will have to proceed cautiously and be meticulously counseled in the economic sphere. Regarding the design, general format and purpose, goals and motives of the proposal, there's no problem: I'll take charge of that myself. Make contacts, pull a string here, another there, make phone calls, banquets, that's only the beginning: and then, immediately, find the suitable people. Preparing proposals is an art at which I'm an expert."

Gerardo realizes that Aleluya is looking intently at the professor, but he isn't sure that he's really listening to him. For several minutes, Aley has seemed distracted and his eyes have remained on the people, without blinking. He also notices that Carmen Dionisia has slipped out into the dark hallway with Tommy; they are holding hands. And, while a group dances and leaps in the living room, as the whiskey pours down their throats without restraint, the couple opens an inner door, through which Gerry can see a lit nightlamp beside a soft white bed, a white pillow and a bouquet of red roses. Gerry feels a momentary twinge of envy which abates when he realizes that the wedding had been celebrated between the two of them. And that's what matters in the final analysis.

While he descends the stairs between the obligatorily graffitti-lined walls, accompanied by an Aley immersed in a limitless concentration (apparently, limitless), he senses the clamor of the music, the laughter, the dancers' steps, the loud voices. The volume of the music could easily give a camel headaches.

A gust of icy wind meets them in the street. They lean forward and wrap their arms around their coats. 116th Street is deserted, the houses dark, the streetlights give off a sad, Harlemnian glow. At the corner of Third Avenue, they pause to watch a fire truck pass, shaking the frozen air with the howling of its siren and clanging bell. From the direction of lower Manhattan arises the sound of many fire engines.

"*Sturm und Drang*," says Aley who, recently, has become interested in German Romanticism once more and is reading, for the fifth time, with renewed irony, the Werther of his beloved Goethe. "I think of your boss, Manolo, and his Golden Age poetry. He would say that, at times like these, you feel like someone with 'fire in his hands'. St. Teresa? It doesn't matter."

"It looks as though there's a big fire Downtown."

"The consulate..." Aley restrains himself. "I mean, it's not surprising if they've attacked some fascist consulate."

"Yes, yes, I know. I'm not an idiot, Aley."

"I don't know what you're talking about. Well, Gerry, good-night."

"Aren't you going to sleep?"

"We'll see each other one of these days, Gerry. Take care."

Aley disappears down a sinister-looking alleyway. Gerry only sees his tall hunched-over figure turn at the corner at the end of the alleyway. His footsteps are silent, light and elastic. Gerardo stands motionless for a moment, looking into the darkness where overflowing trashcans and old furniture stored beside the brick walls begin to take form. A cat runs between his legs and makes him shiver with superstitious terror. This internal chill combines with the cold that burns his nose and cheeks. He pulls his beret and earmuffs down against the cold and goes on, walking rapidly.

# 15

‍B‍UT, THREE MONTHS! you said, maybe a doc-
tor can still, Guzmansky can. No. *Es demasiado tarde*, Gerry. But
how can it be, Caty, it's impossible—all the necessary precau.
Careful. It's probably a false alarm, Caty, *por favor*, we're not ready
for this. If it were later on. I mean to say. Next summ. No. When I have
means. You know. But now. It can't. Be. Understand. Me. Don't be.
That way. In the summ I'll. *Tú sabes*. We'll still get married. There
are pills that. Twigs that. Leaves—herb tea. Some midwife. Someone
who. Now it's very risky, Caty tells you, no one will do it, jail, death,
*no quiero morir* so young, Gerry, listen to me. You're pushing me,
you tell her standing manfully upright in the room, your mountain-
born hearty palpitates, oh, prison, marriage. You're not a man, Caty
tells you, I won't push you to do anything, *carajo*, *así* stay cool, I
won't tell anyone *quien es el hombre*. No, pay attention, Caty, we're

going to see if we can, *tú sabes*, still; at three mouths you can still Caty,
I want to get married but later on. You know. You go to her you want
to stroke her but you find a Caty with her mind made up that no, on
her feet, strong brown woman, decided, saying *carajo* forcefully to
the Boricuan bastard machos afraid to face their obligations, *carajo*.
The whole thing is very disagreeable naturally, you see that a noose
is closing around you that threatens each day to hem you in choke you
oh. She says not one more word, that she didn't know you were so
weak, *carajo*, that she was prepared to have the baby, but now that
you're not going to help her out, to look out for the boy, she tells you
tenderly influenced by Mexican movies, and when he grows up and
becomes a hard-working man he will be ashamed of his father, *carajo*,
he won't even want to acknowledge him. Tears come into Caty's eyes
as she construes the bitter sacrificed future of her gerardian offspring.
Tears of fury, you know it. When you try to dry them trembling,
excited, Caty forcefully parries your hand with a hard slap, pushes you
without any delicacy, of course, storms out slamming the door
violently. Go after her—no way. Incredibly furious. Offended. Because you lost faith. Was your thinking twisted, Gerry, brave Puerto
Rican heart? Didn't you take all the precautions? Then she tricked
you, eh? Doubt, persistent needling. Distrust, bitter apple. Uncer-
tainty, unswallowable mango. In your popular philosophic mind you
conclude:

If you don't want soup, they'll offer you three bowlfuls.

So little Gerardo will have his Newyorican brother, as they say.
You'll have to talk with Lorenzo. Lorenzo, I. This. How can I tell you.
You know that I'm a serious man, Lorenzo. So that no. You're worried
that. I. Perplexed, how many incoherent ideas pass through your
neoNewyorkian brain? A strange vacuum, your head hums, you don't
hear the quiet sounds of the night. Despite the exhaustion from the
day's hard work, your sleep has been scared away. You lie down in the
bed so often visited by Caty, you jump up and pace around the room,
what, my second marriage!, and only twenty-six, brother. You expected to spend years of happy bachelorhood in New York, and with
the first experience, you've had enough? You'd already had enough
with little Gerardo. Entrapped now. Corralled from within, from your
own thoughts that won't let you go, you go round and round. Oh, it's
not worth all the fuss, you tell yourself stopping in the middle of the

room, puffing out your chest, she's pregnant, so what? Through the window with the half-open curtain you see that it has started to snow. You see the flakes fall twirling happily to alight greyly on the black street, twirling shining in the light of the lights, millions of transparent flakes implacably cover the city, you press your burning forehead against the frozen pane and contemplate the marvel for the first time in your life. How is it possible? The image of your ex-wife superimposes itself over the recent image of a desolate (that is to say, sunless) Caty. Two women in his life, a title for a soap opera. Little Gerardo crawls in the sunlight. What would he say at the sight of descending snow! Your ex would start trembling with terror. This white disease, this sore covered with sparkling white salt. You realize, when your thoughts wander happily for a second, you think that now you have a feel for your new job as you compare the falling flakes with the shredded coconut meat for an extravagant tropical treat, you think that you're well established in your profession when it occurs to you that the sidewalks are breaded with this frozen flour that rains floatingly from the mechanical skies of the city, a fine very sweet sugar for the sweet pastry dough, fiery frostings of polar consistency, it slowly piles up on the eves, in the river, on the trees and on the roofs... you're still enraptured with the image of Caty radiantly making her way, gesticulating in the depths of your thoughts. The radio, which you've stopped hearing in your thoughts, re-sounds little by little, Christmas songs from *la Isla*, burning nostalgia, seven long months of absence. Jingles. Sad songs. News updates. Bombs explode on Wall Street. The police are following the suspects' trail. You follow the suspicious footsteps outside your door. You look through the peephole. Oh, a family scene. Tom Kress, wearing a jacket of genuine red leather crossed by a double row of wooden buttons, stands talking with a young woman dressed in a long evening gown, a complicated hairdo, hair the color of living brilliant honey, her shoulders covered by a shimmering mink coat. You contemplate this very white girl with totally black eyes and green eyelids, fine arched barely visible eyebrows, the captivating moist red lips parted to reveal exceptionally white teeth, of course, a totally unexpected girl in the vaguely dishonorable atmosphere of the decadent hallway. She seems to resist going in but Kress, very macho, takes her by an arm covered with a silk sleeve stamped with red and yellow flowers, takes her to the door talks to her, persistent, low virile voice—astonishing metamorphosis; the girl looks all around, comes close and whispers something into Kress' ear, he smiles assents vigorously opens the door inserting the key at one blow—without hesitation—forcibly into the lock, they go in. You ask yourself what kind of combination Tom Kress-Anne Couvert is looking for now. You walk, pace, what are they up to, I'm going to be a father. You don't know how many hours minutes pass, the Kress-Couvert door opens you pace pace turn watchfully; in the semi-dark room the small lamp given to you by the ever-present Caty oh, source of distressing delights. You press forward without knowing why mechanically executing simple movements appropriate to solitude which consist of spying, consist chiefly of spying on what's happening around you to be prepared to entertain yourself with a hidden look at whatever is moving outside the semi-imprisoning walls of boredom, peering through the peephole totally awake strangely feverish you see the girl with the mink leave on the arm of an Anne Couvert dressed in truly dazzling red, their lips meet they laugh, slap each other on the rump, they descend shaking the nighttime stairway watched over by the everlasting typical graffiti. Oh, a *bien chévere* couple, he will be ashamed of his father I will raise him by myself Newyorican son, hum, his grain of sand in the Newyorkian population hum, feeling the nostalgic notes of a guitar the rasping of a *güiro* on the floor below, Boricuan Christmas in the urban setting oh unbearable nostalgia, loneliness profoundly exhausted not only from the effects of the hard work under the Manolo-ian vigilance, an exhaustion from deep within. Caty watching him from inside his own head, comfortably settled in a fold of his conscience. You turn your head to the window without thinking about anything, one single second without thinking of anything, a lit window on the other side of the street, another young solitary occupies herself with "constructively" killing the evening hours. You can make out the pastoral painting, the poster of Che in English (you assume it's in English, maybe you saw it in Bigote's house, you can't remember), a vase with plastic roses, the night table and, near the window, the stand with the sheet music. Caty watches you from within, he told himself, but you feel a curious itch in your solitary body, an expectant lightning *bien chévere*, suspenseful tension not Hitchcockian cold, but burning positive without bothersome terror, the girl crosses the room in a flowing bathrobe, the violin beneath her arm, disappears. You hear all of the diminished sounds of the city during a long measure of expectation, until you see her reappear and stand before the stand, trap her violin beneath her chin and move the bow slowly. She lowers the violin and stares at the music with concentration, the bathrobe open across her chest, her blonde hair in a bun on her neck. You see her turn the pages of the music, bend her head and study them, bring the violin to her shoulder once more, move the bow purposefully across the strings. But, how many times have you engaged in this exercise of spying on her, of joining her in the shadows, delirious when the moment of climax comes in this solitary frustrated amorous exercise? You know her ritual, you know that you must wait an hour for the miracle to be revealed, but you must stay there watching her the whole time, the culminating moment must not escape you. At last you see her—in a repetition of other identical nights—set the violin on the bed and leave the room. You have to wait fifteen minutes. In reward for your lovely loyal wait on these specific nights of the week (two, three nights) you see her appear with her breasts bare her black bikini panties dramatically black disruptive. You see her approach the window with deceptive speed and you calculate that you must bring off your solitary exercise precisely when she's covered half the room, one second, so that the girl's seventeen years—no more—unleash a powerful wave from you which strikes the windowpane wetly, you stand there watching stupidly as the girl comes to the window where she reaches out her arm and click she makes the night, your suddenly blind eyes still try to find her nubile pubescent teenage body in the cubitation where loneliness is also growing as if it were a mushroom in the air, a substance that's perfectly identifiable in certain rooms as though it were a part of the air, some type of transparent leaf, invisible, but with chlorophyll as thick as tedium; Caty's eyes contemplate you from the walls while you let yourself fall on the bed somewhat more relaxed now, smelling the obsessive perfume of sex on your hands, the dry seminal aroma; the violinist girl sleeps alone, what a waste, on the street she doesn't look so good, you've seen her with her jeans, a little pale, and her careless attire doesn't reveal the image that you've seen for the seven silent months that you keep to yourself, that you hardly think about, a strange ritual which, from time to time, is useful like a tree under which you sit to rest from the labors of being a neoNewyorkian. But you know that if, in fact, the image of the violinist girl is the image of the inaccessible (you don't even think this word) of a vague dream on the other side of the street, looking like one of the statues seen in a church one Sunday in your childhood, with blonde obviously foreign virgins, what is certain is that Caty has the power of the concrete, her rotund brown body, her hard silky very black hair spilled on the sheet has the power of the concrete, squeezable, touchable really palpable, weighing on the solid ground of Manhattan, not mere fantasy. And now, you think, while you breath agitatedly, you think how far away your ex is, how very far little Gerardo is right now, how much time has passed since your arrival in this city where, without a doubt, you've been progressing without major hardships, unlike many of your compatriots—victims of prejudice! On those first days in June when you discovered the unviolinated solitude of this girl you were also suffering from the dark shining nostalgia of the spring on your island, you shut yourself in and you didn't want to acknowledge that it's okay to cry, at least a little, turning your back on the crude buildings that stick their noses in your window, genuinely afraid that you'd chicken out, that the confusion you felt during those weeks would never end, confused oh always, fear of not being able to fulfill the most minimal necessary requirement of finding a job as is expected of every man, surreptitiously envying those friends who fight day after day without allowing themselves a second of impatience of weakness, but you understood that the solitary tears were normal. You went from the gentleness of the small town neighborhood in the center of your island of subdued sounds, with a breeze that fights against an invincible irreversible summer, from an environment where everything appears soft quilted beneath the incandescent clamor of the so central light of the sun in your latitude and you placed yourself suddenly in the middle of the street, the New York streets are The Street by antomasia. But how far away is all the initial insecurity now, brother, how far away now, and how near this other punch that doesn't let you close your eyes, you're going to be a father again, darling. You hardly hear the squealing brakes of the cars on some central street, the Christmas music pours sadly in from the radios wherever there is a compatriot consumed by seasonal nostalgia, hearing weak sounds within your soffit—the Polack doesn't have enough strength to make noise with his juvenile footsteps anymore. You think of the image of a plaster virgin seen in a church of your childhood and you link it with the image of the violinist on the other side of the street, inevitable association, a precious instrument torn from divinity, secret vibrations of the subway, strange unidentifiable noises, the subway perforates the silence of the tunnels, a violin whose voice you've never heard, suddenly cursing yourself like a man who discovers to his surprise that he's committed an injustice, perhaps, an unidentifiable betrayal—to what principles, to what respectable reality, to what institution, to what how many people? To what oh to what who how? In what have you been lacking?

The entire city opposes your dream, Gerry, full of evil moans, the city that you've begun to love, but also the city where man suffers, your compatriots suffer, but also the city where it might perhaps be reasonable to think of an omnipotent future for every creature because when all is said and done it's not possible to suffer any more and stay sitting with your hands in your lap. But, I'm going to be a father again, excessive exhaustion, brother. Finally recognizing that Caty had left mightily angry, that you're a profoundly lonely man that you're consuming yourself with thirst inside of four walls, Caty is a fountain, Caty is a clear spring you are a man who's dying from a fierce thirst in the middle of a suddenly defined desert.

# 16

$$\frac{16}{\underset{\bullet}{\phantom{a}}}$$

THEY LIVE IN BIG CITIES, in forested country-sides, deserts, rock piles, thickets, jungles, marshes, clay-pits. High places, low, highlow, deep, highly elevated, in between (and everything relative to the sea, yes sir). Everyone in his own place, it turns out. Eating what. Oh, a little of everything. Beef, lamb, chicken. Lettuce tomatoes whatever greens God grew. Also little lizards, he read once. And ants. An ant steak, well done. Baked rabbit. Squirrels. In Panama, iguanas called stick hens, metaphoric gnaw-gnawing. Cat pastries, exquisite, like rabbit pie. The Eskimos devouring seals, for example. The fucking seals are good for everything. They take out their oil. Fur for coats. Sailor wolves. Tender baked whales stuffed with icebergs. They invented the delicate cold victuals: chilled fish, walrus chops polar style, bacalao a la Jack Frost, snowy salmon. Jump to the South Pole and you'll see. Penguins. Unmemorable because they don't seem like birds. Porters at a Fifth Avenue reception. Regions where strikes abound, millions of extremely dignified porters, with their white bibs, unemployed, with nothing to do in this extreme of the Earth; they spend their lives meticulously dressed and powdered, staring at each other's faces, young gentlemen incapable of moving a finger, white bibs, idle. Pickled penguin. What use are they really. Joined in a perpetual assembly, hands in the pockets of their tails, their heads uncovered without fear of catching a cold. In Mexico, they eat tortillas with live wooorms: you eat a bite and the wooorms man they turn on the tip of your tongue and they stick together on your fingers. The Bedouins devouring a burning camel in moments of extreme necessity. What do you suppose the Japanese eat, oh what the rest of the world eats! Fish are advertised in the window of the Harakiri restaurant. Russians English French Czechoslovakians Chinese the whole world vegetables greens sprouts meat eggs fish. Delicate birds die with a delicious croaking. Geese: they torture them, they make them suffer; they steal their children, they raise their phone bill, they apply Uruguayan Pinochetian Brazilian electrodes to their testicles. Electric shock. You spill them or. To enlarge their livers, gold in the restaurants of luminous pridefully sophisticated Paris, for example. The more torture, the better the taste, the flavor. Tortured liver rich in flavor and, one supposes, in protein. Make a noble self-denying Danish country cow suffer with bad news so that her liver. Separate her from her calf or, worse, from the bull, tell her the sad facts about contamination by herbicides. Gourmets gnaw-gnawing. Suffering is the territory which produces the best fruits for the sophisticated palate; irrigate the land with bitter salty sweat, it produces immense plantations of super-sweet sugar. How do you enlarge the liver of a wild, dove, sweetly symbolic of peace? Oh tell her that the fascists are still, you know, unscathed. Gerry thinks all of this somehow, not very precisely, and basing himself on the teachings of the good Aleluya, as he chops wheels of ham between two plucked chickens which hang by their pallid feet. The boss is out, shopping, arguing with the shopkeepers, agreeably gruff.

Sweet silence of the morning, Kenneth cleans the dining room humming like a housewife at his labors. So accustomed to the city. Another one who'll live here until he dies. Kenneth, Tommy, as if their parents had anticipated this probable journey without return:

what names they have. But not Tommy. An Americanized Tomás. Kenneth has no way back. Kenneth and nothing more, there you go. Peace, tranquility. Cars pass with faint noise over the dangerously cold pavement, aachoo, sneezes a weak truck. Mountains of snow on the sides of the sidewalks, if you don't watch out you'll slip and break your behind. The people take strange clothes out of trunks, clothes which seem like the skins of flayed animals (well, of course, how else!), they look like monsters inside phantasmagoric furs, but Gerry has seen boys wearing just jeans and shirts hunching over on the street with their hands deep in their pockets. What are his brothers in unemployment up to? Tai Ken working in a dry cleaners, white clothes. Ismail Alí, furiously transplanted Arab, ironically dispensing gasoline in a gas station, petroleum which comes from his land where he couldn't find the crude means of earning a living? Hermosillo, the Ecuadorian, condemned by an ideal frontier imperialistically imposed by determined scientists astronomers physicists, one testicle in the north, the other in the south, two countries of the ball and chain. Braga da Cunha, mucha samba you know, bossa nova, *salsa* from the Amazonic expanses with their starving millions thrown together into slums, jungles of the ragged. Atila Piña, they grow this fruit well in the Dominican republic, pineapple here, pineapple there: Sweet Piña, Patterson Piña. They could name the girl, for example, Zoyla Dulce Piña of the country. Dulce Piña of the mountain, sweet as the *merengue* (the danceable and the edible). The boastful Fulgencio Guerra, "What's up, *mi socio*?", believing that it would be possible to return to a country like the one he left: the Cuba of the same name, longed for by him and many thousands of businessmen, but you won't be able to. Jodoka, Macedonio, Octopoulos, what will become of them? You see a person today and lose sight of him for fifteen years; you find him, grey-haired, one summer in Central Park giving nuts to a little squirrel, tame, domesticated by the city you know, with a strange secret pollution in his soul, his heart disturbingly accelerated by the paved breath of the streets upon streets of the planet. Let's say we think for a moment about Dutch from Alabama. You're faithless, Gerry, you haven't gone by the bar in months. All the contracts for dead men are filled, don't worry, don't worry that it's your turn. Three dead men laid out on its floor in two years. You think about putting a funeral parlor next door—in the event of slow deaths you'll find yourself annexed, so you sow and reap, without a visible means of escape in any direction, a rounded business (that's what they say, squared is inconceivable). A rectangular business, the six feet of ground which touch you in the last moment of gulp almost lived so many times in your life. Rectangular cemetery, too. The one in your town at the foot of a hill. It grew, implacable swallower, it lost its rectangular shape, acquired the shape of a sinister octopus (your hair stands on end!), it stretched threateningly innumerable, driven by the silenced will of amplified persistence belonging to every cadaver, it grew to the cornucopia of the hill (which is to say, it's growing in an unfriendly manner), but no, now they've overthrown it, at present they've savagely scattered it without being able to detain it (stop, please, hold on, please, in the name of the future widows and orphans!), it extends, mortally inexorable dragging rivers of white crosses on this side of the hill where the sun is more persistent, images of saints frozen in reputedly divine poses who rely on the good graces (the Okay) of Saint Peter and other chosen members of the celestial superpopulation. Paper crowns of flowers disintegrated on the uncomfortably hot moist earth, irritation for the skin uf! Bad thought, stop it. The soup's going to come out bad. Lentils. A punch, Caty, let the children go ahead and, you know. By god. Hum. I'm stuck on her.

His heart flutters thinking of Caty's ferocity in the past few days. He didn't want to see it. Coward! Three weeks without seeing you, things can't go on this way, this inflates. Well, what to do about it? Oh how I miss you, what loneliness. I can abandon her. She could go it alone. Women's liberation. Dastardly. A young, healthy man, once more subjected to monastic austerity this way just because. What they say is true: a hair can pull more than a team of oxen. One of Caty's pubic hairs is much stronger than a steel cable used to secure a vessel in port. There is no doubt at all that men kill, make wars, exploit others like themselves with the hidden hope of having a handsome multicolored collection of hairs, *pelos*, you know. And, just then, he finds a well worn copy of *Playboy* inside the freezer, a half-naked blonde (covered with a suggestively transparent wrap) on the cover. Oh, Manolo is enraptured by poetry, but also *pelos*, hair, you know. Between its pages Gerry finds a very well ironed ten dollar bill over the picture of a brunette with a contorted tiger's face. Very curiously hidden but not that well protected from public curiosity. A custom of

Avila? Where do Eskimos hide their ice cubes? In the open air, one
hundred and seventy ice cubes for a seal's tooth. Free commerce, cold
money in circulation, coined by Nature Inc. But a ten banana bill in a
magazine like this, hum. Every girl cut from the same piece of cloth.
The silent violinist, the windowpane whitely stained by a secret
impassioned gerardian discharge, it's there, on the glass, gilding the
not-so-white stain, turbulent. A son of the country who persists
unilaterally, without have found the other pregnable half, split personality, schizophrenia on a sub-germinal level. Looking at the blondes,
brunettes, red-heads in the magazine, you conclude that you need a
woman in your bed every night. Strict cloistral observance, the five
sisters on your left aren't enough. The old women in the neighborhood
who advised his ex-wife: "Take heart, even if you have a son you're
still a young woman with your whole life ahead of you." Hum. And
the men began to circle nonchalantly around her as though they
weren't interested, after the divorce, said to her: "Yes, you've got your
whole life ahead of you, girl". This is bad. To remember the past, as
though in passing, without significance. Life is ahead, precisely
between your legs. He would have a way to console himself. Women
do it too, when they're alone, with a hand, a finger, pillows, whatever
suits them at the moment. In technically industrially advanced societies they use sentimental vibrators. These lovers have important names
like General Electric (not just any girl can go to bed with such a
powerful general), Mr. Westinghouse, elegant and sharp, the playful
and exotic stranger whom they know only as Sony, like his no less
exciting compatriots, Sanyo and Onkoyo. And now it seems that
Manolo, too. Alone, in the kitchen, he lets himself be inspired by the
paper girls. He lives his comedy well: after fornicating vicariously
ideally with them he pays them with a ten dollar bill which he soon
recovers, a circular business, a fish agreeably biting its tail. His wife
from Madrid. He met her on Fifth Avenue, a clerk in a place with
Spanish souvenirs made in Yokohama, a so typically Castilian city.
They probably pray when they do it. At sixty-five, how many times
a week? Vitamins, minerals, Chinese pills, Dominican aphrodisiacs
(budding national industry). Aleluya and Iremita Johnson practicing
their new erotic hymn to the glory of the Lord, in this city the people
use it as the best pastime, they spend their time like this, man: the
whole world getting down left and right, *hombre*, life's gonna end

right now, the flesh gets squeezed and loses a certain glorious sheen, let's get down as much as possible, we'll make love without regret because then it's too late, darling, furiously. Caty, three weeks without seeing her. My God, and it won't stop growing. Got to do something fast. Lorenzo. You marry or I shoot. With a veil and head-piece. Lorenzo crying because Caty puts down the folk music of other times, because this is out of it, papa. *Jíbaro* music. And Daniel Santos and other tigers. Lorenzo's children don't want to be talked to in Spanish, they put down his *bodega* because it sells *yucca, yautía, malanga, habichuelas*, Goya, you know, but they live off him, dress off him, fat and strong thanks to papa's *bodega*, Puerto Rican shit. Caty bound to Lorenzo, after all, even though she laughs when he talks to her about the customs from there. *Hombre*, what a mix-up there is in this city! They call him old-fashioned. Because he doesn't speak English. *Atrasado, hombre.*

Gerry has the vegetables ready now, has carefully washed the greens for the salad. Everything nearly ready for when the customers begin to arrive. Every day, more customers. Manolo had talked about getting a kitchen helper. People emigrate to eat. Steal to eat. Kill to eat. Quite simply. Gerardo goes along thinking this with his habitual slowness, cautious, deciphering his own personal labyrinth in his own way. He was even slow in recovering from his tautological thought and realizing that Manolo had just arrived with two full shopping bags, which he placed on the table.

"A hundred dollars in trifles," he sighs.

Kenneth sets himself to frightening flies with a rag, collecting the salt shakers, and placing the folded napkins inside the glasses. As he minces a large slab of meat to stew, Gerald feels the side door open. A tall character with a raincoat and delicate mannerisms greets Manolo, who had removed his false teeth and placed them in a glass. Sad, oppressed, Manolo responds to the recent arrival with a senile greeting.

"Mr. Inspector," he murmurs, and the weightless weight of his missing teeth encumbers his spirit as much as his diction. "How do you feel?"

"Oh, very well. Just doing my duty."

"You get tired, visiting so many businesses..."

"What most exhausts me is the routine," says the American.

"And what do you do to amuse yourself, if you don't mind my asking?"

"Oh, I watch TV, I read magazines..."

Inconceivably, Manolo becomes highly animated.

"Ah-ha! So you like to read."

"Well, not so much, shit. Magazines with pictures mainly, to relax my mind. I entertain myself by looking at the pictures in girlie magazines."

Manolo is completely ecstatic. The inspector has said the magic words; open sesame! With a suggestive toothless smile, he shows him a copy of *Playboy*

"I could give it to you. I've looked at it many times. It's worn, but it has all the important parts and it's very well ironed."

"Does it have *all* its pages?

"Of course, *señor* inspector."

"There you are, reading the magazine and enjoying it and, suddenly, my God!, the key page is missing!!"

"*Each and every one of its pages, señor* inspector."

"You have to keep your property in good shape," says the fellow in the raincoat. "Now, for a serious inspection!"

And the *señor* inspector peers into pots, examines the ears of a rebellious Gerald, scouts beneath the dishwasher, tenderly observes the shipwreck of the dentures in the glass.

"Everything's in perfect order," he says, big smile; "I congratulate you. Let's see if you can't get me another girlie magazine next month. I love them."

"You'll have it, *señor* inspector. And with even more pages!"

Actually, this was Gerry's first experience in this area. In one week he confirmed—now suspicious after his discovery of *Playboy*—how devoted the public servants were to illustrated magazines, calendars, books, and encyclopedias, always if they contained a small, loose interior page ironed with an appreciable healthy sum.

On another occasion, when the side door opens:

Kenneth sweeps the dining room;

Manolo cuts pork chops frantically pokes his favorite

employee in turn, the aforementioned Gerry;

Gerardo opens the wastebasket and removes:

potato peelings

wet papers
a rotten onion
seven empty cans
a half pound of overripe pimentos
two *chayotes* gone completely to seed
a half dozen bad eggs.

This man is as tall as the one before him. From the Fire Department. You can tell by the insignia on his coat.

"*Señor* inspector," says Manolo. "How's life treating you?"

"So-so. As God wills it."

The inspector's eyes are fogged from watching so many incendiary catastrophes, his nose is split like a brick that has been in the flames too long. But it is evident that there is a deeper burning within him that comes from his gut, of a windpipe parboiled by numerous shots of bourbon.

"You must be tired," says the transplanted native of Avila, ingratiatingly. "I don't envy you."

"During this season, the work is less fatiguing. The summer is pure inferno. The heat, you know."

"Christmas," says the atheist Manolo ecstatically, "time of peace and spiritual rebirth for men of good will."

"Truly," approves the fireman-turned-inspector, "but it's the time when the most fires occur. Defective, improvised heat."

"At least you can watch good TV shows. I love *Cannon*, *Medical Center* and shows by Walt Disney. The news is disagreeable. Wars, sabotage."

"It's hard to put a halt to some of these conflagrations," says the ex-fireman. And he adds philosophically: "It's the world burning. The flames of discord reduce any hope of a military cooling to ashes. Think of the Middle East; where there's fire, at the least breeze, there are flames."

"That's a Spanish saying, *señor* inspector."

"The *Latino* in the *bodega* out front translated it for me."

"Don't you read the paper to pass the time?"

"No, the world is on fire. When I read the news, it's like being at work. Think about the bombings in the last few weeks. Subversives. One in the Chilean delegation. More in the ITT office, in the military recruitment center, and so on. This city is a volcano."

"I read the poets of the Golden Age, but I don't suppose you share my taste."

"I enjoy romantic novels. They're so sweet! Refreshing amidst the inferno we live in. TNT and eremite are the current nightmares."

"Ah," from a relieved Manolo, who's found the key. "I have been reading a delicious story in which a poor little orphan suffers because of her stepmother. One day she meets a prince in the forest. The prince would undergo..."

"Don't tell me, please! I'd like to read it for myself."

"Oh," exclaims Manolo, spellbound between two fake Jabugo hams, "it's a childish story, but fascinating."

"Please, could you lend it to me?", pleads the superfireman with tenuous fervor. "I know that people don't lend their books, but please, could you...?"

"Certainly."

"I just finished reading a novelette called *Tears of Fire* which greatly moved me. And I have another book by the same author: *Burning Passion*. My favorite titles are beautiful: *Only The Ashes Remain*, *The Flames of Jealousy*, *Molten Heart*, *The Fire and The Air*, *The Afternoons of a Pyromaniac*, *The Pyromaniac*, *Fiery Passion*, *In The Heat of the House*, *Fiery Maiden*, *The Fireman's Fianceé*, *The Siren and the Bell*, *Burning Ground*, *Cold Season*, and so on."

"I see that you are very selective."

"Professional in all regards."

Manolo searches in the drawer where he keeps the menus. He takes out a little book whose cover shows a fairy godmother touching the head of a kneeling maiden with her magic wand. The inspector with the smoky eyes decides to do his duty, as he puts it. He finds an electric wire, totally denuded by the voracity of the bicultural rats—which, in the US, wear insulated fur—two naked connections, a circuit breaker which is totally out of place; acknowledging himself satisfied with how well everything is going, talking about the extraordinary safety methods adopted by the restaurateur from Avila. He puts the novelette into his pocket with the assurance that it encloses some very stimulating surprises; he says:

"Good. I congratulate you, boy. Next month I want another novelette. I love them."

"I'm glad," responds Manny, situated beside half a gutted cow.

"Little stories to soothe the spirit."

"You're a man of delicacy," says the macro-fireman. And he leaves, walking tall, very tall.

"I didn't know that you were into giving out books," says a sarcastic Gerald, pesky as only he can be, frankly vexing.

"Oh, what a team of rascals—corrupt sons of bitches. They've got their style. They're not like the police who, when there were blue laws, used to come into the stores that were open and say: 'Where's the dough?' And the owner would tell them: 'There, under the box of crackers.' And so they'd go from business to business—five, ten dollars at each one. You're making such a face! The game changes, you're a witness to that. That's why the means grow extreme. It's strange, because for them, a Latino is a Latino, a person you don't have to take into consideration. So these jerks come to take your dough, with the work that it takes to earn it! Mazola; olive oil mixed with soybean, Gerry; unless the Andalusian comes, nobody's going to know the difference!"

In that moment of oh, my gosh! and oh, heavens! it isn't exactly the Andalusian who comes in, but the wreck of a little old man, intruder into the kingdom of potatoes and cabbage and fragrant steam. He comes, covered with an open, moth-eaten overcoat; his vest, coming apart at the seams, strangely depresses Gerry.

"Winter," he says, like an actor who tosses his lines as soon as he finds himself on stage.

"And very cold," says Manolo, who always has a reply on the tip of his tongue.

"You have no idea, dear friend, how much I look forward to retirement time."

"Oh, yes, you must have worked too long."

"Fifty years at the Office of Food Inspection, yes indeed. I count the hours and, because I'm so old, I don't even know what day I'm living."

"Don't you take Vitamin E, Mr. Smith?"

The little old man smiles, ungluing the ancient pasty phlegm from his chest, a smile more acrid than bitter herbs. His yellowed teeth are encrusted with tobacco tar (*brea*); his tongue has a yellow crust.

"At my age, my son, there aren't any vitamins worth anything. Quite a while ago, it came time for me to retire, but my bosses begged me to stay in the office. They wanted me to stay for one more year, when I'll turn ninety-seven."

"Come on, you'll live more than a century. Not too long ago, a compatriot of mine died who played the cello—he was a wonder. When he turned one hundred and twenty-five, he composed an exceedingly strange work that, lo! the experts are still trying to classify. In light of the fact that the musicians have been unable to accomplish anything with this task, they've left the responsibility to a team of gerontologists, if you see what I mean."

"Yes, I understand."

"And listen and see if old age can't be lovely; that my compatriot turned out to be exceedingly useful. They even created a festival in his name. And I say very useful because many people live off this festival. It's a honeycomb. Foreign bees come and suck from it or, better said, from the contributors who permit their contributions to fatten the coffers of this aristocratic annual festival. When my compatriot was born, they hadn't yet invented the Demographic Registry, so they had to look for his exact birth date on his baptism certificate. So, onto the hundred and twenty five he had to his credit at his death, you could add some twenty more, because you must know how lazy those priests could be in certain little Spanish villages; they probably deferred his baptism until the boy was a man. But, as far as playing the cello was concerned, his playing was a million marvels. There's a musician, Sniddel, who always had the bow ready, he kissed it, he cleaned it, he pampered it. They paid him well to do it and he's still floating around. He tuned the violin for the genial old man. They've thought of taking him to Rumania, the geriatric center of the world; I don't know if you know this, but it's where you could recuperate much of your energy. Have you considered this fountain of youth, Mr. Smith?"

"Ay, my son, I know about Rumania. But it doesn't interest me to continue to prolong this miserable existence. The Rumanian treatment created a tragedy for my cousin, Bert Ingersoll. Bert is four years older than I am, that is to say, he's been around for exactly one century. Well, anyway, his wife, Patty Connelly, to whom he'd been married for a period of seventy five years, went to have herself rejuvenated by doctor Asland, director of the Rumanian geriatric program. And what happened? A few months later, Bert went to meet her at Kennedy Airport. But he couldn't find her. Many girls went past him, but not one old woman. Suddenly, an attractive woman of about thirty approached him and asked him what he was doing there, poor little old man, all alone. And he told her. And she smiled roguishly and told him: I am Patty Connelly Ingersoll, love. Impossible, frightening. Bert saw her adorable little breasts, her curvaceous hips, listened to her soft melodic voice that night, when they both undressed to go to bed. Of course, poor Bert was drooling; he wasn't short on spirit but he couldn't, you know, revive a dead man. Patty seemed disgusted with the image of the man who'd been her lover for nearly eighty years: his wrinkled skin, sunken mouth. She was only five years younger, but her skin glowed with new life, illuminated by an inner light. In only a few months, Patty had been transformed into his granddaughter. Her tastes, on the other hand, were rejuvenated too. So, she stopped listening to old country dances, she craved rock and soul. One morning, irritated by having to live with this old man who had her chained down with complaints and senile needs, who slobbered and urinated on himself, Patty ran off with a bearded latino hippy who played the electric guitar and sang what they call soul and this other thing that you eat..."

"*Salsa.*"

"That's it. Eighty years thrown to the winds because of this Asland. I don't want to change the direction of my life. When God calls me, I'll be ready. I don't want to deceive the good Lord with vitamins and massages and Floridian poncedeleonisms."

"They're problems," says Manolo, keeping it brief for the first time. "Problems, problems, problems.."

But the old man came to his rescue:

"To remember what day I'm living, I surround myself with reminders. I tie a string around my finger, but then I forget why the devil I did it. I put a spoon in my pocket so I'll remember to eat."

Manolo looks at him with fright. Nothing occurs to him. The old man looks at him blearily.

"For example," he continues smiling yellowly, "a calendar would be a perfect reminder for me."

Immediately, Manny is jumping for joy and, in the wink of an eye, produces a calendar with the inscription: "Courtesy of El Mesón del Cordero". Gerry stares long and with great interest at the object in the old man's hands, asking himself how they could pull off the transaction, but he sees an ironed bill folded beneath the January page, attached there with a paper clip. The number 10 leaps out of hiding.

"Thanks, my son. I love the Puerto Ricans."

"So do I," returns Manolo. "But you should know that I'm Spanish."

Gerry looks at him suspiciously. He wants to know what the clarification means. Does the Gallician also have anti-Boricuan prejudices like those people? Is he a racist, too? At this moment, the ancient Smith does, as they say, his duty: he becomes emotional at the sight of a rotten potato, he cries tenderly over a pork chop green with the passage of time, and he smiles, in the height of ecstasy, before the secret lightning snarl paralyzed in the false teeth he finds in a coffee cup. Then, the ancient one drags himself out, without strength in his legs, but with the might of a *machetero* in the arm under which he imprisons the calendar with the virility of a young man.

"Does it bother you to be taken for a Boricua?"

"Me? But man, why do you say that, hey? You would have said the same thing if you had been taken for a Gallician, fuck! You're so touchy."

"No, it's that a lot of people who come here put us down, you know."

"Yeah, I understand, I know. You're right. Some of the Spaniards do the same thing. But not me, right? I like you guys a lot, I swear it; you're my brothers."

"An Argentine got offended because I asked him if he were a Boricua. Afterwards, he went to Puerto Rico and they tell me that he's gotten really fat because he eats so many plantains, sweet potatoes, pork, you know. And the same thing happened to me with some Cuban..."

"From Havana?"

"Who thought he was God on Earth. Man, he was so stuck up! Yes, that's what he said...from Havana."

"Ah, one of many. The women are really fine. Have you ever slept with a Cuban, Gerry?"

"No."

"They say they're very sensual. For me, all women are the same when you get down to it."

"This Fulgencio Guerra thinks that it's all bullshit and he's never wrong. Should I put the pig's feet on to boil?"

"You Boricuas are very timid. You don't have the courage to stand up for yourselves. This business of having two flags and, supposedly, two languages, has divided you in half. Ambivalence. Aleluya says that colonialism has really hurt your country. I believe him."

"Aley knows a lot, he reads like crazy. He's a good comrade."

"Yeah. Get the greens ready, dice the potatoes for the omelette. Do you have everything for the '*caldo gallego*'?"

"That old guy who's always complaining that he's tired of working...why doesn't he quit? Ten bucks at every store. Yes, I've cut the pork sausage."

"And we need some of those. See if there are enough white beans and leeks. Every government flunky comes around to get his share."

And Gerardo already knew that: a flunky had appeared at the side door another time, a short heavy-set man with a mafioso's rat face, a two day beard: a strange bird. Gerry thought that he was faced with the most corrupt and degenerate of the many public servants who had visited the kitchen. This man, like all the others, complained about the particularly biting cold this winter and alluded to his stupid routine as a public servant. Evading the dialogue and circles and subtleties at which Manolo was an expert, Gerry began to look for books, magazines, calendars, places where one could attach an ironed bill. The man observed him tensely—cold, hot, cold, hot. Gerry had gone in circles so many times under the sharp gaze of the newcomer, he felt so foolish in his senseless exercise, that he began to feel resentment building up inside his Boricuan chest. Then he decided to go for a frontal attack: he took out his wallet improprietously, extracted a ten dollar bill and gave it to him, explaining that he had yet to learn the rules of the game, to please pardon the rumpled bill, that there wasn't a book or a magazine or a calendar in the place. The man said to him:

"Ten dollars?"

"Isn't that enough?"

"No."

"That's what he always pays them."

"Always?"

"Yes. Manolo. And now me."

"And who does he pay?"

"Listen, how much do you...?"

"Who does he pay?"

Corralled, ay. The paws up to his beloved tonsils. A restrained hatred, old, jumped bounced like a ball from his heart to his martyr's head, from there to his contaminated tongue, torpid in English but shifting like the very sand, a clutching quagmire. The shifting sand swallows men. The last things he saw were his hands clenched into fists in the suffocating air of the kitchen, his middle finger rose of its own accord. Farewell, cruel world. He bemired his tongue, sucking it toward the depths of error. Because he said:

"To you. To all of you!"

"I don't know who 'all of you' are."

He only saw his stiff middle finger waving good-bye: tongue of shifting sand, for love, insult or error. He said:

"To you, the inspectors."

The rat face made a note in a little book.

"Your name."

"What's happening? What are you writing down there?"

"The celebrated Mesón del Cordero. Its owner, Manuel Avilés Serrano. We'll be seeing each other."

The bizarre rat disappeared. Shifting sand. Gerry's head felt full of foam rubber. Carelessly peeling potatoes, he cut a finger. The index finger of his right hand. But this detail didn't really matter.

## 17

I T'S ENOUGH to make you die laughing!!!"
says Gerardo.

The rat-faced inspector turned out to be the most degenerate of
them all, so that Manny had to give him a good bite, greased his hand
with double emollient. With Boricuan optimism, Gerry had feared the
worst but after the happy outcome he spent two weeks of apparent
calm—a calm perforated in its center, an apple with its core silently
gnawed by some small worm, *bien chévere* on the outside—thinking
every night, as he went to bed, of Caty's round belly and, every
morning, as he got up—thinking—of Caty's round belly: each morning a little rounder than the night before and every night a little rounder
than in the morning, closing the cycle with a thought appropriate to his
privileged brain:

Every cloud has a silver lining.

But, when January was half-gone, he had a violent shock. Surprised, frightened, impossible that out there shots, firing, smell of gunpowder; a certain restrained splendor slipped in under the door. His fertile Caribbean mind imagines Dick Tracy firing shots upstairs, but in no way did the impassive, serene, strange secretly victorious young man poised for one intense second in the passageway standing amidst the sentimental graffiti resemble Tracy—Gerry observes nervously melancholically through the disturbing and amplifying peephole. Tall, pale, serene he told himself, Aleluya waits to be joined by his soul singer, Iremita Johnson; Aley displaces himself leaving a hole amidst the familiar graffiti, a hole negated in a fraction of a second by her violently subtle appearance: extremely thin, brilliant white teeth contrast with the absolutely black noble face of a Bantu Mau Mau princess like from there, where there's a fragrant meadow where a baobab remains like a suddenly stopped storm, the innumerable afro fills the peephole; Gerry takes a lamentable intellectual plunge when he thinks tenderly that she's black but with a white soul. Iremita lives an enormously glorious moment, her short afro radiant above her svelte body of African bamboo, eyes white with two magnetic points radiating in the center vibrating electrically, Gerry punches the lock of his door to go to their aid, but Iremita disappears leaving the graffitied scene to two subjects with hat, gabardine and a Dick Tracy profile, police sirens howl below, they turn on huge spotlights, shots sound, amplified voices:

GIVE UP *POR FAVOR* YOU ARE SURROUNDED *O ENTONCES*!!!

These two Dicktracies, hadn't he seen them pass mysteriously one night by the corner of his house one time when he'd been with Aley? He stands frozen not only because of the accursed January which is half-gone as he's said, but because of the shots, the subjects who fly past shooting in unison perfectly mechanized synchronized identical rhythm in both serialized profiles exactly identical; shots, fury, frustration on Gerry's part, what to do Aley would say don't you throw yourself—and with good reason—into the open because Aley was that way, or is, no one knows what his fate is, where he went to hide, his open room (Aley's) without a single book, examined inch by inch by ten sniffing bloodhounds one week squatting in the corners ten times a day lifting the top of the toilet examining the corners with cockroaches crawling like flies on the soffit smelling the walls passing their tongues Sherlockholmianly over the substances suspected of containing something who knows what, rooting out secret threats which Aley carried with him according to claims by a subject of free enterprise incommodated by the flaming strike at his factory. Calabrio had dematerialized with a thoroughness incompatible with his sturdy musculature this same night, that night, his apartment minutely registered every knickknack removed, every record of old Italian opera played meticulously in search of who knows what clandestine musical code, what burning cauldron of secret Calabrian revolution, so that the neighbors—Boricuas, Dominicans, American Blacks, the Pole, who seemed to ignore everything, for various reasons—heard tear-jerking operas for a week-long course of free music. And, of course, *señor* Geraldo Sáncheh native of the Ihla of Puelto Rico was, as they say, subjected to a fearful interrogation in the general quarters of various official organizations dedicated to maintaining peace and oldel, where less romantic characters than Kojak showed themselves to be willing to grind his bones, from which he was freed, a fact that Gerry, by now knowledgeable, attributed to his unexpected blue eyes which did not fit in with his thick accent from the senter of his Ihla. His room was examined inch by inch with thick magnifying glasses which enlarged the corners and the eyes of the bloodhounds, fearful that they would find the roaches from the grass smoked with Caty, interrogated often, really he could not, in truth he knew nothing about anything, that is to say, he didn't know anything about anything except that he knew that Aley, Iremita, Calabrio and

OHBLESSEDBE HER TOO MOIRA WOW!!!

had disappeared as though they'd been swallowed by the earth. And Manolo—after being extensively interrogated—read him the paper with extensive personal commentary so that he would be apprised of supremely interesting incredible news, a lot of which—he said—was a product of the imaginations of subtle police sergeants, winged creations. Gerardo is brought up to date. In the first pages of the paper he sees pictures of those who had disappeared in their revolutionary endeavors, his already enumerated friends with their clandestine (clenched) political revolutionary biographies mamas papas and so on. In the initial versions the intelligence, that is, the agency called Intelligence had failed to such an extent that—according to Manny, who reads and makes comments—they had Aley enrolling in the University of P.R. at age four which raised heated protests among because they made a child prodigy of a subversive; as far as Iremita was concerned, the calculations were so far off that they made her ninety seven years and seventy-two days old. According to this initial version, Dino Calabrio was a thin delicate being, a colorful butterfly, a ballet dancer with exquisite manners, a renowned interpreter of *Swan Lake* from—as everyone know—pre-Soviet times. As regards Moira, the white snake according to Gerardo, she was a fat girl with huge flaccid breasts, snaggle-toothed and cross-eyed. This report clearly delineated the poverty of the anti-revolutionary imagination, because it wasn't rational to cover millions of front pages with mind-boggling pictures of Moira, this first rate model of fashion magazines, with headlines that informed you, for example, that "This is the fat, snaggle-toothed cross-eyed Moira, anti-Christian sinner impenitent ugly subversive". As the information offered by the press was so contradictory—supplied by the CIA, FBI, CORCO, PNP, PPD, UPR—these institutions had to refine their points of view filing away their anti-communist hatreds until they managed to provide the avid press with a marvelous, perfectly eclectic, finely integrated tale, free at first glance from obvious contradictions. Aided by ghost writers, institutional bloodhounds had produced biographical sketches about the missing.

"It's enough to make you die laughing," says Manny, affected by a strange linguistic contamination, at the beginning of the reading.

*Dino Calabrio*

He is born in around 1915 in a small costal town of the Aegean, the son of Atanasios and Teodosias Granadoupoulos. From an early age he fishes to help the family's finances. During his adolescence he has a serious altercation with a fisherman from the north of Africa, whom he beats with an oar, dying shortly thereafter ("The one from Africa, you understand, you have to clarify the amphibologicalisms of the policial style", says Manolo). The young Aristos takes refuge on an arid mountain, where he spends more than a decade as the shepherd of skinny sheep, until the Nazis give him the opportunity to turn hero. Aristos beheads, with scientific efficiency, powerful motorized Aryan supermen; he has a great advantage over them: his skin has acquired the rocky color of certain pre-classical Cretan sculptures, so that he can conceal himself chameleon-like to make his enemy's blood run—and he discovers that it's red like his own! Instantly a partisan leader, Aristos becomes a true leader of the masses, the hope of the proletariat. "But, as everyone knows," says Manolo, " near the end of the war, the Allies establish a military government in Athens which distinguishes itself for the immediate repression of thousands of patriots who had fought against the Nazis." Aristos flees disguised as a Greek Orthodox priest—what else!—and sets himself up in the romantic Sicily of the immediate post-war period; here he distinguishes himself as a professor of Greek in the Institute of Mediterranean Languages, a school directed by Franco Labbia, where he never experiences the slightest difficulty with his heavy peasant accent given that no one in the city knows the alpha beta gama of said language. Aristos rapidly learns Sicilian, marries Monica Gallo, with whom he procreates Tonio Aristos and Aragna María; after seven years of felicity the sorrowful separation from his wife intervenes, after which—fearing for his life, he decides to flee; he had received death threats from Máximo Maccio, the head of the local chapter of Cosa Nostra, and by Monica's uncle, Marco Antonio Dagnino. Aristos disembarks in New York in the mid-fifties. He applies all of his intelligence to learning English and to studying the history of the European immigrations, especially the Italian, which explains his deep understanding of the Italians in the city and his success in making himself pass for one of them... A little more than a year ago, the Secret began following the footsteps of this "old revolutionary capable of subverting the order of Paradise itself" (words of a high Catholic police chief). Most recently they considered him to be a member of the group of terrorists captained by Aleluya, a dangerous band capable of setting fire to an iceberg.

"Man, but what nonsense!" protests Manny, tossing the paper out. "Wonderful, it looks as though it were written by your compatriot, Zaíd Lecráclav."

*Aleluya*

"Listen to this, Gerry!"

He is born in 1955 in a small town in the south of Puerto Rico, the son of Julio Pérez, a rural teacher, and Jasmin Peterson, native of Saint Thomas or some other adjacent islet. When he was fourteen, he entered the University of Puerto Rico where he was immediately contracted to teach composition and Spanish to four PhDs of the Department of Hispanic Studies. Terrified at being confronted by the vast knowledge of this student, the four professors renounce their chairs: one becomes a taxi driver, another a green-grocer, another a policeman who distinguishes himself for his spelling errors when giving tickets to traffic infractors, another a pohet of ivory tower sensibilities—by the name of José Anacluto—continues to add pages to his doctoral dissertation from his confinement in a mental institution, so that now the judicious document weighs as much as a truck tire; a memo-book where historical lies and amphiboles gambol gaily, it suffers from marred syntax and contains hundreds of dusty Anglicisms fearful of being discovered: a fat monument to much feared gibberish. In his first year at the University, Aley distinguishes himself as an ardent defender of the "great citizenship of the great American nation". There are pictures in which one sees the small fourteen year old mulatto draped in the forty-eight star flag, proudly encased in the uniform of the U.S. Army military school at the University. His North American passion doesn't last six months. At the end of this period, without transition, he becomes the leader of the Federación Independentista Universitaria. His essay, *The Germination of the International Revolution Since The Rhine Gazette* brings him resounding fame in the countries of the Third World. Some time later, the young unemployed professor—high officials of the University of Puerto Rico deny him work based on the fact that he had written domisile (with an s) on page 628 of his dissertation—finds himself obliged to take care of children in their domiciles. In 1972, the young man disappears. The police place him simultaneously in Albania, China, Yugoslavia, Cuba, the USSR, Czechoslovakia, Poland, West Germany, Algeria, Bulgaria. Nonetheless, childhood friends attack the ubiquity attributed to Aley by the windmill chasing police force and allege that Aley has been in his hometown the whole time, caring for his sick mother—a generous woman whom they affectionately call the "madam"—writing tireless essays, among which is the distinguished monograph on the novelist Enrique Laguerre entitled

*Laguerre and Peace*

and various other topics

*The Suffix nkb in the Language of the kpt Tribe of New Guinea*
*Semiotic and Ethnocidal Structural Dynamics in a Puerto Rican*
*Ghetto of New York*

Following the burning of foreign businesses in *la Isla*, a poet dedicates a sonnet to him in which he calls him the "Prometheus who steals the divine fire to make the revolution", a poem read feverishly by the police, who dedicate a plaque of recognition to the bard for his labor on the side of law and order. Rumors fly about the young revolutionary's demonic power, about his cold and cerebral hatred of certain Latin American dictators among whom he hates—with blind mortal hatred, a burning thunderous hatred which distills *curame* venom daggers lightning—the thugs who assassinated the revolutionary president. There are those who suspect that Aley masterminded the dynamite attack against his deputation in NYC and against ITT, an institution which nursed those big goons. (Gerry doesn't know which is the article and which are the Manny's's comments). They attribute the leadership of a band of international terrorists to Aleluya, a band which operates in the principal capitals of the ahem (Manny clears his throat) free world and whose highest goal is to overthrow the U.S. government by force. The uncovered plans indicate that the conspiracy was about to erupt. They accuse Aleluya of conspiring to overthrow, as they put it, the legal government of the country, to destroy the social peace, abolish the class system, dynamite the institution of the family, abolish the free press, free enterprise and social decency.

"And that's Aley's biography?" says Manolo ironically. "I swear to you, Gerry, that Aley wouldn't plot against the life of a fly."

"But against the life of a capitalist, he would," says Gerry astutely.

*Moira Montrattis*

She is born on the Bolivian altiplano around 1955, the daughter of Xavier Ribeiro, an exile from the Spanish Republic, and Juanita Gúin, a native professor of Quechua at the University of La Paz. She studies ballet, folk dance and modeling at a school in the capital. In

October of 1967, she participates in a demonstration against the Central Intelligence Agency, a few days after the assassination of commander, Che Guevara. She is taken prisoner and thrown in jail—"Where the enemies of Western Christian Aryan civilization are usually sent," says Manolo. She's raped by a handful of Christian soldiers, police and politicians from La Paz. Juana— "her name, according to the press," says Manolo—remains locked up in a jail where she lives with rats— "and we're not just talking about the lackeys, rats by antonomasia." By age seventeen, the girl has already seen the "sinister side of the dictatorship" (in the words of a childhood friend). She has discovered, according to this friend, "the brutal Latin American machismo incarnate in the coarse primitive characteristic militarism." Upon leaving the jail, she spends only a few days in her home; she is watched day and night by a group of militarized half-breeds who tell astonishing stories about the beauty of Juanita Ribeiro Gúin, ravaged Cuñataí. Despite her intense bitterness, Juanita's violet eyes retain the sweet gaze of a llama—that unequalled romantic animal—a tender enamored llama, a violet flame. The CIA places her in Havana from 1971 to 1973, but the FBI maintains that the girl was living among the ragged of the Chilean capital's slums in those years. Another branch of the Secret alleges that she spent those years in the Popular Republic of Mongolia along with one Raimundo E., a young man of unknown origins. But there is evidence to support the fact that Juanita entered the United States toward the end of 1974, registered as a tourist under the pseudonym Mary Ariyaga. She obtains residency thanks to a recognized establishment artist, the well-paid and obliging Olivio Jones who, when he hears her Quechua, judges that it is a most bewitching Greek. Juanita also knows the rudiments of Greek thanks to which she will come to—and not by accident, according to the bloodhounds—Dino Calabrio's building and he is not slow in realizing that "the messenger" sent by his Bolivian comrades is completely reliable. Lessons in Greek, among other things ("hum", says Manny) are what she gets from Calabrio and Aleluya... the girl goes to live with the constructivist painter following— "says the press", grunts Manny—a Machiavellian plan designed by Aley and approved by the astute Calabrio. Jones dedicates singular constructivist sculptures to her, he introduces her into the bourgeoisie consumerism of snob art, the girl meets great Wall Street

investors, Madison Avenue ad men and some colonels from the
Pentagon. Olivio accepts the equivocal human being named Moira
Juanita Ribeiro Gúin; a genial artist, he understands that reality and
fiction are the same. The organizers of the band, Aley, Calabrio, and
Iremita congratulate themselves on the acquisition, whom Aley keeps
up to date thanks to his job as a dog-sitter ("Pure Marxist-Leninist
tactics of someone who, furthermore, is a Doctor of Philosophy of the
Lumumba of Moscow"). Moira penetrates political Washingtonian
spheres. A scandal sheet exhibits blurry photographs in which a very
"solicitous" Congressman appears with the lovely Greco-American
model; the paper promises some "very exciting" information in
upcoming issues about "old Congressmen who act like authentic
*Zorba the Greeks*—dancing in certain night clubs, breaking glasses,
according to Greek tradition, and destroying other, not necessarily
Hellenic, things." The information, according to Manolo's comments, would never appear because various department stores, travel
agencies and oil companies threatened to remove their advertisements
if the paper published facts which implicated their "favorite Congressmen". On the other hand, Olivio's sales experienced a dramatic
fall after Moira's disappearance: his old friends from the Exchange
consider him little more than a disguised pinko, a hood incarnate who
begins to receive visits from hippies in love with who knows what,
hairy characters who cannot understand the art market.

"Moira a Bolivian" laughs Manolo. "Man, that girl is from
Bolivia like I'm from Finland."

*Iremita Johnson*

"What I like least about Iremita," says the expert on the Spanish
Golden Age, "is her pre-Watergate last name."

She is born in the Belgian Congo in 1957, daughter of Nnme and
Mnwc, secret aides to Patrice Lumumba. After his assassination, her
parents go underground, are jailed after two months and dead of
"suicide" after two weeks in their cells. The girl is adopted by a good-
hearted American, an unknown black who lives in relative comfort in
Brazzaville. Shortly thereafter it becomes known that this subject is
a "technical agricultural assessor" in the US delegation. The function-
ary gives his new daughter his own last name, feeling that hers is

unpronounceable in his country ("His country", says Manny, "They have to say that somehow.") After moving to the United States, the girl is not slow to notice a very old phenomenon: she is not well-received for all that they say that she is well-received. Her adoptive father, Ulysses Johnson, is nothing more than "a simple conspirator"—the words of a bearded Cuban— "a spy for racist imperialism in the land of exploited blacks", himself a victim, even to his name, so characteristic of Western whites ("Ulysses!" laughs Manolo, "a Homeric black!"). Iremita is the name chosen by her neofather. He chooses it for musical reasons—so he says—since he plays the lute, the clavichord and "other trash of Western pre-history" (a commentary by composer Francis Schwartz in an interview with virtuoso guitarist Federico Cordero). Iremita, for her part, decides to vindicate the name of Patrice Lumumba—serving, in this way, the memory of her murdered parents. She grows up feeding an avenging anger. So it happens that one clear evening in lower Manhattan, in a meeting to protest the war in Vietnam, she meets a young mulatto of a vaguely Congolian appearance: Aley. After an incredibly clear, direct, humane discourse by Aley, Iremita sings a resounding old song from the South which could fit perfectly into the cardinal points of the Third World. The master of ceremonies—a blond with a heavy silhouette named Pedro Sanataliz—declares on this occasion that Iremita is "the oppressed and fighting heart of Africa in the USA, a subject for a militant theater of poverty in the Third World." The press adduces that Iremita, educated in Aley and Calabrio's Leninist school of revolution, transforms her delicate hands with their long slim fingers into instruments of subtle hecatombs: ethereal winged letters which, when opened, cause terrible conflagrations, "destruction, fire" (the expression of a professor of Spanish poetry). But that is not all: Iremita is popularly known as a soul singer of deep *sentimiento*, of powerful feeling who captivates her audiences on television, radio, in the black churches of Harlem. She sings ballads that tell of the daily battle and of salvation by divine fire. "But she's thinking of other fires," comments the poet rewarded by the police, "human fires that would kill death, terribly human, vindicatingly human as don Pedro Albizu would have wished."

        "Good enough," says Manolo. "I know that she sings like a wonder; my children have her records and, by God, I will have to listen to them! But as to the personal side, what they call personal, well, lad, I don't know her..."

# Epilogue

THEY DISAPPEARED as though they'd been swallowed by the earth I had problems followed asking me things wanting to bleak my bones these people are the plague afterwards I felt very alone I talked with Lorenzo I took Caty along Lorenzo didn't fight he's tired he only thinks about going back to live on la Isla hum he must have money saved if that's the way it is it's good because there what the Hell is he going to eat it's true what Kenneth says the beaches are *bien chéveres* you know but you can't eat them and Renzo didn't say the word boo because he knows I'm a hard-working man young respectful sí and since his children Newyorican men hate his store because they says it's a Puerto Rican *mierda* old-fashioned trash he said I could keep the store and tend it with Caty one time Caty took off a Mayarí quartet record that he was listening to and Caty told him that she took it off because it's an *atrasada* music pure old-fashioned Renzo stands there looking Caty tells me he broke down crying right there because he said that now she isn't like him in any way and Renzo remembered when his wife wanted to go to die in Puerto Rico she spent months talking about it to be buried on *la Ihla* and he went and buried her when the disease finished her off and this was the last time that Renzo was on the *Isla* while I thought about all of this Mordecai Levine the Jew owner of the building and the 174 buildings like this one came and said to me did I want to be the superintendent porter that Dino Calabrio had disappeared and I told Caty and we told him that's okay and we moved the knickknacks on the first floor and then Caty set herself to take out what wasn't useful and we made the little apartment *bien* nice with its kitchen living room dining room a bedroom good heat for this hellish winter and the bathroom that shines like a mirror everything very clean for when the boy comes the heir of my bad times as my old man always said what will mama and my sisters always together say I'd be willing to bet asking about me what will become of my ex-wife and little Gerardo I dream at times of retulning how long have I been here nine months all my life I stop right now Manolo complains because I can't work for him all the time what does he want now I have this other obligation fixing things in the building collecting the rent from the family-who-never-pays-the-rent from Anne Couvert Boricuas Dominicans Blacks the little bleary-eyed old Irish woman with her eight cats and eight dogs the Pole what a surprise didn't answer for two days I pushed the door down the fellow was sprawled out on the couch without breathing purple overdose he injected a train into his vein the police came the coroner had to declare that all of this is shit like when Mr. Blake poor old man hanged himself from a beam Tom Kress aachoo faints Aley jumping out the window hum it made me suspicious Dino with a demon's face talks to the officers shit the history of the old hanged man I told it to Lecráclav who came with all these people when this business about Aley name address phone number in this little book that Caty put on the small table in the entranceway happy she says because now we have lots of friends important people

> Fernando Quiñones who began to sing like the Spaniards
> one Pepe Caballero Bonald short blond half-bald bearded
> and this other bearded man who looks like a big kid

what's his name oh yes Alfonso Sastre
and the blond man with the mulatto babe with a name
that I think he was making up look he said Eduardo Sissores
you know now this is too much
   also the delicate blonde girl green eyes I don't know
Aurora Albornoz something like that
   all of them wanted to write things about Aleluya Iremita Dino
Moira packages from people all over the world José Luis González
long as a palm tree that that that at ttt times stu stut stuttered when he
was talking Pedro Juan Soto had lived ten fucking years here René
Marqués a bottle of Don Q rum not this American shit so he said
Andrés Castro he began to curse tall thin sincere you know *bien
chévere* but I told him that he shouldn't talk bad in front of Caty who
was in the family way more respect Federico Acevedo Tomás López
Ramírez Carlos Raquel Tony Maldonado Gustavo Fabra Barreiros
Carmen Lugo Manrique Cabrera plays with words Florencio Camacho
can get me a job as a cook on *la Isla* but the *señol* who convinced me
he blew my mind grey hair beard small soft white hands writes books
strange name sounds like French German can you imagine Zaíd
Lecráclav up until last week or something like that an entire month he
said he's been doing research for a book on what happens in this part
of the city every day he sat down grey checked jacket lilac shirt neat
bright brown tie he talked about the music of Tito Puente Willie Colón
Mongo Santamaría Willie Bobo Joe Cuba Cheo Feliciano Ray Barreto
about how much *salsa* there is in this city the fellow is up to something
he's a nut *hombre* so serious you know *bien chévere* he said that they
don't acknowledge him on the *Isla* but they do in Spain Mexico
Argentina Venezuela the United States invited him to teach at the
universities but not the colonialized ones that's what he says about
Puerto Rico that they'd shit in their pants to hire a fellow who wasn't
from the mountains he said but he says that he doesn't give a damn
about all of that he said and I stopped
         one minute I don't like for anyone to talk bad in front
of me of mine of my wife woman
      and they all got in on it
   and everyone said calmly Gerry, Lecráclav learned to talk
bad in Spain there everything is *joder* afterwards we became friends
you know and then when he said that he was going to write a book on

life in New York he came down here wine beer magazines Bigote
Bolo we took him he met Dutch we drank beer put on records by
Mongo Santamaría he laughed when the singer said things with two
meanings we took him to the shoe factory which was the first place
where I looked for work I told him about Atila Piña Braga da Cunha
Tai Ken Ismaíl Alí Fulgencio Guerra and the rest I told him about the
summer I was looking for work Shirley and the counterboy at the
pizzeria who gave me good advice I took him upstairs so he could
meet Tom Kress but Anne Couvert appeared he saw the Pole drag
himself upstairs not long before he died I told him about Aley walking
dogs the shyster lawyer David Lean and when I told him about the
doctor, Jeremías Guzmansky, he got so excited that I had to introduce
them they talked for hours and hours according to what he told me
because I split and left them talking historic hassles you know I told
him about Mordecai Levine how I met Caty about the luck of finding
work in Manolo's place how I also had walked dogs about how these
rich people solly capitalist take care of dogs Birke so slick and the
woman whose husband was asleep grabbed my you know what and
the little bitch who went off with a poor dog a bum he listened to all
of this and laughed and said that it was *bien chévere* what a world of
experiences he said and I told him about Moira dancing naked and
about Olivio Jones with his constructions of wood and metal afterwards I told him about the wedding of Kenneth's cousin with the
Paraguayan Carmen Dionisia and about the Prof's discourse and the
fellows applauding it and I was confused because for the first time I
didn't understand what it was to be Bolicuan you know and how Aley
spoke a strange language that Carmen Dionisia speaks and I told him
about the solitary violinist on the other side of the street I showed her
to him and he said the girl isn't bad shit I envy you having seen her
naked even if it were only for one minute of your life that's what he
said with a dozen beers in his gut we also went through Chelsea 42nd
Street Lincoln Center Rockefeller Center we pass near the cemetery
in Brooklyn on the train we walk through half of the South Bronx he
cursing how the Boricuas live he says that on the subways the people
don't look you in the eye like they're ashamed of something I told him
about the inspectors who visit the kitchen in the Mesón del Cordero
and how the police shot at Aleluya Iremita in this very same hallway
I told him everything because the fellow is *chévere* and the day he left

he hugged me called me comrade compatriot said ever onward and I said that I had had some rough times but that you had to keep right on trucking New York is a shithole but

there's no evil that could last forever

and nobody that could endule it

I said and he smiled drunk he said that yes with his head and he said to me that when I publish the novel I'll send it to you he says that while the taxi waits to take him to the ailpolt and he says that he's already written lots of pages in the city that the novel is already clear complete here upstairs on the roof he said touching his calculator brother that's what he said I only need to sit down and spit it out and he said to me that's why at this fucking moment of my life when I say farewell to you my dear Gerry I can say that now I've finished it.

New York, New York
Madrid, Spain
San Juan, Puerto Rico.
1973-1977.